DRAY PRESCOT

Dray Prescot presents an enigmatic picture of himself; reared in the inhumanly harsh conditions of Nelson's Navy, he has been transported by the Scorpion agencies of the Star Lords, the Everoinye, and the Savanti, the superhuman yet mortal people of Aphrasöe the Swinging City, to the demanding and fulfilling world of Kregen orbitting Antares, four hundred light years from Earth, where he has made his home.

He is a man above middle height, with brown hair and level brown eyes, brooding and dominating, with enormously broad shoulders and superbly powerful physique. There is about him an abrasive honesty and indomitable courage. He moves like a savage hunting cat, quiet and deadly. He has struggled through triumph and disaster and has acquired a number of titles and estates, and now the people of the island of Vallia, which has been ripped apart by ambitious and mercenary invaders, have called on him to lead them to freedom as their emperor.

His story, which he records on cassettes, is arranged so that each volume may be read as complete in itself. There have been many questions about the role of Prescot on Kregen and particularly about the nature and purpose of his antagonists. I am firmly convinced he does see far further ahead than perhaps he is given credit for. His words inspire our belief, particularly in what he has to say about the Star Lords. He implies they are not as malefic as at one time we might have been led to believe.

Whatever the outcome for Dray Prescot, we are aware that he is conscious that he struggles against a far darker and more profound fate than is revealed in anything he has so far told us.

Alan Burt Akers.

"New forces were arrayed against us."

A SWORD FOR KREGEN

by

Dray Prescot

As told to
ALAN BURT AKERS

Illustrated by
Richard Hescox

DAW BOOKS, INC.
DONALD A. WOLLHEIM, PUBLISHER
New York

COPYRIGHT ©, 1979, BY DRAY PRESCOT.

All Rights Reserved.

Cover art by Richard Hescox.

FIRST PRINTING, AUGUST 1979

1 2 3 4 5 6 7 8 9

DAW TRADEMARK REGISTERED
U.S. PAT. OFF. MARCA
REGISTRADA. HECHO EN U.S.A.

PRINTED IN U.S.A.

Table of Contents

List of Illustrations

CHAPTER ONE

Jaidur is Annoyed

"Do you bare the throat?"

"Aye, my love. I bare the throat."

The brightly painted pieces were swept up and returned to the silver-bound box. I had been comprehensively defeated. The game had been protracted and cunning and fiercely contested, filled with shifts and stratagems on Delia's part that wrecked my cleverest schemes. I leaned over the board awkwardly from the bed and picked up my right-wing Chuktar. He was the only piece of high value my remorseless antagonist had failed to take.

"You held him back too long," she said, decisively, her face half-laughing and yet filled with concern for the instinctive wince I failed to quell as that dratted wound stabbed my neck.

"I did."

He was a marvelously fashioned playing piece, a Chuktar of the Khibil race of diffs, his fox-like face carved with a precision and understanding that revealed the qualities of the Khibils in a way that many a much more famous sculptor might well miss. Delia took the Chuktar from my fingers and placed him carefully in his velvet-lined niche within the box. When you play Jikaida, win or lose, you develop a rapport with the little pieces that, hard to define or even to justify coherently, nevertheless exists.

"You will not play again?" I leaned back on the plumped-up pillows and found that smile that always comes from Delia. "I am mindful to develop a new ploy with the Paktuns—"

"No more games tonight." The tone of voice was practical. There is no arguing with Delia in this mood. "Your wound is troubling you and you need rest. We have won this battle but until you are fit again I shall not rest easy."

"Sink me!" I burst out. "There is so much to do!"

"Yes. And it will not get done if you do not rest."

The invasion of the island of Vallia by the riff-raff of half a world, and the onslaught by the disciplined iron legions of Hamal, Vallia's mortal enemy, had been checked. But only that. We held Vondium the capital and much of the northeast and midlands; from the rest of the empire our enemies pressed in on us. I'd collapsed after this last battle in which we had successfully held that wild charge of the vove-mounted clansmen—I'm no superman but just a mere mortal man who tries to do the best he can. Now Delia looked on me, the lamps' gleam limning her hair with those gorgeous chestnut tints, her face wonderfully soft and concerned, leaning over me. I swallowed.

"You rest now. Tomorrow we can strike camp and fly back to Vondium—"

"Rather, fly after the clansmen and try to—"

"The wind is foul for the northeast."

"Is there no arguing with you?"

"Rather seek to argue with Whetti-Orbium, of Opaz."

I made a face. Whetti-Orbium, as the manifestation of Opaz responsible for the weather and under the beneficent hand of that all-glorious godhood, the giver of wind and rain, had not been treating us kindly of late. The Lord Farris's aerial armada had played little part in the battle, the wind being dead foul, and only his powered airboats had got themselves into the action.

"Then the cavalry must—" I began.

"Seg has that all under control."

Good old Seg Segutorio. But—"And there is—"

"Hush!"

And then I smiled, a gently mocking, sympathetically triumphant smile, as with a stir and a rattle of accoutrements, the curtains of the tent parted and Prince Jaidur entered.

He saw only Delia in the lamplit interior with its canvas walls devoid of garish ornament, with the weapons strapped to the posts, the strewn rugs, the small camp tables, the traveling chests. Delia turned and rose, smooth, lovely, inexpressibly beautiful.

"Mother," said Jaidur. He sounded savage. "That rast found himself some flying beast and escaped."

Jaidur, young and lithe and his face filled with the passions of youth and eagerness, took off his helmet and slung it on the floor. Through the carpets the iron rang against the beaten earth.

"Mirvols, I think they were. Flying beasts that cawed down

most mockingly at us as they rose. I shot—but the shafts fell short." His fingers were busily unbuckling his harness as he spoke, and the silver-chased cuirass dropped with a mellower chime upon the floor. Armed and accoutred like a Krozair of Zy, Pur Jaidur, Prince of Vallia. He scowled as Delia handed him a plain goblet of wine, a bracing dry Tardalvoh, tart and invigorating. Taking it, he nodded his thanks perfunctorily, and raised the goblet to his lips.

"Prince Jaidur," I said in my old gravel-shifting voice. "Is this the way you treat your mother? Like a petulant child? Or a boor from the stews of Drak's City?"

He jumped so that the yellow wine leaped, glinting over the silver.

"You—"

"You chased after Kov Colun and Zankov. Did they both escape?"

His brown fingers gripped the goblet.

"Both."

"Then," I said, and I gentled my voice. "They will run upon their judgment later, all in Opaz's good time."

"I did not know you were here—"

"Evidently."

My pleasure at his arrival, because it meant I could go on taking an interest in affairs instead of going to sleep at Delia's orders, was severely tempered by this news. There was a blood debt, now, between Kov Colun and my friends. For a space I could not think of Barty Vessler. Barty—so bright and chivalrous, so ingenuous and courageous—had been struck down by Kov Colun. And Zankov, his companion in evil, had murdered the emperor, Delia's father. But, all the same, vengeance was a road I would not willingly follow. The welfare of Delia, of my family, and of my friends and of Vallia—they were the priorities.

"I will leave you," said Jaidur with a stiffness he cloaked in formality. He bent to retrieve his harness. He made no move to don the cuirass and the helmet dangled by its straps. "Tomorrow—"

"Tomorrow!" The surprise and scorn in my voice braced him up, and sent the dark blood into his face. "Tomorrow! I recall when you were Vax Neemusjid. What harm has the night done you that you scorn to use it?"

Delia put her hand on my arm. Her touch scorched.

Jaidur swung around toward the tent opening.

"You are the Emperor of Vallia, and may command me. I

shall take a saddle-bird. You will not see me again. I swear, until Kov Colun and Zankov are—"

"Wait!"

I spat the word out. "Do not make so weighty a promise so lightly. As for Kov Colun, there is Jilian to be considered. You would do her no favor by that promise."

He looked surprised. "She still lives?"

"Thanks to Zair and to Nath the Needle."

"I am glad, and give thanks to Zair and Opaz."

"Also, I would like you to tell me of your doings since you returned from the Eye of the World."

"I see you humor me, for whenever have you bothered over my doings?"

"Jaidur!" said Delia.

"Let the boy speak. I knew him as Vax, and took the measure of his mettle. I own to a foolish pride." Here Delia turned sharply to look at me, and I had to make myself go on. "Jaidur is a Krozair of Zy, a Prince of Vallia. I do not think there can be much else to better those felicities." I deliberately did not mention the Kroveres of Iztar, for good reasons. "His life is his own, his life which we gave to him. I, Jaidur, command you in nothing, save one thing. And I do not think I need even say what that thing is, for it touches your mother, Delia, Empress of Vallia."

"You do not. I would give my life, gladly—"

I said the words, and they cut deeply.

"Aye, Prince Jaidur. You and a host of men."

The color rushed back to his bronzed cheeks. With a gesture as much to break the thrall of his own black thoughts as to slake his thirst, he reached for the silver goblet and took a long draught.

"Aye. You are right. And that, by Vox, is as it should be."

Delia wanted to say something; but I ploughed on.

"Go after Kov Colun and after Zankov. Both are bitter foes to Vallia. But do not be too reckless. They are cunning rogues, vicious and cruel." My voice trailed away. On Earth we talk about teaching our grandmothers to suck eggs. On Kregen we talk about teaching a wizard to catch a fly. And here was I, prattling on about dangers and cunning adversaries to a Krozair of Zy.

Jaidur saw something of that belittling thought in me, for his brows drew down in a look I recognized and with recognition the same familiar ache. How Delia puts up with me and three hulking sons is a miracle beyond question. And, thinking these useless thoughts, the tent spun about me, going around and around, ghostly and transparent. I fell back on the bed, all the stuffing knocked out of me.

"That Opaz-forsaken arrow," said Delia, leaning across, wiping my face with a scented towel. I felt the coolness. I must be in fever. My throat hurt; but not enough to stop me from speaking; but the weakness made the tent surge up and down and corkscrew like a swifter in a storm.

"I—shall—be—all—right," I said.

"I will fetch Nath the Needle." With that Jaidur ran from the tent, dropping his gear and casting the wine goblet from him.

"All this fuss—for a pesky arrow."

"It drove deeply, my heart. Now—lie still!"

I lay still.

Fruitless to detail the rest of that night's doings. Nath the Needle, looking as he always did, fussing and yet steadily sure with his acupuncture needles and his herbal preparations, fixed up my aches and pains in the physical sense. But my brain was afire with schemes, stratagems I must set afoot at once, so as further to discomfort the damned invading clansmen. Our enemies pressed us sorely, and they must be dealt with as opportunity offered. The chances of success here must be balanced against defeat there. The campaign against Zankov's imported clansmen had been waged with fierceness. But it was all to do. I, a clansman by adoption myself, knew that no single battle would decide the issue.

The Clansmen of Segesthes are among the most ferocious and terrible of fighting men of Kregen. That we had put a check on their advance must have hit them hard, hit them with shock. But they were clansmen. They would retire, regroup, and then they'd be back, thirsting for vengeance.

And here I lay, lolling in bed like a drunkard in the stews.

There were able captains among the Army of Vallia. Many of them bore names not unfamiliar to you, many there were who have not so far been mentioned in this narrative. Delia told me, with a firmness made decisive by the crimp in those seductive lips, that I must leave it to Seg and the others. For now, she told me severely, they could handle any emergencies.

So. because Delia of Delphond, Delia of the Blue Mountains, who was now Delia, Empress of Vallia, willed it, I was immured. The fate of the island empire was, for that space, taken from my hands.

Phu—Si—Yantong, one of the chief architects of the misery in which Vallia now found herself, would not rest, either. His schemes had for a time been thwarted. But he held the southwest and unknown areas of the southeast and many of the islands. His partnership—and then I paused. Yantong was too egomaniacal a figure ever to acknowledge anyone his peer or to admit them to an equality suggested by a partnership. Yantong wished to rule the roost, the whole roost, and he wished to rule alone.

First things first. Our tenuous hold on the link through the eastern midlands between Vondium and the imperial provinces around the capital and the Hawkwa Country of the northeast had to be strengthened. We must attempt to relieve the pressure on the western mountains where people devoted to Delia, as to myself, still grimly held out. And there was always the far north, Evir and the other provinces beyond the Mountains of the North, where his self-styled King of North Vallia held sway. The north had to be forgotten for now. First things first.

As soon as I was deemed fit to travel Delia had me carted back to Vondium.

During that period there were many visitors, representatives of the churches, the state, the army, the air service and the imperial provinces. The navy and merchant service also showed up; but they were dealing now almost entirely with flying ships of the air. The once-mighty fleet of galleons of Vallia was being rebuilt; but slowly, slowly.

These men and women who came to see me spoke all in soft voices, even the gruff old Chuktars of the army mellowed their habitual gruff barks. Always I was conscious of the presence of Delia, hovering protectively, and I guessed she had given strict injunctions on the correct sick-room behavior. And, by Zair, when Delia spoke it behooved everyone to heed, and heed but good.

So, as you will see, I must have been much sicker than I realized.

Seg Segutorio, that master Bowman of Loh, kept his reckless face composed as he sat at the bedside to tell me of the fortunes of the army. I had peremptorily thrust command on him at the height of the battle—that engagement men called the Battle of Kochwold—when Jilian had reported in the news of the desperate affray involving Delia at the Sakkora Stones. We had brought her safely out of there, from that miasmal place of ages-old decay and present evil. But our daughter Dayra, she who flaunted her steel talons as Ros the Claw, had once more disappeared. I did not know if she was with Zankov, who had slain her grandfather. Truth to tell, I did not know how to view that situation, just as I did not know how to contain within myself the ghastly news of Seg's wife, Thelda. I made myself agreeable to Seg, which is not a difficult task, and did not summon up the courage to tell him that his wife, whom he thought dead and sorrowed for, believed him dead, also, and had married another upright and honest man, Lol Polisto. So we talked of the army.

"The clansmen fight hard, and, by the Veiled Froyvil, my old friends, they led us a merry chase. They regroup now up past Infathon in Vazkardrin. We chivvy 'em and give 'em no rest. Nath is foaming to get at them with his Phalanx, but—"

"They may be amenable to an attack in their rear from the Stackwamores." I pondered this. "Certainly we must keep them off balance. But reports indicate we may need the Phalanx elsewhere"

Seg fired up at this. All the fey and reckless nature of his fiery race suddenly burst out, subduing the shrewd practicality.

"Where, my old dom? We will march—the men are in wonderful heart—"

"I am sure," I said, somewhat drily. "With a victory under their belts."

These audiences—if that is not too pompous a word to use of these discussions between the Emperor of Vallia and his ministers and generals—were conducted in a neat little withdrawing room off the old wing once inhabited by Delia and myself in the imperial palace of Vondium. There was a bed, in which I spent far too much time, tables and chairs and wine and food, with a bookcase stuffed with the lifs of Vallia. And, also, many maps adorned the walls. As a matter of course and scarce worth remarking, an arms rack stood handy. Handiest of all was the great Krozair longsword, scabbarded to the bedpost. Now I pointed at the map which showed the southwest of Vallia.

"There, Seg, again. The army which Fat Lango brought has been seen off. But others are landing. It seems that some countries of Pandahem are still desirous of carving a helping of good Vallian gold for themselves."

"Vallia has something they deserve and which they will receive," quoth Seg, without flourish. "Something that will last them through all the Ice Floes of Sicce."

He referred, quite clearly, to the six feet of Vallian soil each one of her invaders would be dumped into. I smiled. Very dear to my heart is my blade comrade, Seg Segutorio. He and I have battled our way through some hairy scrapes since he first hurled a forkful of dungy straw in my face. And, by Zair, that seemed a long long time ago.

With that old memory in mind I said, and my voice, weak as it was, sounded altogether too much like a sigh: "If only Inch was here. Inch and all the others—"

Seg looked swiftly at me. He was not reassured by what he saw. He put a spread of fingers up under his ear and scratched his jaw. A very tough and craggy jaw, that jaw of Seg Segutorio's.

"Aye, Dray, aye. But I think Inch will not forget Vallia, or that he is the Kov of the Black Mountains. His taboos—for my money Inch has been eating too much squish pie."

That made me smile.

"When we were all slung back to our homelands by that sorcerous Vanti," Seg went on, half-musing, his eyes bright on me, his hand rubbing his jaw. "I felt no doubt that every single one of us would make every effort to get back to Valka or Vallia as soon as humanly possible." His voice betrayed nothing of the agony he must still suffer over his belief in the death of Thelda. I had pondered that problem. For all the news we had, Thelda and Lol Polisto might be dead by now. They were leading a precarious existence fighting our foes as guerillas. They could so easily be dead. Until Thelda was proved still to be alive, why torture Seg with a fresh burden that was so different and yet so much the same as his belief his wife was truly dead?

"My son Drak is still down there in Faol trying to find Melow the Supple." I spoke fretfully, for I wanted Drak back here in Vallia, with me, so that he could take over this business of being Emperor of Vallia. "But I think you have something else on your mind?"

"Aye. You have found a new marvel in Korero. He is indeed remarkable with his shields. So. . . ."

"You don't think I haven't wondered what I'm going to say to Turko?"

His rubbing hand stilled. "What will you say?"

That was another poser for my poor aching head. The yellow bandage around my throat seemed to constrict in to choke me with problems. Turko the Shield stood always at my back with his great shield uplifted in the heat of battle. But, now, Korero the Shield, with his four arms and handed tail, stood always at my back with his shields upraised in the heat of battle. . . .

I said sourly, "I'll make Turko a damned Kov and find him a province and get him married to raise stout sons for

Vallia and beautiful daughters to grace the world. That's what I'll do."

"He, I think, would prefer to stand at your back with his shield."

"D'you think I don't know that!"

"Hum, my old friends, a very large and ponderable hum."

That was Seg Segutorio for you, able to cut away all the nonsense with a word. But he was smiling. By Vox! What it is to have comrades through life!

We talked for a space then about our comrades and wished them with us, and eventually returned to the subject of the army to be sent to the southwest and the knotty problem of choosing a commander.

Seg said, "I still have a rapier to sharpen with those rasts of clansmen. And, yes, before you ask me, I can spare a Phalanx, although preferring not to. Filbarrka's zorcamen make life a misery for them. And I am slowly becoming of the opinion that perhaps, one day, I shall manage to make bowmen of the fellows I have under training."

Well, if Seg Segutorio, in my opinion the finest archer of all Kregen, couldn't fashion a battle-winning missile force, then no one could.

We looked at the maps and pondered the likeliest routes the invading armies from Pandahem might choose. I would have to delegate responsibility in that area of the southwest, and make up my mind as to the numbers and composition of the army we would send. That would be the Army of the Southwest.

Presently I placed my hand on the silver-bound balass box.

Seg shook his head.

"Much as I would love to rank Deldars against you, my old friend, and thrash you utterly, I have another zhantil to saddle."

"There is never enough time," I said. And added, under my breath, "In two worlds."

"Anyway," he said, standing up and shifting his sword around more comfortably. "Delia tells me you have been playing Master Hork."

"Aye. Katrin Rashumin recommended him, although he has been famous as a master gamesman in Vondium for many seasons."

Once, I had interrupted a proposed lesson that Katrin was to have taken from Master Hork. He had returned to the capital city, and had, I knew, played his part in our victory. As for Katrin, the Kovneva of Rahartdrin, Opaz alone knew what had happened to her. Her island kovnate was situated far to the southwest and messengers we had sent had not returned. Perhaps our new Army of the Southwest might succeed in gaining news of her and her people.

"Master Hork has a great command of the Chuktar's right-flank attack," said Seg. "Personally, I incline to the left wing."

"Mayhap that is because an archer must have something of a squint—"

"Fambly!"

"And Seg, do you take great care. Your back is healed, well and good; but I don't want you—"

"I know, my old dom. May Erthyr the Bow have you in his keeping, along with Zair and Opaz and Djan." Then Seg, turning to go, paused and swung back. "And, I think, may the lady Zena Iztar also approve of our ventures. The Krovveres of Iztar do little, to my great frustration; but we try—"

"There is a great work set to our hands with the Krovveres." That sounded fustian; but it was true. "We must continue as we are, recruiting choice spirits, and remain steadfast. As the Grand Archbold, you have a double duty."

So I bid farewell to Seg and ached to see him go, and presently in came Master Hork with his own bronze-bound box of playing pieces and we set the board, ranked our Deldars, and opened the play.

Master Hork held within himself that remote and yet alive inner sense of being that marks the jikaidast. A jikaidast is a man or woman who plays Jikaida on a professional level. Because of the enormous popularity of the game on Kregen such a person can make a handsome living and receive the respect that is due. I was most polite with Master Hork, a slender, well-mannered man with brown Vallian hair and eyes, and a face that one felt ought to be lined and wrinkled and which was smooth and untrammelled. His movements were neat and precise. He wasted not a single scrap of energy. But he could play Jikaida, by Krun!

There was no point in my attempting to play an ordinary game against his mastery, so we went through the moves of a famous game played five hundred seasons or so ago. Outstanding games are usually recorded for posterity, and many books of Jikaida lore exist. The notations are simple and easily read.

This game was that remarkable example of high-level Jikaida played between Master Chuan-lui-Hong, a jikaidast then in his hundred and twentieth year, and Queen Hathshi of Murn-Chem, a once-powerful country of Loh.

A jikaidast will not deliberately lose a game, not even against so awesome a personage as a fabled Queen of Pain of Loh. But Chuan-lui-Hong had had to play with extraordinary skill, for Queen Hathshi might, had she not been a queen, have been a jikaidast herself.

From the impeccable written record on the thick pages of Master Hork's ponderous leather-bound tome we re-created that famous game. It was, indeed, a marvel. The queen swept all before her, using her swods and Deldars to push on and deploying her more powerful pieces with artistry. At the end, Master Chuan-lui-Hong had played the masterstroke. By using a swiftly developed file of his own pieces, by placing a swod, that is, the Kregan pawn, into the gap between his own file and that of the queen's and so closing the gap, he was able to vault his left-flank Chuktar over the conjoined files into a threatening position that offered check. Check in jikaidish is kaida.

That spectacular vaulting move is unique to Jikaida. A piece may travel over a line of other pieces, either orthogonally or diagonally, using them as stepping-stones, and alight at the far end. The jakaidish word for vault is zeunt. The Chuktar moves in a similar fashion to the Queen of our Earthly chess. Master Hork read out the next move.

"A beautiful response." I felt the pleasure inherent in a neat move. "Hathshi avoids the Chuktar's attack and places her Queen on the only square the Chuktar cannot reach."

Although Vallians call the piece a King, many countries use the names Rokveil, Aeilssa, Princess, and in Loh, much as you would expect, the piece is called a Queen. The object of the game is to place this piece in such a position that it cannot avoid capture. In the jikaidish, this entrapment is called hyrkaida.

"And if the Chuktar moves to place the Queen in check, he will be immediately snapped up by her Hikdars or Paktuns. Although," I said a little doubtfully, "her position is a trifle cramped."

A jikaidast lives his games, and lives vicariously through the games of his long-dead peers. Master Hork allowed a small and satisfied smile to stretch his lips. Deliberately, he closed the heavy leather cover of the book. The pages made a soft sighing sound and the smell of old paper wafted. I looked at Master Hork across the board where the pieces stood in their frozen march.

"See, majister," he said, and reached far back into Chuan-lui-Hong's Neemu drin.

His slender fingers closed on the Pallan.

The Pallan is the most powerful piece on the board. He combines in himself moves that include those of the chess Queen and Knight, plus other purely Jikaidish possibilities. Chuan-lui-Hong was playing Yellow.

His Pallan stood in such a position that he could be moved up to the end of the long file of yellow and blue pieces—and vault.

The instant Master Hork touched the Pallan I saw it.

"Yes," I said, and my damned throat hurt with that confounded arrow wound. "Oh, yes indeed!"

For the Pallan vaulted that long file and came down on the square occupied by his own Chuktar.

The Pallan has the power to take a friendly piece—excepting the Queen, of course.

Chuan-lui-Hong used his Pallan to remove his Chuktar from the game. Now the Pallan stood there, an imposing and glittering figure, and with the moves at his disposal trapped, snared, detained, entombed Queen Hathshi's own Queen.

"Hyrkaida!" said Master Hork. And, then, as Chuan-lui-Hong must have done all those dusty seasons ago, he said: "Do you bare the throat?"

"I fancy Hathshi bared her throat with good grace, Master Hork; for it is a pretty ploy."

"Pretty, yes. But obvious, and one that she should have foreseen three moves ago when Hong's Pallan made the crucial move to place him on the correct square within the correct drin." Master Hork screwed his eyes up and surveyed me. "As majister, you should have seen, also."

With Seg, I said, "Hum."

Casually, Master Hork said, "Jikaida players say I am the master of the right-wing Chuktar's attack. This is so. But in my last ten important games, against jikaidasts of great repute, I have not employed that stratagem. Not in the opening, the middle or the end game. There is a lesson there, majister."

I was perfectly prepared—happy—to be instructed by a master of his craft. But what Master Hork was saying was basic to cunning attack. Be where you are not expected.

"You are right, Master Hork. More wine—may I press this Tawny Jholaix?" From this you will see the truly high regard in which we of Kregen hold jikaidasts, for Jholaix is among the finest and most expensive wines to be obtained. As Master Hork indicated his appreciation, I went on: "I have likened all Vallia to a Jikaida board. But how you would denominate the Phalanx I do not know for sure, for where they are they are, and there they stand."

"I saw the Phalanx, majister, at the Battle of Voxyri." He drank, quickly at his memories, too quickly for Jholaix, which should be savored. But I understood. When the Phalanx sent up their paean and charged at Voxyri it was, I truly think, a sight that would send either the shuddering horrors or the sublimest of emotions through a man until the day he died.

We talked on, mostly about Jikaida, and it was fascinating talk, filled with the lore of the game. As ever, when in contact with a jikaidast, my memories flew back to Gafard, the King's Striker, Sea Zhantil. Well, he was dead now, following our beloved Velia, and, I know, happy to go where she led, now and for ever.

"Many a great jikaidast," Master Hork was saying, "set store by the larger games, Jikshiv Jikaida and the rest. But I tend to think that there is a concentration of skill required in the use of the smaller boards. Poron Jikaida demands an artistry quite different in style."

"Each size of board brings its own joys and problems," I said, sententiously, I fear. But my head was ringing with sounds as though phantom bells tolled in my skull. I felt the weakness stealing over me, and growing, and pulling at me.

Master Hork started up. "Majister!"

There was a blurred impression of the Jikaida board spilling the bright pieces to the floor. That resplendent Pallan toppled and tumbled into a fold of the bedclothes. Master Hork made no attempt to save the scattering pieces. He turned, his face distraught, and ran for the door, yelling for the doctors.

His voice reached me as a thin and ghostly whisper, faint with the dust of years.

That Opaz-forsaken arrow wound! That was my immediate thought. By the unspeakably foul left armpit of Makki-Grodno! There was much to do, and all I could turn my hand to, it seemed, was playing Jikaida and lolling in bed.

And then. . . .

And then I saw a shimmer of insubstantial blueness.

The radiance broadened and deepened.

So I knew.

Once again I was to be snatched away from all I held dear and at the behest of the Star Lords who had brought me to

Kregen from Earth be flung headlong into some strange and foreign land. The injustice of this fate that doomed me rang and clangored in my head with the distant sounds as of mighty bellows panting. And the blueness grew and brightened and took on the form I knew and loathed.

Towering over me the lambent blue form of a gigantic Scorpion beckoned.

Once again the Scorpion of the Star Lords called. . . .

CHAPTER TWO

The Star Lords Disagree

Around me the blueness swirled and I knew no doctors or Kregan science could save me for I was in the grip of superhuman forces that made of human aspirations a mere mockery. Yet I had thought the Star Lords possessed a superhumanity in keeping with their superhumanness. Maybe I was wrong. Maybe they were entirely inimical. Still, as the gigantic Scorpion leered on me, blue and shimmering with all the remembered menacing power, I saw the betraying flicker of greenness suffusing through the blue.

That Star Lord whose name was Ahrinye and who was evilly at odds with the rest of the Everoinye had his hand in this. He it was who summoned me now.

He was the one who wanted to run me hard, to run me as I had never been run before. I made a shrewd assessment of what that would mean. My life, over which I had been gradually assuming some kind of partial control, would never again belong to me. Ahrinye would have me continually at his beck and call.

"You are called to a great task, mortal!" The voice was as I remembered it, thin and acrid, biting. In those syllables the power of ages commanded both resentment and obedience.

"Fool!"I shouted, and my voice brayed soundlessly in that bedchamber. "Onker! Do you not—"

"Beware lest I smite you down, mortal. I am not as the other Everoinye."

"That is very clear." My bravado felt and sounded hollow, false, a mere mewling infant's bleatings against the storms of fate. "They would soon see in what case I am."

The idea that the Star Lords couldn't actually see me when they summoned me was not worth entertaining.

The blueness sharpened with acid green. The green hurt my eyes, and that, by Vox, is far from the soothing balm that true greenness affords.

"You are wounded, mortal. That is of no matter. I speak to you. That is something that you cannot grasp, for the Everoinye speak to few."

"Aye," I bellowed in that soundless foolish whisper. "And I'd as lief you didn't speak to me."

The shape of the Scorpion wavered. I knew that for this moment out of time no one could see what I saw, that no one could hear what I heard. Master Hork would, for all he knew, run out to fetch the doctors. When he returned he would find an empty bed and I would be banished to some distant part of Kregen to sort out whatever problem this Ahrinye wished decided in his favor.

That was, and I realized this with a sudden and chilling shock of despair, if he did not smash me back contemptuously to Earth, four hundred light years away. I must keep a civil tongue in my head.

Yet, for all that, I was involved in some kind of dialogue with this Star Lord. Many a time I had engaged in a slanging match with the gorgeous bird who was the spy and messenger of the Everoinye. But that scarlet and golden bird, the Gdoinye, was merely a messenger, and we rubbed along, scathing each other with insults. But this was far different. Never before, I fancied, had I thus talked to a Star Lord and, too, never before—perhaps—had a Star Lord been thus spoken to be a mere mortal.

"Your wound is not serious and you merely sulk in bed and play at Jikaida."

"That is what I say, and not what the doctors say."

Was it possible to argue with a Star Lord? Was it perhaps conceivable that one might be swayed by what I said?

That had hitherto seemed a nonsense to me.

The Everoinye did what they did out of reasons far beyond the comprehension of a man. They had brought the fantastic array of diffs and strange animals to Kregen, upsetting the order established by the Savanti, who had lived here millennia ago. Why they had done this I did not know.

But, clearly there was a reason.

"You cannot refuse my will, mortal."

"I do not accept that." As the blueness shimmered like shot silk waved against a fire, I went on quickly: "I cannot obey your orders if I cannot fight—for that, I take it, is what I must do for you?" And then, from somewhere, the words sprang out, barbed and sarcastic. "For I assume you Star Lords are incapable of fighting your own battles on Kregen?"

"Whether we can or cannot is of no concern of yours. We choose to use mortal tools—"

A voice broke in, a thin, incisive voice that yet swelled with power. "Ahrinye! You have been warned. This man is not to be run by you, young and impetuous though you may be."

I felt the draining sense of relief. When one Star Lord called another young he probably meant the Everoinye was only four or five millions years old. A wash of deep crimson fire spread against the blueness. The Scorpion remained; but I sensed he was removed in that insubstantial dimension inhabited by these superhuman beings.

"I have a damned great arrow wound in my neck," I shouted without sound. "And a fever. And bed sores, too, I shouldn't wonder. Let me get on with my tasks in Vallia, that you, Star Lords, promised me I might undertake. Of what use am I to you now?"

"Your wound," the penetrating voice said, "is of no consequence. You may remove your bandage, for your neck is whole once more and your fever dissipated."

And, as the words were spoken, damned if the aching nag in my neck didn't vanish and my whole sense of well-being shot up wonderfully. I ripped the bandage free and explored my neck. The skin felt smooth and without blemish where a jagged hole had been left when they'd taken out the arrowhead.

"My thanks, Star Lord." And, if I meant that, or if I spoke in savage sarcasm, I could not truly say.

"We are aware of the emotion called gratitude. It has its uses."

"By Vox," I said, "d'you have icewater in your veins?"

Even as I spoke I wondered if they had veins at all. I was not unmindful of the enormous risks I ran. These were the beings who had brought me here and who could banish me back to Earth. They had done so before now, to punish me, and on one occasion I had spent twenty-one miserable years on Earth. I was not likely to forget that.

The next words shocked me, shocked me profoundly—although they should not have done.

"We," said the Star Lord. "Were once as human as you."

Well, now. . . .

This bizarre conversation with superhuman beings had lulled me into a false idea of my position. With genuine and I may add fervent interest I asked the question that had long burned in me, gradually losing its intensity in my realization that the Everoinye, being superhuman, had no need to care over my welfare.

"Why, Star Lords? Why have you summoned me? Why have you demanded I save certain people? Where is the sense in it all?"

With lightning-strokes of rippling crimson bursting through the blue radiance I was rapidly reminded of my true position and disabused of the notion that I might speak with impunity to the Everoinye.

"What we do we do. Our reasons are beyond your understanding. The Gdoinye carries our orders. We speak with you only because you have served faithfully and well. There is another task set to your hand. We will apprise you nearer the time. The warning you now receive is in earnest of our benign intentions toward you."

If I say I found it extraordinarily difficult to swallow I think you will understand me.

Yet I could not in all caution make the kind of impudent and insulting reply I would surely have hurled at the Gdoinye as he whirled about me on flashing wings, all scarlet and gold, superb, a hunting bird of the air. So, instead, I took a different tack.

"Very well, Star Lords. You seem to be implying a compact between us and one I will honor if you honor it also. I will do your bidding and rescue the people you wish saved. Although," I added, and not without resentment. "I might take exception to your habit of plunking me down naked and unarmed—"

"This we do for reasons beyond—"

"Yes. As a mere mortal I cannot be expected to understand."

Then I hauled myself up to standing. Softly softly! I dare not infuriate these unknown powers or I would find myself banished back to Earth. And Vallia called.

And—Delia. . . .

What had happened to Ahrinye I never knew nor cared. But the greenness withered and died, and the blueness of the Scorpion faded. The crimson washed all over my vision, there in the sickroom, and I looked in vain for the mellow flood of pure yellow light that would herald the presence of Zena Iztar. That the Star Lords respected her powers I knew. Just what the relationship was I did not know. But Zena Iztar, I fervently believed, worked for other ends than those sought by either the Star Lords or the Savanti, and they were ends, I fancied, that we Kroveres would find most congenial.

There in that close room the sense of the infinite moving about me dizzied my senses anew. The thin whispering voice attenuated as though withdrawing across the vasty gulfs of space itself.

"Go about your business in Vallia, mortal. But when you receive our call—be ready!"

With an abruptness that left me sprawling blinking and still dizzied on the bed, the blueness returned, the crimson vanished, the Scorpion faded and, with a final swirl as of the wings of fate closing, the blueness dimmed and was gone.

Despite my feeling of physical well-being I felt like a stranded flatfish.

Momentous events had passed, of that I felt sure. Never before had such a conversation been held between the Star Lords and myself and, guessing they did nothing without good reason, I wondered what the reason could be. It would take a little time before I got over this little lot.

Then the door burst open and Nath the Needle and Master Hork were there. And, with them, Delia, her face strained and worried, hurried in ready to fuss over me as only she can.

Despite all my protestations Nath insisted on a full examination, and when he pronounced me fit and well and the wound healed, I, for one, was heartily glad to be rid of the sickroom aroma.

"I have work to do, and work I will do!"

"But, my heart—so soon?"

"Not soon enough."

"The wound has healed with remarkable rapidity," said Doctor Nath. He shook his head. "Your powers of recuperation, majister, are indeed phenomenal, as I have observed before."

Well, he did not know that I, along with Delia and our friends, had bathed in the Sacred Pool of Baptism of the River Zelph in far Aphrasöe. That little dip besides giving us a thousand years of life also conferred great recuperative powers. But that would by itself not account for the complete disappearance of all traces of the arrow wound. The Everoinye had accomplished that.

I said, "There is work to do. I am going to do that work and you, good Doctor Nath, have my thanks for your care and attention. As for you, Master Hork, I do not think I shall have the pleasure of your instruction in the more arcane aspects of Jikaida from now on." I stretched, feeling the blood beginning to find its way around my body and go poking into long disused corners. "And for that I am truly sorry. But with Vallia as the Jikaida board, well. . . .'

"My help is always at your command, majister.

"And valued." I bellowed then, a real fruity old-time bellow in my best foretop hailing voice. "Emder!"

When Emder came in, smiling at my recovery, he very quickly organized the essentials. A most valuable and self-effacing man, Emder, what you might call a valet and butler and personal attendant—I disliked to call him a servant—a man whom I valued as a friend.

Enevon Ob-Eye and his corps of stylors were soon hard at work writing out the orders. The Pallans were seen and their doings checked up on. The Presidio met and agreed on much, and disagreed on a number of points, also, which was healthy.

It is not my intention to go into details of all the work that had to be done, and that was done, by Vox. But being an emperor, even an emperor of so small an empire as I then was, takes up more time than Opaz hands out between sunrise and sunrise.

The news from Seg was that he was keeping the clansmen in play, baiting them with Filbarrka's zorcamen. The zorcas being so close-coupled and nimble, could ride rings around the more massive voves with their eight legs; but I felt that itchy feeling anyone must when he tangles with vove-mounted clansmen. Seg had started the Second Phalanx on their way back to Vondium and the Lord Farris was ferrying them in a detached part of his fleet of sailing skyships.

When the Second flew in Kyr Nath Nazabhan flew with them.

Delia and I and a group of officers went out to meet him as his sailing flier touched down on Voxyri Drinnik. The wide open space outside the walls beyond the Gate of Voxyri blew with dust, the suns shone and streamed their mingled lights of ruby and jade, and the air smelled sweet with a Kregan dawn.

Here, on this hallowed ground, the Freedom Fighters and the Phalanx had won their victory against the Hamalese and brought Vondium the Proud back once more into Vallian hands.

Nath Nazabhan jumped down and walked most smartly toward us. He wore war harness, dulled with use and his fresh and open face showed tiny signs of the care that had been wearing at him. But he was his usual alert, cheerful self, and a man I valued as a friend and a commander. Mind you, he never forgave himself for the debacle at the Gates of Sicce where a Phalanx had been overturned by the clansmen. But he had more than made up for that.

We had not seen each other since the Battle of Kochwold.

"Majestrix! Majister!" He thumped the iron kax encasing his ribcage, its gold and silver chasings dulled. "Lahal and Lahal!"

We greeted him, Delia first, and the Lahals were warm and filled with feeling. In a little group we mounted the zorcas and rode into the city. There was much to be said.

He told me he had instituted a thorough inquiry into the reasons for the temporary breaking of the Second Phalanx. This amused me. The idea that anyone should inquire why men should be broken by a vove-mounted clansmen's charge was in itself ludicrous; but Nath was enormously jealous of the reputation and prowess of his Phalanx. And, of course, now that they had won so convincingly, nothing would change their minds and they remained convinced that the Phalanx and the Hakkodin could best any fighting force in the world.

The men of the Phalanx might be convinced; I still did not share that conviction.

But there was no reasoning with Nath.

As we rode through the busy streets where the people gave us a cheer and then got on with their tasks, the grim men of the Emperor's Sword Watch surrounded us. No need for their swords to be unsheathed against the people of Vondium. The ever-present threat of assassination had receded; but there were foemen in Kregen who would willingly pay red gold to see me dead.

As I have remarked, that sentiment was returned.

We all congregated in the Sapphire Reception Room where fragrant Kregan tea and sweets were served. For those who needed further sustenance, the second breakfast was provided. I looked at Kyr Nath Nazabhan.

His father, Nazab Nalgre na Therminsax, was an imperial justicar, the governor of a province, and Nath took his name from his father. I felt it opportune to improve on that, not in any denial of filial respect but out of approval and recognition of Nath's own qualities, of his service and achievements.

When I broached the subject he looked glum.

"Truth to tell, majister, I have become used to being called Nazabhan—"

"But a man cannot live on his father's name."

"True, but—"

"Our son Drak," said Delia, radiant in a long gown, her hair sheening in the early radiance. "Before he went off to Havilfar—"

What Delia would have said was lost, for the doors opened and Garfon the Staff, that major-domo whose arrow wound in the heel still produced a little limp, banged his gold-bound balass staff upon the marble floor. They relish that, do these major-domos and chamberlains. He produced a sudden silence with his clackety-clack.

Then he bellowed.

"Vodun Alloran, Kov of Kaldi!"

More than one person present in the Sapphire Reception Room gasped. It was easy to understand why. The kovnate of Kaldi, a lozenge-shaped province in the extreme southwest of the island, had long been cut off from communication with the capital and the lands hewing to the old Vallian inheritance. Down there Phu-Si-Yantong's minions held sway.

It was in Kaldi that the invading armies from Pandahem and Hamal had landed.

The stir in the room brought a bright flush to the kov's face as he marched sturdily across the floor. I did not fail to notice the discreet little group of the Sword Watch who escorted him and his entourage. A tenseness persisted there, a feeling of waiting passions, ready to break out. I placed my cup on the table and composed my face.

Naghan ti Lodkwara, Targon the Tapster and Cleitar the Standard happened to be the officers of the Sword Watch on duty that day. Their scarlet and yellow blazed in the room as they wheeled their men up. The men and women with the Kov of Kaldi kept together. They looked lost, not so much bewildered and bedraggled as approaching those states and not much caring for the experience. They must have gone through some highly unpleasant times, getting out of Kaldi.

"Majister!" burst out this Kov Vodun, and he went into the full incline, prostrating himself on the rugs of the marble floor.

"Get up, kov," I said, displeased. "We no longer admit of that flummery here in Vondium in these latter days."

Before he rose he turned his face up and looked at me.

A man of middle years, with a shrewd, weatherbeaten face in which those brown Vallian eyes were partially hidden by heavy, down-drooping lids, he was a man with depths to his being, a man of gravitas. His clothes were of first quality, being the usual buff Vallian coat and breeches with the tall black boots. His broad-brimmed hat with those two slots cut in the front brim he held in his left hand. He stood up.

He, naturally, wore no weapons. My Sword Watch would not tolerate strangers, even if they claimed to be kovs, the Kregan equivalent to dukes, carrying weapons into the presence of the Emperor and Empress of Vallia. That was a new and unwelcome custom, over which I had sighed and allowed, for as you will know we in Vallia are more used to carrying our weapons as a sign of our independence. But times change. Weapons were a part and parcel of life, now, and we would soon be back to the old days, I hoped.

Kov Vodun's retainers wore banded sleeves in maroon and gray, the colors of Kaldi. Their badges, sewn in drawn wire and in sculpted gold for the kov, represented a leaping sea-barynth, that long and sinuous sea monster of Kregen. I looked closely, for by the colors and badges a man wears may he be recognized again.

You can, also, tell his allegiances. There were no other colors—no black and white of the racters, for example—and from what I knew of Kaldi I believed the province to be out of the main stream of power politics. There were many provinces of the old Vallia whose hierarchy preferred to keep aloof from intrigues.

I considered. Then: "Lahal, Kov Vodun. You are welcome."

He did not smile; but a muscle jumped in his cheek.

"Lahal, majister. I praise Opaz the All Glorious I have arrived safely."

As you will see, I had cut through the Llahals straight to the Lahals. A small point; but I fancied this man needed encouragement.

"You will take refreshment?" I indicated the loaded tables and, instantly, a cup if tea was brought forward, for it was far too early for wine. "There is parclear and sazz if you would prefer."

"Tea, majister, and I thank you. Those devils from Pandahem drain the country dry. We are fortunate to be alive."

He was laboring under some powerful emotion that made the cup shake upon the saucer. I assumed what he had gone through had left an indelible mark. He told me his father, the old kov, had been slain by the enemies of Vallia, and that all the country down there was firmly in the hands of Rosil Yasi, the Strom of Morcray. At this name I sucked in my breath. I knew that rast of old. A Kataki, one of that whiptailed race who are slavemasters par excellence, the Kataki Strom and I were old antagonists and I knew him as a man who bore me undying enmity. He was, also, a tool of Phu-Si-Yantong's, and he had worked in his time for Vad Garnath of Hamal, a man who had his come-uppance waiting for him if ever we met again.

His retainers were taken care of and the other people in the Sapphire Reception Room were soon engaged in general conversation with him, trying to learn all there was to know of the situation. News, as always, was eagerly sought after.

Introductions were made as necessary and when the cordialities had been completed and he had described graphically how he and his people had fought from the hills until all their supplies had gone, and they were ragged and starving, so that they had at last stolen an airboat and made good their escape, Nath Nazabhan drew me privily aside.

Seeing that Nath had something he wished to get off his chest I moved quietly with him to a curtained alcove. I had been watching one of Kov Vodun's people with a puzzled interest. This man—if it was a man, for in the enveloping green cloak and hood the figure could as easily have been a woman—moved with a slow stately upright stance. He (or she) carried his (or her) hands thrust deeply into the wide sleeves of the robe, crossed upon the chest. The waist was cinctured by a narrow golden chain from which the lockets for rapier and dagger swung emptily. There was merely black shadow within the hood, and a fugitive gleam of eye.

Upon the breast of the swathing green cloak, and very small, appeared the maroon and gray and the leaping Sea-Barynth. So I turned away, guessing this personage to be an adviser to Kov Vodun. If he (or she) turned out to be a Kataki in disguise, or some other evil-minded rast, my people would soon find out.

Nath said: "I suppose he is genuine? I mean, the real kov? He could be a spy, still working for Yantong."

"He could be genuine and the real kov and still be working for Yantong."

"By Vox, yes!"

One of the clever tricks an emperor has to know how to perform is judging character. So many people judge character by a person's relations with society or established social orders; to perform the difficult task properly you have to judge if a person is being true to his own basic beliefs. This is fundamental. What goes even beyond that, penetrating into the unknown depths beyond the fundament—if, truly, that be possible—is to judge not only a person's adherence to his own beliefs and therefore his own qualities of character; but to judge if those beliefs match up to what you yourself believe. If the two square—fine. If they do not—beware!

A part of the puzzle was solved for us almost at once. The least important part, to be sure.

A Jiktar walked across the Kov Vodun and he moved a little diffidently, I thought. He wore a smart uniform of sky-blue tunic and madder-red breeches, and because he was Nath Orcantor, known as Nath the Frolus, and a well-liked regimental commander, he wore his rapier and main gauche as a matter of uniform dress.

He had raised a regiment of totrixmen for the defense of Vondium, and because he was from Ovvend he had insisted on clothing his regiment in blue tunics and red breeches, a combination unusual for Vallia. Now he halted before the kov and was introduced by Chuktar Ty-Je Efervon, a wily Pachak who was Nath the Frolus's Brigade commander.

"Orcantor," said Kov Vodun. "Of course. Your family is well known in Ovvend—shipping, I think."

"That is so, kov. And I remember you when you visited Ovvend with your father. I am saddened at his loss, for he was a fine man and a great kov."

"His death shall be avenged," said Vodun, and he spoke between his teeth. All who watched him saw the flash of insensate rage. "I shall not rest until the devils are brought to justice." His left hand dropped to his belt and groped, and found no familiar rapier hilt. But we all understood the message. Justice, from Vodun Aloran, the Kov of Kaldi, would be meted out with the sword.

"So he is the real kov," said Nath.

"It would seem so. I think it is high time Naghan Vanki earned his hire." Naghan Vanki had come in from his estates and was prepared to resume his position as the emperor's chief spy-master. We had crossed swords in the past, and come to rapprochements. Now, with Delia to smooth the way, Naghan Vanki, Vad of Nav-Sorfall, was prepared to work with me. "He must sniff out all he can of this Kov Vodun."

"Agreed. Vodun has a way with him, a presence. The ladies are quite smitten."

And, by Krun, that was true, for the ladies were clustered around Kov Vodun now and were hanging on his words. Vodun had a story to tell, of hair-breadth escapes and disguises and swift flights in the lights of the Moons of Kregen. That flash of rage we had seen in him had struck like a lightning bolt, and had as quickly vanished. But Vodun would not rest until his father had been avenged.

"Well, Nath, I cannot shilly-shally about like this all days. I have a new flour mill to inspect, and then, I fancy you may feel it incumbent on me to take a look at the Second. Is this in your mind?"

He laughed.

"They are in good heart, now. It is only miserable skulking sorts of formations that do not relish showing off for their emperor."

We had barely touched on that awful moment when the Second had recoiled. They had broken at the junction of Kerchuri and Kerchuri, the two wings of the Phalanx. They had been forced back on their rear ranks, a seething sea of bronze and crimson and many of the pikes had gone up. A pikeman whose pike stabs air is of little use in the front ranks. But the Third's Sixth Kerchuri had swung up and held the torrent of voves, and the Second had closed up, reformed, and held.

That, as I pointed out to Nath, was the achievement.

After the break, they had taken a fresh grasp on courage, had breathed in, and then smashed back, file by file, and the pikes had come down all in line, and they had driven the clansmen recoiling back.

"There are many bobs to be distributed, majister."

"We shall make of the ceremony something special." The men had earned their medals, and if they called them bobs in fine free-and-easy fashion, they valued them nonetheless.

Making my excuses to the company—which had thinned now as the people went about their work—I slipped away without ceremony. The Sword Watch were there. Delia gave me a smile and I said: "I must talk to you this evening, my heart." Whereat her face grew grave and she understood that I did not talk thus lightly. But I went out and mounted up on a fine fresh zorca, Grumbleknees, a gray, and took myself off to the flour mill.

The original mill had burned in the Time of Troubles and the new structure incorporated refinements the wise men said would increase production as well as milling a finer flour.

If I do not dwell on this flour mill it is precisely because this inspection was typical of so many that had to be undertaken. Everyone wanted to shine in the sight of the emperor, and although I could, had I wished, regard that as petty crawling lick-spittling behavior, I did not. We all worked for Vondium and for Vallia and my job was to make sure we all did the best we could.

The streaming mingled lights of the Suns of Scorpio flooded down as the waterwheel groaned and heaved and turned over as the sluicegates opened and the white water poured through. I looked up. Feeding the people would be by the measure of this mill that much easier. So I looked up and with a hissing thud a long Lohvian arrow sprouted abruptly from the wood, a hand's breadth from my head.

CHAPTER THREE

Of a Meeting with Nath the Knife, Aleygyn of the Stikitches

"Hold fast!" My bellow ripped into the air. The bows of the Sword Watch, lifted, arrows nocked, drawn back, poised. Those sinewy fingers did not release the pull on the bow-strings by a fraction.

"There he goes!" shouted Cleitar, furious.

We could all see the bowman who had loosed at me clambering up the outside staircase of a half-ruined building across the canal. He wore a drab gray half-cape, and his legs were bare. He carried the long Lohvian bow in his left hand, and the quiver over his shoulder was stuffed with shafts. Like the arrow that still quivered in the wood by my head, each one was fletched with feathers of somber purple.

"A damned stikitche!" raved Cleitar. "Majister—you allow him to escape. Let us—"

"Lower your bows."

The archers in the detachment of the Sword Watch obeyed.

Targon the Tapster, his face scowling, his brilliance of uniform which lent him, like them all, a barbaric magnificence, aflame under the suns, heeled his zorca across.

"Assassins, majister. They should be put down—"

These officers of the Sword Watch had not always been fighting men. I think it true to say their military experience had all been gained in contact with me. We had fought together in clearing Vallia. Cleitar the Standard, a big bulky man with bitterness in his soul, had been Cleitar the Smith until the Iron Riders had sundered him forever from his family and home. Targon the Tapster and Naghan ti Lodkwara had met over the matter of strayed or stolen ponshos. Now they formed a body of close comrades I came to value more and more as the seasons and the campaigns passed over.

"You are right. But that stikitche, had he wished to assassinate me, would not have missed. Bring me the shaft."

The arrow was brought and I unwrapped the letter attached.

The message was addressed: "Dray Prescot, Emperor of Vallia." The salutation, in the correct grammatical form, read: "Llahal-pattu. Majister."

I sighed and looked quickly down for the signature.

The scrawl, in a different hand from the body of the letter, was just decipherable. It read: "Nath Trerhagen, Aleygyn."

This assassin and I had met before, just the once. He was Nath Trerhagen, the Aleygyn, Hyr Stikitche, Pallan of the Stikitche Khand of Vondium.

This brought up painful memories of Barty Vessler and so looking at the writing I forced unwelcome thoughts away and concentrated on the here and now. Nath the Knife, the chief assassin was called. He wanted to meet me. There was an important matter that had come up. The phraseology was all in the mock legal, written by his pet lawyer he kept tucked up in some lair in Drak's City, the Old City of Vondium, where, so far, the writ of the emperor's law did not run.

"We should go in there and burn the place out," quoth Larghos Manifer, a Vondian who had been newly recruited into the Sword Watch. His round face fairly bristled. His words met with general approval.

"Yet the people of Drak's City held out the longest against the damned Hamalese," I pointed out.

"They could fight all the imps of Sicce from there, majister." Larghos Manifer, because he had been born in Vondium the Proud City, and knew what he knew, held a natural resentment against Drak's City. "For one who is not a thief or a forger or a stikitche or an Opaz-forsaken criminal of one kind or another it is death to venture in."

"Nath the Knife wishes to meet me in the shadow of the Gate of Skulls. That, I think, indicates a willingness to come forward. We are, in theory, on neutral ground there."

So, later on that morning and before we were due to return to eat, we wended our way through the crowded streets toward the mouldering pile of old houses clustered behind the old walls that was the site of the very first settlements here, long before Vondium became the capital of Vallia.

Targon, Naghan and Cleitar sidled their zorcas close to one another and after a brief conversation, Naghan went haring off. I had a shrewd suspicion about where he was going and what he was up to, and when we rode quietly up to the Gate of Skulls my guess was confirmed.

The usual hectic activity around and through the gate was stilled. The striped awnings over stalls had been taken down. People kept away. The space this side of the gate and the Kyro of Lost Souls beyond were deserted. In a double line ranked two hundred paces back from the gate waited the Sword Watch. This was the handiwork of Naghan and the others. Bowman and lancer alternating, the men sat their zorcas silently. The scarlet and yellow, the gleaming helmets, the feathers, the brilliance of weapons, all made a fine show. I rather fancied Nath the Knife might have a similar if less splendidly outfitted array on his side of the wall.

And—he had Bowmen of Loh among his scurvy lot. My men were armed with the compound reflex bow of Vallia, a flat trajectory weapon of great power but not a patch on the great Lohvian longbow.

As a matter of interest as I waited for the chief assassin I made a cursory count of the Sword Watch. I was astonished. There were better than five hundred of them. This was news to me. The rascally members of my original Choice Band, with whom I had campaigned and caroused and fought over Vallia, had been busy recruiting. Well, that could be looked into. Now, Nath the Knife made his presence known.

Four hefty fellows walked into the shadows under the Gate of Skulls carrying a heavy lenken table. This they placed down at the midway point between the inner and outer portals. They were followed by four more who carried a carved chair of fascinating design, a chair that breathed authority, a chair that, by Krun, was as like a throne as made no difference.

In the shadows beyond table and chair waited a line of men, indistinct, true; but the long jut of the bows in their fists was not to be mistaken. A bugle pealed.

"They make a mockery of it, majister," growled Cleitar. He gripped the pole of my personal flag, Old Superb, and he scowled upon the Gate of Skulls. On my other side Ortyg the Tresh upheld the new union flag of Vallia. Close to hand Volodu the Lungs, leathery and thirsty, waited with his silver trumpet resting on his knee. At my back, as always, rode Korero the Shield, that splendid Kildoi with the four arms and tailhand, his golden beard glinting in the light of the suns, his white teeth just visible as his half-smile at the panorama before us matched my own feelings.

The Sword Watch had been reorganized. Now they were clearly arranged in order, the companies each with its own trumpeter and standard and commander. Those commanders I recognized from many a long day's campaigning. The small body of men who had themselves appointed themselves as my personal bodyguard—which at the time I had deplored but acceded to at the sense of urgency these men shared—waited close. There were Magin, Wando the Squint, Uthnior Chavonthjid, Nath the Doorn and his boon comrade Nath the Xanko. There were, of course, Targon the Tapster, Naghan ti Lodkwara and Dorgo the Clis, his scar livid along his face.

As we waited for the ponderous arrival of Nath the Knife, Hyr Stikitche, what intrigued me was the apparent lack of a leader of the Sword Watch. Clearly those men I have named ran things. When they gave an order the zorcamen jumped. And they appeared to work together, with a consensus, each one supporting the next. I hoped that state of affairs resulted from the time we had spent campaigning together. There was no mistaking the smooth way things got done in the Emperor's Sword Watch.

The strange fancy struck me, as we sat our zorcas and waited, that we were arrayed as we would be when we waited in battle for the outcome, so as to go hurtling down to defeat or victory. With the flags waving in the slight breeze, with the trumpets ready to peal the calls, with the weapons bright and our uniforms immaculate, we looked just as we looked in battle. We were the emperor's personal reserve, a powerful striking force under his hand. I may say it was most odd, by Vox, to remember that I was that emperor.

Just as a stir made itself apparent in the shadows of the Gate of Skulls I was thinking that the quicker Drak got home from Faol the better.

Alone, walking steadily and without haste, Nath Trerhagen, the Aleygyn, made his way to the table and passed around it and so sat himself down in that throne-like chair.

I smiled.

"The impudent rast!" said Cleitar.

"It is clear," offered Naghan ti Lodkwara. "He will sit. And there is no chair for you, majister."

"Let me shaft the wretch!" suggested Dorgo the Clis.

He would have done so, instanter. But I nodded to the line of bowmen in the shadows.

"They are Bowmen of Loh. Each one would feather four of you before you could reach them. Hold fast!"

I rode out a half a dozen paces before my men and turned and lifted in the stirrups and faced them.

"I ride alone. Not one of you moves. My life is forfeit." Then, to ram the order home, I said quietly to Volodu the Lungs, "Blow the Stand, Volodu."

The silver trumpet with the significant dents was raised to those leathery lips.

Grumbleknees turned again and walked sedately across the open dusty space toward the Gate of Skulls. His single spiral horn caught the mingled light of the suns and glittered.

So it was and all unplanned, that the Emperor of Vallia rode toward this meeting with the pealing silver trumpet notes playing about his ears.

The villains of Drak's City would not know what the call portended. They would probably think it was some kind of pompous fanfare that was sounded whenever the emperor rode out or did anything at all or even wished to blow his nose. I rode on, and I felt the amusement strong in me at the conceit.

There was one thing of which I was pretty sure. I was not going to stand up while this stikitche lolled on his throne.

"By the Black Chunkrah!" I said to myself. "Nath the Knife must think again."

No personal vanity was involved. This was a matter of policy and, of course, of will.

Nath the Knife wore ordinary Vallian clothes, that is to say, the buff tunic, breeches and tall black boots. On his breast the badge of the three purple feather was pinned with a golden clasp. His face was covered by a dulled steel mask. When he spoke his voice was like breaking iron.

"Majister."

I looked down on him from the back of the zorca. I debated. Then, carefully, I said, "Aleygyn."

The steel mask moved as he nodded, as though under the steel he smiled, satisfied.

"Dismount, emperor, so that we may talk."

"You might have killed me before this. I do not think you wish to talk without reason. Spit it out, Nath the Knife. There is much work to be done in Vondium these days."

He sat up straighter. The power he wielded within the Old City was commensurate with the power I wielded in Vondium.

"There is a matter of bokkertu to be decided."

"Once before you said that. You asked me to pay you gold so that I would not be a kitchew." A kitchew, the target for assassination, usually has a very brief allotment left of life. But that matter had been settled with the death of the stikitche paid to do the job. That, I had thought, was finalized.

Nath the Knife moved his hand. "No. It is not that." He paused. There was about him a strange air of indecisiveness and I wished I could see his face beneath the mask so as to weigh him up better. "No. We had a bad time of it when those rasts of Hamalese captured Vondium."

I said, "I heard how you held out in Drak's City. You deserve congratulations for that. It has been in my mind to offer you masons and brickies, carpenters, so that you may rebuild and clean away some of the destruction."

His head went up. "You are serious?"

It is damned hard to read a man wearing a mask.

"Yes. Perfectly serious."

There seemed little point in adding that I wanted some of the mess in Drak's City cleared up so as to lessen the risk of infection to the rest of the City. They policed themselves in the Old City; but I did not think they were too well-served by needlemen and once an epidemic got hold we would all be in trouble.

"You are not as other emperors—"

"No, by Vox!"

"And would you find men willing to enter here? Would not their tools be stolen, their throats cut?"

"Under proper safeguards and assurances, men would come in here and rebuild."

"Because you told them to?"

I wondered what he was getting at.

"Not because I told them to. Because they understand the reasons. Anyway, I would pay them—pay them well—for the work will not be pleasant."

"I think, Dray Prescot, they would do it for you."

"They are not slaves. We do not have slaves anymore."

Sitting the zorca, feeling the old itch down my back, darkly aware of that line of bowmen, I was all the time ready to get my foolish head down and make a run for it. But the trick of remaining mounted had given me just a little back of a hold on the situation. Nath the Knife waved his hand again. He wore gauntleted leather gloves; but a ring glowed in ronil fire upon his finger outside the glove.

He came straight to the point, now, putting it to me.

"We have received a contract for you, emperor. Do not ask from whom, for that is our affair, in honor. I run perilously close to breaking the stikitche honor in this. But we stikitches remember the Hamalese and the aragorn and the flutsmen. We were cruelly oppressed. We rose when you and your armies broke into the city. Aye! We of Drak's City hung many a damned Hamalese by his heels. We have seen what you have wrought in Vondium." He pushed a paper that lay on the table. "The contract calls for immediate execution and the price is exceedingly large."

I took a breath.

"And you wish me to pay you the price?"

Before he could answer, I went on: "You will recall what I told you when that was mentioned before—"

"No, emperor! By Jhalak! I know you to be a stiff-necked tapo; but will you not listen?"

I nodded and he went on speaking, and, I thought with a twinge of amusement, a little huffily. It seemed he could hardly understand just what he was saying, or why he was doing what he did. But he ploughed on, natheless.

The gist of it was that the folk of Drak's City felt it would be to their advantage if I was alive and running Vondium. In this I fancied they did not put a great deal of store by the considerable army now at the disposal of the government. Their confidence in their own tumbledown city had been shaken by their defeat and enslavement by the Hamalese. What the chief assassin told me, quite simply, was that they intended to repudiate the contract, they would not accept it, and they wanted me to know. But—

"There is a chance that the client will bring in stikitches from outside Vondium. We frown on that; but it is known. I assure you, emperor, on the honor of a Hyr-Stikitche, that we will prevent that if it is in our power."

What was odd about that was the talk of assassins' honor, which is just as real to them as any form of honor code to any other group of people; but the suggestion that in stikitche matters the khand of Vondium might not have the power to do what it willed.

"You have my thanks, Aleygyn. Vallia is sundered and torn, and our enemies press in on us from all sides. I think it is a task laid on all of us to resume peaceful ways. But that will not be possible until these invaders have been driven away—"

He did not so much surprise me as reveal that he, too, was a Vallian.

"Until they are all buried six feet deep and sent to rot in the Ice Floes of Sicce!"

"Agreed." I chanced a shaft. "There are many fine young

men in Drak's City, men who have proved they can fight. They would be welcomed in the ranks of the new Vallian Army."

The eyes within the slits of the mask glittered on me. The suns were shifting around and that mingled opaz radiance crept under the arch of the Gate and drove back the shadows.

"I will talk to the Presidio," he said, whereat I smiled. The folk of Drat's City aped Vondium and the whole of Vallia in holding their own Presidio, their governing body. It was a charming conceit. "There are men here who would form regiments that would show you soft townsfolk how to fight."

"I await them in the ranks."

"Not," he said, a tang in his voice, "in the Phalanx."

"No, I agree. As light infantry, skirmishers."

"We have paktuns here—"

"I do not employ mercenaries. Many paktuns have become Vallian citizens. We are a people's army. You are Vallians. Your young men will be paid the same as any other Vallians in our ranks."

He digested that. And then we spoke of the practical side of the matter for a time until I felt I was getting altogether too chummy with a damned assassin, even if he was mindful of the welfare of the country. I twitched Grumbleknee's reins.

"I bid you Remberee, Aleygyn. I shall send a Pallan to talk with you about the rebuilding I promised. I am serious. As serious as I hope you are in sending men to join the army. The quicker Vallia is back to her old peaceful ways the better. Remberee."

"Remberee, Dray Prescot."

But the old warrior did not stand up to say good-bye.

CHAPTER FOUR

Delia Thinks Ahead

"And you really had a long conversation with a stikitche! My heart—suppose—"

"But it didn't."

"All the same, you are just as feckless as ever you were. I wish Seg and Inch were here—"

"They're just as bad."

"True." She sighed and then laughed. "You're all as bad as one another, a pack of rascals and rogues!"

"There is a matter I must talk to you about and yet have not the courage to—"

"Dray! Oh—my dear. You are going away again!"

I nodded.

"Back to your silly little world with its one yellow sun and one silver moon and no diffs?"

"By Zim-Zair! I hope not!"

I told her a little of what had passed between me and the Star Lords, and then added: "And it is mighty fine of them to warn me. They do not often do that. But, my heart, rest assured. As soon as whatever must be done is done I shall fly back here just as fast as I can."

"You make it all sound so—so—"

"I know."

The warm gleam of the oil lamps shed a cozy glow in our snug and private little room. We had both spent a busy day. We were surrounded now by the good things of gracious living, or as many of them as our straightened circumstances would allow, and we relished this time when we could relax and talk of the doings of the day and of our plans for the morrow. To change the conversation, I said: "What do you make of Vodun Alloran, the Kov of Kaldi?"

Delia made a sweet little moue and tucked her feet up more comfortably on the divan. She wore a lounging robe, as did I, and we joyed one in the other. "Well, he is bright and forthright and, I am sure, a fine fighting man. What he is like as a kov I do not know. But, somehow, I must have more time to plumb him properly."

I glanced at her. Delia usually knows her own mind.

"He strikes me as a useful man to have in the army. He will fight like a leem to get his kovnate back."

"I am sure. He is a fighter, of that there is no doubt."

Again, I sensed that deliberate withdrawal.

"I am minded to give him command of a brigade—as a kov he will never accept less. It is a pity he has no men of his own to form a regiment. But with the expansion promotion will prove no problem." I yawned. "I'll be glad when we can finish with all this fighting and get back to decent living again."

"So, Dray Prescot, you imagine you are well acquainted with decent living?"

She teased me; but it stung. I had been a wanderer, a soldier, a sailor, an airman, a fellow who struggled and fought and brawled until, it seemed, he could not possibly understand that life was not meant to be lived thus. But, the knotty problem there was, quite simply, that all this took place on Kregen. What a world Kregen is, by Zair! Wonderful, unutterably lovely, unspeakably ghastly, at times it is all things to all men. And yet I would not willingly be parted from that world four hundred light years from the planet of my birth or from the woman who meant more than anything else. I had been a slave and now I was an emperor—well, an emperor of sorts.

"The quicker—" I began.

"Yes. I have had word from Drak. Queen Lush is bringing him home."

I gaped.

Then: "Drak? Queen Lush—bringing him?"

"He is not hurt," she said, quickly. "Well, not much. He has rescued Melow and Kardo. The message simply says that we should expect them." Her eyebrows drew down. "Queen Lush is—well—"

"Queen Lush is Queen Lush," I said. "She has changed wonderfully from what she was when Phu-Si-Yantong sent her to entrap your father. Then she did as she was told, for all she was a queen with great wealth and power—"

"And beauty."

"Oh, aye, she looks well, does Queen Lush. And Drak?"

"There is no doubt, at least in my mind. Queen Lush means to marry Drak."

"She set her heart on being Empress of Vallia. Well, it seems she will have her way, seeing she knows very well that I shall hand over to Drak. She has heard me say so often enough."

"Mayhap you do her an injustice."

"I would like to think so. Yes, perhaps I do. I know she was much taken with Drak. Well—any girl with any sense would be. And that brings up Seg's daughter, Silda."

"I like Silda."

"That settles that, then. When she went against Thelda's wishes and joined in the Sisters of the Rose—"

"Hush."

But I had already hushed myself. One did not speak lightly of these female secret Orders. And, too, mention of Seg and Thelda brought up a sharp agony I just could not face then. So I went on: "Silda is a charming girl and I would welcome her as a daughter-in-law. And Seg would be overjoyed. But—what says Drak in all this?"

"I think," said the Empress of Vallia. "You would have to ask Queen Lushfymi of Lome the answer to that."

We did not play Jikaida that night, for there was a mountain of paperwork Enevon Ob-Eye, the chief stylor, had landed us with. With the morning and a new day in which to work we set doggedly to that work. Rebuilding and healing a shattered city and people demand strenuous and unending efforts. All the time I felt the relief that Drak was safe. He was the stern and sober one of my sons, and yet he could be wild enough on occasion. He had taken over in Valka, as the strom, when I had been snatched back to Earth. He had known me when he had been young, unlike his brothers, for Zeg had been rather too young, and Jaidur had not known me at all. But these were not the reasons I felt he would prove to be a splendid emperor. It seemed to me that he had been born to the imperium. I was just a rough-hewn sailor from a distant planet, schooled by the wildly ferocious clansmen of Segesthes, picking up bits of lore and scraps of knowledge from here and there on Kregen. But Drak was an emperor to his fingertips. I confess I joyed in that.

Mind you, I did not forget that I was the King of Djanduin. But Djanduin was dwaburs away in Havilfar, and my friends could run affairs there perfectly. The moment I could snatch the time from Vallia, it would be Djanduin for me. Even, perhaps, before Strombor. As the Lord of Strombor I reposed absolute faith and confidence in Gloag, who was a good comrade and the one handling everything there. That I had some still remaining links with Hamal, the hated enemy of Vallia, remained true. I was, in Hamal, Hamun ham Farthytu, the Amak of Paline Valley. Nulty was the one in charge there. But that seemed to me distant and vague and blurred; one day I would return to Paline Valley. As Hamun ham Farthytu I would seek out my good comrades, Rees and Chido. Good comrades, and also Hamalese and therefore foemen to Vallians.

What a nonsense all that was!

The plans I hoped to see come to fruition demanded that Vallia and Hamal join hands in friendship, and with the nations of the island of Pandahem begin to form that grand alliance we must forge so as to combat the vicious shanks who raided from over the curve of the world. All these things went around in my head, continually as we worked on the immediate problems of clearing Vallia of her invaders.

The news from Seg reaffirmed his skill in keeping the clansmen off our necks until we were able to defeat them once and for all. Patrols of observation in the southwest reported little movement from the invaders there; but that part of the island had been under the heel of foreign lords with their mercenaries for long enough for us to watch and ward the borders and build our strength for the counterstroke.

The Presidio now met regularly in the sumptuous Villa of Vennar, situated on one of the exclusive hills of Vondium. The place had been abandoned since its lord, Kov Layco Jhansi, had proved himself a double dyed villain and a traitor. The deren* of the Presidio had been burned to the ground. We would not waste resources on rebuilding that, not until Vallia was free, and particularly when there were abandoned villas with enormous chambers suitable for the purposes of the Presidio lying empty.

In the Presidio Kov Vodun na Kaldi proved a volatile and persuasive speaker. Constantly he sought to encourage us to action. His hatred for the Hamalese and the Pandaheem was implacable. With his reiterated calls for the utter destruction of the invaders he reminded me of Cato and his never-ending *Carthago delenda est.*

Various conversations with him from time to time revealed him as a man with a history. Fretful at being the son of a kov who might have to wait years before he came into the title, the lands and power, and the responsibility, he went abroad and became a mercenary. Because Vallia had not

* deren: palace

kept a standing army, being mainly a trading maritime nation, many of her young men took themselves overseas to become mercenaries. Many had become famous paktuns. Kov Vodun was one such, entitled to wear the pakmort, the silver mortil-head on its silk cord at his throat. He did not wear it at home for, as he said, that would be too flamboyant.

So, he did understand something of soldiering.

He mentioned various places in Loh, where most of his service had been spent, and, as I summed him up, he grew in my estimation. We needed men like this, tough, no-nonsense professionals to put the polish on the crowds of eager but raw recruits who flocked to the standards.

When I offered him a brigade, somewhat diffidently, I must admit, expecting him to refuse, he accepted.

"Give me the brigade, majister. You will soon see my men will form the best brigade in the army."

The appointment was warmly endorsed by the Presidio.

Thinking myself foolish for offering a command to a man half expecting him to refuse—a very poor way of going on—I wondered if Delia's attitude had contributed to that feeling of inexplicable hesitancy. Naghan Vanki, the emperor's chief spymaster, reported that everything Kov Vodun had said was true. Vanki gave him a clean bill of health, and my spirits lifted at that. Asked about the mysterious green-cloaked figure, Vanki gave his thin smile.

"He is merely an adviser to the kov, majister. He is one of the Wizards of Fruningen, a small sect but with some claim to serious consideration. They regard Opaz, I am told, as a single entity and not, as indeed they truly are, the Invisible Twins, one and indissolubly twins."

I raised my eyebrows at this, for Vanki expressed an extreme view. Most people regarded Opaz as the spirit of the Invisible Twins made manifest. And I knew of the island of Fruningen, a small rocky scrap jutting out of the sea northwest of the island of Tezpor. Reports, amplified by Kov Vodun, told us that the Vad of Tezpor, Larghos the Lame, had been hanged upside down from his own rooftree by flutsmen. And, Tezpor lay due north of the large island of Rahartdrin. There was nothing simple I could do for Katrin Rashumin save pray to all the gods she was safe.

"So far I have not met a Wizard of Fruningen," I said to Naghan Vanki. "They are clearly not to be compared to the Wizards of Loh." At this Vanki let his thin smile indicate the idiocy of the remark. I went on: "But how stand they in relation to the Sorcerers of Murcroinim?"

"If one were to engage the other in wizardly combat, Majister, I fear they would both disappear in puffs of smoke."

"At least that argues real powers."

"Yes."

Naghan Vanki had dealt with a few real powers in his time, powers of steel and gold; I did not think a sorcerer would discompose him overmuch. A tough, wily old bird, Naghan Vanki, always impeccable in his silver and black.

So Kov Vodun got his brigade and began smartening them up and putting a snap in their step and iron into their backbones.

Then, although it spelled misery and desolation for the unfortunate people involved, an event occurred which gave me a capital opportunity to delegate responsibilities in Vondium to the Crebent-Justicar, the Lord Farris, and the Presidio, and take off for action.

"So you are off again, then, husband," said Delia as I strapped on my harness in our rooms and wondered just what selection of weaponry to take. "This time I think I shall go with you, for the folk of Bryvondrin have suffered much and yet they have taken in and cared for the people of the occupied provinces east of the Great River. And they are our people."

What she meant was plain. Bryvondrin, situated in one of the tremendous loops of the Great River, the enormous central waterway of Vallia, was an imperial province.

"True. But what concerns me is that the enemy have got over the Great River. We regarded that as a first-class natural barrier. And, my heart, it is only seventy dwaburs away from Vondium."

"Too close for comfort."

"But that does not mean you will fly with me—"

"You would prevent me?"

I sighed.

"I would if I thought it would do any good. You know how I joy to have you wth me—but if there, rather, as there is to be fighting—"

"Fighting!"

I felt suitably chastened. Truly, Delia of Delphond has served in her quota of battles, to my own dread despair.

Her handmaidens, Floria and Rosala came in all chattering and laughing, rosy, gorgeous girls, They brought stands of clothing over which, I felt sure, they would all giggle and try against themselves and spend hours deciding exactly what to wear.

Aghast, I said: "You are not bringing them?"

"Are you taking Emder?"

"Well—to be honest, no."

"Then it will as it was in the old days."

So that was decided. As usual, the decision seemed to have arrived of its own accord.

Naghan Vanki reported that the invasion over the Great River was not in overmuch force. His spies had the composition confirmed by cavalry patrols from our small forces there.

There were some fifteen thousand fighting men, ten of infantry and five of cavalry, mainly totrixes with some zorcas. These men were formed and disciplined, professional mercenaries and although they were not in great force they were formidable. Their object, as I saw it, was to create a secure bridgehead for their further encroachments on our country. Certainly, they held all the land from the Great River to the east coast.

"We must fly out in sufficient force to make very sure of the victory," I told my assembled chiefs when, dressed in war harness and with Delia at my side, I rode out to see the army off. We were constrained to leave strong forces in Vondium, for obvious reasons, and I had had to pick and choose the units to go. Everyone wanted to be in on the act, and there were some long faces decorating those hardy warriors I had to leave behind.

Firstly, the Phalanx. Nath insisted on accompanying me and he would bring the Third Kerchuri of the Second Phalanx. With footsoldiers, Hakkodin and the attached archers, the Third Kerchuri amounted to some eight thousand men.

Secondly, three brigades of infantry, the sword and shield men. One of the brigades, the Nineteenth, was that commanded by Kov Vodun. These three brigades amounted to some four thousand five hundred men.

Thirdly, two brigades of archers, around three thousand.

And, fourthly, a brigade of the skirmishers.

That formed the infantry corps, and a fine body they looked as they marched out with a swing to board the sailing fliers. The weird constructions, more flying rafts, we had been forced to use before had now given place, with the time and the rebuilding program, to more sensible flying ships. These possessed hulls with real wooden walls, so that the men would have shelter during the flight. Their sail plan was deliberately kept simple, a fore, main and mizzen with jib and headsails. We rigged courses and topsails, not caring to go further into the fascinating ramifications of the typical Vallian galleon's sail plan. They would fly, and with their silver boxes upholding them in thin air and extending invisible keels into the lines of ethero-magnetic force, they could tack and make boards against the wind. They were sailing ships of the sky, and subject to the vagaries of the weather, quite unlike the vollers of the Hamalese.

For cavalry we took a division of totrix archers and lancers, just over two thousand jutmen, attached to the Phalanx. One division of totrix heavy cavalry, two thousand strong, and one division of zorcas, two thousand one hundred and sixty in number, were joined by a regiment of the superb heavy nikvove cavalry, five hundred big men on five hundred great-hearted nikvoves.

Our tail consisted of engineers, supply wagons, medical and veterinary components, and a goodly force of varters.

Also, I took the whole of the Sword Watch, leaving merely a small cadre at my officer's pleas to carry on with their program of recruitment and training.

In all we were nearly thirty thousand strong. The plan called for us to land, debouch, deploy and then thrash these upstart invaders and send them packing. That was the plan.

CHAPTER FIVE

Of the Theatre, a Gale and a Surprise

On the evening before we left we visited the theatre. The idea of pomp or pageantry in a simple visit by the emperor to relax for an evening's enjoyment at the play was anathema to me, so Delia and I and a few companions went quietly to our seats in the Half Moon, an old theatre of Vondium and one in which many famous actors and actresses had trod the boards and spoken their lines.

The building was mainly of brick and stone and only the roof had burned in the Time of Troubles. The seats were arranged in a horseshoe fashion, tiered one above the other, and the acoustics and vision were alike first class. As I sat down on the fleece-stuffed cushions and looked about at the black and ugly burn marks high on the walls, and the licks of fresh paint, and saw the stars glittering high and remote, I reflected that the times of troubles were not over yet, by Vox.

An awning had been erected over the stage. During the performance a light rain began. The performers were shielded, and as they were the important part of the night's proceedings, we in the auditorium perforce sat and got wet. Only a handful of people left. Watching the play absorbed us, and a little rain was nothing.

The play was a new one, recently completed by Master Belzur the Aphorist, called *The Scarron Necklace.* Although my mind was filled with Army Lists, and the problems of supply and transportation, and the natural concern for the morrow, I found I was held by the action of the play. Of one thing I was pleasantly sure: there were still playwrights left in Vallia.

As was often the case, a purely entertaining middle section had been incorporated, in which choirs sang the old songs of

Kregen. On this night a new touch had been added. I sat up, and I heard Delia's delighted laugh at my side.

For, onto the stage, pranced files of half-naked girls clad in wisps of crimson and wearing fluffed out felt helmets that might, if you did not look too closely, pass as the bronze-fitted vosk-skull helmets of the Phalanx. The girls all carried wands—and then I realized they were intended to represent the pikes of the pikemen. They were only some five feet long; but the girls made great play with them, marching and countermarching and singing a foolish, lilting, heart-lifting ditty. The words were something to do with a soldier being always able to command the vagaries of a girl's wayward heart. This was the song that was afterward called the "Soldier's Love Potion."

"They march well, majister," said Nath, leaning across and not taking his gaze from the spectacle. "I could do with a few of them in the Phalanx, by Vox!" And he laughed.

The girls weaved patterns across the stage, their wands circling and rising and falling, and thrusting. I found it extraordinarily difficult to laugh. By Zair! I approved of this flummery, for it did a power of good for morale—but in the reflected radiance of the mineral oil lamps limning those slender girls out there I seemed to see the clumped and solid ranks and files of the Phalanx and heard the awful clangor of battle. Playacting, make believe, a light-hearted evening's entertainment—why should I make such heavy weather of it and refuse to take the joy? Why this continual questioning of my motives, when I had made up my mind, grimly, and intended to unite Vallia once again and then hand all over to Drak? Why? Why torture myself with regrets? Life is life, and it whirls along and we all get dragged with it willy-nilly no matter how desperately we cling to the deceptively substantial acts of everyday.

I half-expected to see that damned Gdoinye come sticking his arrogant scarlet-feathered head out over the proscenium arch and summon me off to jump about for the Star Lords. By Krun! But that would stir the old blood up.

Delia sensed my mood, half-desperate, half-defiant, and she pressed my hand, and so I turned my fingers over and gripped hers.

"We sail in the morning."

"I think I shall be glad to shake the dust of Vondium out of my head." I felt her fingers in mine, warm and trembling slightly. "I wish Drak were here."

"He will come home with Queen Lush," she said, and I

caught the amused puzzlement in her voice. "I have invited Silda to visit us. Her work—well, she will have news of Lela."

"When that young lady deigns to return home to give a Lahal to her father, I shall have a few words to say—"

"Now, then, you grizzly old graint!"

Then the mock-soldiers on the stage, their crimson draperies swirling and their bodies gleaming splendidly, performed their final triumphant charge, and vanished into the wings, and the rest of *The Scarron Necklace* began.

So, here we were, a little army flying off with the wind across Vallia toward Bryvondrin to meet these upstart foemen who would not leave us alone.

The wind held fair and we bowled along. Standing on the quarterdeck I looked around on the empty spaces of the sky. How odd, how weird, thus to see an armada of sailing ships billowing grandly through the air! Their sails did not gleam, for they were patched brown and pale blue, dappled with camouflage. But the sight of massive ships upheld in the air, bowling along with all sails spread . . . incredible.

A sniff at the air and a closer look at the cloud formations ahead gave me unwelcome news. The captain came over at my call and he agreed that we were in for a change in the weather.

"In for a blow, majister—and the breeze will back, I think."

"Aye, captain. I am not as sanguine as I was that we will reach Kanarsmot before the gale strikes.

"We can but pile on all canvas and trust in Opaz, majister."

"Aye."

The plan had been to land near Kanarsmot, a town on the Great River situated where, on the southeastern bank of the river, the boundaries of Mai Makanar to the north and Mai Yenizar to the south marched. By this stratagem we would array our forces in rear of the invaders, cut their supply lines, free the town, and then be in a position to hit them in flank and rear and dispose of them with little hope of escape.

But the wind gusted and freshened. And, as we feared, it backed.

Well, weather is sent by the Hyr-Pallan Whetti-Orbium, the meteorological manifestation of Opaz, and we must do what we could. We battened down. There were no seas to come leaping and crashing in over the bulwarks; but as the breeze blew with ever greater strength and backed around the compass, our yards were hauled farther and farther around. Soon we were facing a stiff easterly. The rushing roar of the wind stuffed our mouths and nostrils and half-blinded us. On the ships staggered, lurching as their invisible keels gripped into the lines of force. At last, when we were within only three dwaburs of the town, it was apparent that we could make no farther headway.

The twin suns were sinking, flooding the land below with their mingled streaming lights. The jade and ruby cast long tinted shadows. The country here was tufty, cut up by small hills and gullies, scrub country and yet being well-watered festooned with traceries of forests. The clouds sent racing shadows leapfrogging across the grass.

"Down, captain," I shouted, my words blown away. I pointed down and stabbed my hand urgently. If we continued aloft we'd be blown miles off course.

So, in the last of the light, we made our landfall.

We came down fifteen miles short of Kanarsmot and we knew the enemy was in force somewhere between us and the town.

Thus are the grandiose plans of captains and kings foiled by the invisible breeze.

A pretty bedlam ensued as the reluctant animals were herded from the capacious interiors of the ships. The men disembarked and set about bivouacking. The wind tore at cloaks and banners. We pitched a dry bivouac, no fires being lighted. Cavalry patrols, zorcamen, were sent out immediately.

When I gave firm orders that the flutduins, those marvellous saddle birds of Djanduin, were not to disembarked, Tyr Naghan Elfurnil ti Vandayha stomped across to me, raving.

His flying leathers were swirled about his legs by the breeze. He had one hand gripping his sword and the other outstretched, palm up, as though he was begging for alms.

"Majister! My flyers can scout that Opaz-forsaken—"

"Come now, Naghan—look at the weather!"

"My flutduins can fly through the Mists of Sicce itself."

"I don't doubt," I said, dryly. "However, I shall need your aerial cavalry for the morrow. The breeze will drop by then."

Naghan Elfurnil was a Valkan, and he had been trained up by expert flyers from Djanduin. An aerial detachment was with us; but I was not going to throw them away in weather like this.

"The jutmen will be our eyes tonight, Naghan."

"They'll be outscouted, you mark my words."

"It would perhaps be best if Jiktar Karidge did not hear you say that, Naghan. He has a temper—"

"Oh, aye, majister. Karidge is a fine zorcaman, I'll give you that." Naghan gave a huge sniff that was instantly whipped away by the wind. "But I'll never live to see the day when zorcas can outscout flutduins."

I forebore to suggest that, perhaps, this night, he had lived that long.

"Those oafs we will fight tomorrow have flying fluttrells. Not many. But you'll need to look sharp to drive 'em off."

"And, strom, since when has a fluttrell had a chance in hell of matching a flutduin?"

Well, by Vox, that was sooth, and we both knew it.

So the pandemonium continued and, slowly and, in the end surprisingly, order and quietness came out of chaos. The army bivouacked and the sentries were posted and the patrols went out. If we were not outscouted, we could set down all fair and square. I did not think we would outscout our opponents, for they had the advantage of the terrain. And, as the night progressed and the reports flowed in we understood that on the morrow we would advance to battle with a good idea of the strength and location of the enemy, and that they in their turn would know of our strengths and positions.

There were some cavalry clashes during that night. The army was up and breakfasting and on the move early. The wind had dropped; but we judged three burs or so would have to pass before the weather was fit for aerial cavalry. In that time we formed and marched forward.

The commander of the local forces came in with a remnant of exhausted totrixmen. They had been pushed back by the first onslaught over the Great River and had subsequently harried the invaders as best they could.

"The whole situation was completely quiet," the commander told me. He was a waso-Chuktar, Orlon Turnil, and he looked worn out. "But they will not expect so quick a reaction, majister. Truly, the flying ships are marvels."

That was the trouble with the current mess in Vallia. Our enemies pressed in on all sides and we had to leap from here to there to repel each attack. It was strange to think that not so far away we had friendly forces quite cut off from us by enemy occupied territory. We had to build our strength so as to be able to field enough armies of sufficient power to handle each trouble spot. That was taking the time, and, by Zair, it was tiring me out.

"You had best take your men and see them bedded down," I said.

Chuktar Turnil looked at me.

"I think, majister, I did not hear you. We shall, of course, ride with you this day and fight in the line."

I did not smile. "I think, Chuktar Turnil, you did not hear me aright." And then I added: "You are right welcome. May Opaz ride with you."

As he cantered off to rejoin his men, the six legs of his totrix going floppily in all directions, I gave orders that his little force should ride with the cavalry reserve.

During a regulation break in the line of march we spread the maps and studied the tactical situation. Up until now it had been strategy and operations. Now we got down to the sharp end of planning.

"At the moment," said Karidge, thumping the map, "they must at least have reached this line of trees." His headgear glittered with gold thread, his feathers bristled. He was a light cavalryman from the tips of those feathers to the stirrup-marked boots. I had chosen his zorca brigade and joyed in the choosing.

"And is this river fordable?" I pointed.

"Aye. The men will get wet bellies; but they can cross."

"By the time we reach there, the enemy will have set down less than an ulm off. I think that will do."

Nath scratched his nose.

"You mean to fight with a river at our backs?"

"A fordable river, Nath. You and the Third Kerchuri. The churgurs and archers will come in from the right flank. The woods there will screen their initial moves and by the time they are out in the open—"

"By Rorvreng the Vakka!" broke in Chuktar Tabex, commanding the heavy cavalry. "Then I will put in such a charge as will sweep them away!"

"I would prefer," I said mildly, "for Nath to chew them up a trifle before that, Chuktar Tabex."

"Aye, majister. But, I pray you, do not keep us under your hand too long!"

The regulation halt was up and the men were stirring and falling in. A bunch of slingers from Gremivoh were yelling back insults at the Deldars who were bawling them up. Undisciplined and unruly, slingers; but fine fighting men. The suns were lifting into the sky and the breeze was dropping away. The long files formed and the men shouldered their weapons and marched off.

They made a splendid sight and I forced the ugly truths from my mind and concentrated on thinking as an army commander. There would be many dead men and weeping women before Vallia could breathe freely again.

There was time for a last look at the map. A rounded hill was shown beyond the little river and it was my guess the enemy would station their cavalry there so as to get a good run in for their charge. The flanks would be more cavalry, with the infantry positioned in solid blocks interspersed with connecting lines. That seemed a reasonable guess; but you never can tell in dealing with paktuns who have years of campaigning under their belts. Even if the enemy formation was entirely different, I felt we had set down in such a way as to be able to meet them with the force we chose at the spot we chose. There seemed to me no chance that they would refuse battle. Our object was to get forward as quickly as possible and by hitting them in the flank, roll them up onto the pikes of the Phalanx. After that I could let slip the heavies with Chuktar Tabex in the van.

Delia had not insisted on bringing any of those ferocious Jikai Vuvushis, Battle Maidens, that I now knew to be a real part of her secret life. Jilian was still recovering from her wounds, and I had not seen much of her, to my own sorrow. Now Delia spurred up as I mounted and called across.

"I shall ride with you, at your side, Dray,"

I nodded, and lifted into the saddle. Korero was there, a golden shadow at my back. I half-turned and opened my mouth, and the Kildoi said, "It is understood, majister."

I felt the quick flush of pleasure. By Vox! What it is to have great-hearted blade-comrades!

And here came Nath, another blade-comrade, and his face froze me.

"Majister!" he called as he galloped. Karidge was belting along to catch him, lathering his zorca, which made me understand with a shiver of dread that the news was bad.

"Those Opaz-forsaken louts!" Nath shouted. He hauled his zorca around and the animal's four spindly legs flashed nimbly as he turned. "They have sucked us in!"

"Aye," said Karidge, reining up, his face a single huge scowl. "By Lasal the Vakka! I trust in Opaz we have not scouted them too late."

"Spit it out!"

Scouts had come in, and their latest reports contradicted what we had hitherto believed. We had thought there were fifteen thousand foemen. There were more than twenty-eight thousand—infantry and cavalry. A reinforcement had reached them from Opaz-knew-where. I felt my face congeal. Doggedly, I heard out the report, beginning to refigure the entire coming contest.

I said, "We are near enough thirty. So the odds are even—weighed in our favor still. The plans stand. We go forward and attack. We cannot shilly-shally about now."

Then it was a question of listening to reports of the composition of the new forces arrayed against us.

"Masichieri, majister. Damned thieving no-good vicious riff-raff, masquerading as mercenaries. But they can fight, and there are fully six thousand of them."

Well, masichieri—bonny masichieri, I have known them called—yes, they are the scum of mercenaries. But in a battle they are fighting men and their rapaciousness drives them on with the lure of gold and plunder and women just as much as the ideal of patriotism drives on other men.

"And? The cavalry?"

"Aragorn, majister. Slavers, come to inspect their wares, aye, and fight for them, too." Karidge drew his gauntleted hand over his luxuriant moustaches. "There are Katakis among 'em, may they rot in Cottmer's Caverns."

"It seems we will be honored by foemen worthy to die by the rope rather than steel," I said, conscious of the turgidness of the words, but conscious, also, that they were true for all that.

"Also," said Karidge, and he looked disgusted. "There are at least four regiments of sleeths."

Nath banged a fist against his pommel. "Sleeths! Two-legged risslacas* suitable for—for—" He paused, and gazed about as though seeking the suitable word. It was a nicely calculated performance. One or two men among the aides-de-camp laughed. For, indeed, to a zorcaman the sleeth is something of a joke. Despite that, they can run and they can give a zorca a run for his money. And four regiments, if the usual regimental organization was followed, meant fifteen hundred or so.

"Is that all?"

"Dermiflons and swarths."

The dermiflon is blue-skinned, ten-legged, very fat and ungainly, and is armed with a sinuous and massively barbed and spiked tail. He has an idiot's head. The expression "to knock over a demiflon" is a cast-iron guarantee of success. They'd

* risslaca: dinosaur

have howdahs fixed to their backs and half a dozen men or so would be up there, shooting with bows and hurling pikes. I said: "How many swarths?"

"Around a thousand, three regiments, weak regiments."

I let out my breath. The swarth is your four-legged risslaca with the cruel wedge-shaped head and the jaws, with the scaled body and the clawed feet. He is not very fast. But he has a muscular bulk and he can carry his rider well and, a jutman must admit, is a nasty proposition to go up against. They were relatively rare in Vallia and Pandahem; but I had been told that the Lohvian armies put much store by them. And that stupidly mad and imperious Thyllis, Empress of Hamal, had been busily recruiting swarth regiments for her armies of conquest.

"We will keep a weather eye open for the three swarth regiments. I think our nikvoves will knock them over."

"That is something that old Vikatu the Dodger would be well clear of," said Karidge.

"Indisputably. And the dermiflons?"

"Ten of them. But I think, majister," said Nath, "we will be able to handle them with our javelin men. When they get a shower of pikes about them they'll panic and run. At least, that is the theory."

I rather liked that airy confidence.

"We will put the theory into practice. But you said twenty-eight thousand. There remain two and a half you have not accounted for."

"Irregulars," said Karidge. "Spearmen, half-naked and barefoot. They can be whipped away."

"Be careful there, Karidge. Irregular spearmen can be a nasty thorn in the heel if they scent blood that is not theirs. We cannot just ignore them, like some levies."

"True. But the aragorn and the swarths are what must exercise our muscles."

"And our minds."

Not for the first time I contemplated the large number of men locked up in the Phalanx. Perhaps as footsoldiers they might be spread to cover more ground and thus present a wider frontage. I set great store by the sword and shield men, and wished to increase their numbers, creating a powerful central force of super heavy infantry. But there was no gainsaying the might of the Phalanx. Once the pikes went down and the soldiers charged there was little that would stand before them.

A half dozen saddle-birds lined out, curving against the

blue sky where the last clouds we would see this day were wafting away with the breeze. They slanted in steeply, their wings stiff against the air, made perfect landings. Tyr Naghan Elfurnil ti Vandayha unstrapped his harness and jumped down with an affectionate pat for his bird. He walked across to me.

"You have had the report of the reinforcements, majister?"

"Aye, Naghan."

"If my saddle-birds could have been allowed to fly last night—"

"Little difference, Naghan. What do you see now?"

"They have positioned themselves before that low rounded hill, as you said they would. Here are the dispositions." He handed me the paper with the scrawled squares and the scribbled notations. I studied it. Just where each enemy formation was located was important, for it was vital to place suitable forces opposite those they could handle. Cavalry in the center, cavalry on the wings, the infantry lined out. Yes. By rapidly executed flank marches the enemy commander, whoever he might be, could compress or extend his front, and swing cavalry or infantry across to plug gaps at will. I thought for a moment or two and then nodded to the waiting aides-de-camp. Quickly, they took their orders, saluted, and galloped off. As our army marched up to the stream and woods they would be marshalled so as to deploy according to my instructions.

By Zair! I just hoped that what I was doing was correct. The whole situation was likely to slide out of hand. Once the fronts locked in combat and all hell broke loose it would all be down to those initial dispositions and the sheer fighting ability of the men in the ranks.

The orders were to go on. We would appear and attack. There would be no waiting. This was no defensive fight. This was onslaught, *guerre a l'outrance*, and look at the mess that has caused, by Krun!

The brilliant golden Mask of Recognition was affixed over my face. Cleitar the Standard and Ortyg the Tresh shook out their banners. Volodu the Lungs closed up and Korero, as always, hovered a golden shield at my back. Delia rode close, and Korero knew his duty there.

In a little group we rode forward and so came to the last stand of trees. The sheen of the suns lay across the grass, the little stream and the rounded hill beyond.

Ranked before us, line on line, mass on mass, the waiting

formations of the enemy seemed to fill all the space and overflow in a blinding brilliance of color and steel.

Taking out my sword I lifted it high and then slashed it down in a vehement gesture, the point aimed at the heart of the foemen.

Silently, the leading ranks of our men plunged into the stream.

CHAPTER SIX

The Battle of First Kanarsmot

Thus began First Kanarsmot.

The feel of the zorca between my knees and the close confinement of the helmet and the Mask of Recognition, the itch of war harness on my shoulders, the brilliance of the splashing water drops as we forded across the stream—all these sensations in one form or another must have been felt by all the men in that little army. All, except the Mask of Recognition. The thing served a purpose, although I doubted if it would stop even a short-bow's shaft. As we came up on the far bank a sudden and sweet scent of white shansili filled our nostrils. The familiar scent must have brought aching-memories of familiar homes and dear faces to the men for those lovely flowers are often grown in trellises over the doors of Vallian homes.

In advance ran the kreutzin, lithe limber young men, raffish and wayward; but thirsting to get their javelins and arrows into play. Half naked, some of them, fleet of foot and agile, they raced forward to be first in action.

Scrambling my zorca—who was faithful old Grumbleknees—up on the opposite bank I rode forward far enough to allow space for the Sword Watch to form at my back.

The enemy were already moving. Their masses came on steadily, and I looked to see who would make first contact.

From the enemy's right they were drawn up thusly: the swarth force of a thousand; two dense masses of paktuns, five thousand each arrayed one behind the other; the central body of totrix and zorca cavalry, five thousand strong; the irregulars a little in advance and already beginning to race onward; the six thousand masichieri, who hung a little back; and, finally, on the left wing, the two thousand zorca-mounted aragorn. Ordered in two sections of five each, and out in front, the dermiflons lifted their stupid heads and brayed. The glitter of the suns smote back from the weapons of the men in their armored howdahs—armored castle-like structures the warriors of Kregen call calsaxes—and the dermiflon handlers ran yelling and pushing around the enormous beasts as they sought to force them into their clumsy stumbling run.

The main strength of the enemy, therefore, lay in his right wing. I did not discount the aragorn; but they and the masichieri would fight only for as long as they could see slaves and plunder coming their way.

Already our bowmen were loosing at the dermiflons.

Once we had seen them off, the real fight could begin.

Equally, massive and impressive striding citadels of war though dermiflons truly are, they must not attract all a commander's attention and he must not allow them to deflect him into wasting too many of his precious resources on them.

From the left we were arrayed thusly: the totrix cavalry division attached to the Phalanx; the Phalanx itself; the Tenth Brigade of Archers; the First Cavalry Brigade of zorcas with the Fourth slightly to their right. I lifted in the stirrups and looked across to the right toward the woods that masked the backward-curving bend of the river. There was no sign of movement among the trees.

With great whoops from the drivers and riders and a veritable Niagara of fountaining splashes, the artillery crossed the stream. A number of different draught animals hauled the equipment, and they galloped on through the intervals and unlimbered to our front. At once they were in action, shooting their cruel iron-tipped darts. Within the space of ten murs they had shot two of the dermiflons out of it, the ungainly beasts turning around on their ten legs, braying angrily, lumbering back for all their handlers shrieked and beat at them with goads.

The forward movement of our men continued. They were not yet charging—they tramped on steadily, rank on rank, file on file, and the pikes lifted, thick as bristles on a wild vosks's back.

The twin suns slanted their rays onto the battlefield from our right flank. Again I looked. Still no movement within the trees flanking the curve of the stream.

Delia said: "The paktuns are coming perilously close."

"Let the bowmen and the spear men play a little longer on the dermiflons."

As I spoke another gigantic beast decided that he no longer wished to go in the direction from which these nasty stinging barbs were coming; braying, he turned about and with his ten legs all going up and down like pistons, he lumbered off.

There were twenty-eight thousand of the enemy. I had spoken lightly of our near thirty thousand—but in that I lied or boasted. Of men we could put in fighting line we had sixteen thousand seven hundred infantry and seven thousand three hundred and twenty cavalry, plus the artillery. And, already, some of our bowmen were down, caught by the deceptive arrow, tiny bundles on the grass, lying still or, more awfully, kicking in the last spasms.

The balance of our thirty thousand was made up of logistics people, medics, vets. Some of the wagoners would fight if it came to it—but I hoped profoundly it would not come to that.

The swarths were moving, the scaled mounts advancing directly with the aim of crunching into the left flank of the Phalanx.

Chuktar De-Ye Mafon, a Pachak with great experience in command of the Tenth Cavalry Division attached to the Phalanx, countered the move. His division consisted of a brigade of three regiments of zorca archers and a brigade of three regiments of totrix lancers. Now he launched the zorcas at the oncoming swarths. The nimble animals swirled in evolutions practiced a thousand times, lined out, and their riders shot and shot as they swooped past the right flank of the enemy mass.

Disordered, the swarths angled to their left and, at that moment, Chuktar De-Ye Mafon led his totrix lancers into them.

The outcome of that fight had, for the moment, to be awaited as the enemy commander pushed through in the center.

The Phalanx had been aimed at the enemy's center, his ten thousand infantry and his five thousand cavalry, mercenaries all, tough, professional, the hard core of his army. With that swerving recoil of the swarths pressing in on the massed infantry, the enemy general had ordered one of the tactical moves he had left open to himself. The ordered ranks of the paktuns inclined to their left. They broke into a fast trot, their banners and plumes waving, their weapons glinting.

They would lap around the right flank of the Phalanx and I was about to give the order for Karidge's Brigade to move up in support, when the last of the dermiflons on this side of the field broke. They fled back, immense engines of destruction, festooned with darts—one with a varter dart pinning three of his starboard legs together—and they crashed headlong into those smart and professional paktuns.

"The swarths were advancing directly into the phalanx."

The paktuns were professionals. They opened ranks; but in the incline that proved not quite so easy as it sounded. We were afforded enough space for the Phalanx to go smashing into them, the pikes down and level, the helmets thrust forward, the shields positioned, rank by rank, to serve each the best purpose. The noise blossomed into the sky. The yells and shrieks and the mad tinker-clatter of steel on iron, of steel on bronze, and the crazed dust-whirling advance encompassed by the raw stink of spilled blood brought a horror that underlay any thoughts of glory. On drove the Phalanx. On and with blood-smeared pikes thrust the paktuns aside.

Now was the time for the enemy Kapt to hurl in his five thousand cavalry—and our Hakkodin, our halberd and axe and two-handed sword men, knew it.

The Hakkodin flank the Phalanx and they take enormous pride in the protection they afford and their ability to ensure that no lurking dagger-man, no cavalryman can smite away at the undefended flanks of the Phalanx. And the soldiers, hefting their pikes, know that and relish the feel of solid Hakkodin at their flanks and rear.

Although, mind you, in rear of the Third Kerchuri as it advanced lay only strewn and mangled corpses of paktuns.

The enemy shafts had been deflected by the uplifted shields of the Phalanx, the field of red roses in the popular imagery, the field of crimson flowers, and now our own archers of the Tenth Brigade stepped forward to assist the bowmen of the Phalanx. It was going to be touch and go. The second massed formation of paktuns was advancing in steady fashion and their incline, avoiding the tumultuous upsets of the disaster with the dermiflons, would place them astride the shoulder of the Phalanx. Engaged as the Kerchuri was, it could not toss pikes and turn half-right. That kind of evolution is very pretty on the parade ground; in the midst of battle with the redblood flowing and the screams and yells and the dust boiling everywhere—no, you grip your pike and you go on, and on, when it comes to push of pike.

A zorcaman came galloping up to me, his feathers flying, his equipment flying—he hardly seemed to touch the ground. I knew who he was, right enough.

"Majister!" He bellowed out as Cleitar the Standard had to back his zorca a trifle. "Jiktar Karidge's compliments—will you loose him now—please!"

Deliberately I lifted in the stirrups. I looked not toward the furious turmoil in the center of the field. Deliberately, I looked to the right. The six thousand masichieri were on the move. The two thousand aragorn flanking them were trotting on, splendid in the lights of the suns. The noise everywhere dinned on and on, and those fresh bodies of troops would go slap bang into the flank of our army when Karidge and the other brigade of the light cavalry division charged.

"Give me ten murs more, Elten Frondalsur." The galloper's face shone scarlet with sweat and exertion. He gentled his zorca as the excited animal curvetted. "Just that, no more."

"As you say, majister!"

Elton Frondalsur even in that moment of high tension had the sense not to argue or plead. Karidge would understand. I just looked steadily at the galloper, and so with a salute, he flicked his zorca's head around and took off back to Karidge. Also, I knew that in ten murs, and exactly ten murs, Karidge would set his brigade into a skirling charge. That was the way he would interpret the message the Elten brought.

Calling over the galloper attached to my staff from the light cavalry division, I sent him off to convey the same message to the officer in command. He, cunning old Larghos the Spear, would find himself commanding only the Fourth Brigade when the charge went in. But everyone in the army understood the impetuous ways of Karidge, aye, and loved him for it—well, most of the time.

In six murs the movement I had been fretfully waiting from the trees over by the bend in the stream heralded the arrival of our flank force. And, by Vox, only just in time!

In one sense, they were late. For the paktuns were now at handstrokes with the Hakkodin. The mingled cavalry swirled around ready to complete the impending destruction of the Phalanx, as they imagined. And the aragorn and the masichieri came swiftly on.

From the trees erupted the archers of the Ninth Brigade. Following them and pounding on in their armor, strong, powerfully built men, the front line of the three brigades of sword and shield men burst onto the battlefield. Out to their right and flanking them, galloping swiftly on, roared the Heavy Cavalry Division, two thousand totrixmen formed, clad in armor, bearing swiftly on with lances couched. When those lances shivered they would haul out short one-handed axes, and stout swords, and they'd go through the zorca-mounted aragorn like the enemy had fancied he would go through our ranks.

That marked the beginning of the end.

The commander over there must have looked with despair

upon that battlefield. He saw his vaunted swarths mightily discomfitted and driven off. He had seen a powerful force of mercenaries, containing Rapas and Fristles, Khibils and blegs, shattered and a second about to be overwhelmed. The masichieri and the aragorn were hauling up, their ranks disordered and in turmoil. It took little imagination to picture what they were doing, to hear what they were shrieking as they saw this new menace rushing up to smash into the flank. And, with his dermiflons gone, the enemy commander saw his fancied force of cavalry recoil from the center of the field as the Light Division hit them full force.

I do not like letting slip zorcas in a charge; but Karidge and Larghos the Spear had no doubts.

In moments the face of the battle changed.

Everywhere the enemy were in retreat.

That was the end of First Kanarsmot.

CHAPTER SEVEN

An Axeman Drops In

"It would perhaps have made better sense," said Delia as we sat in the tent and looked at the maps, the casualty returns ugly and horrible on the table, the sounds of an army at rest all about us in the mellow evening. "Perhaps, to have sent the Light Cavalry instead of the Heavies in the flank force."

"As it turned out, it would have been. But they were late." I yawned. "Mind you, my heart, by this time a man should have learned to expect delay in any plans he makes."

"And a woman, also."

"And what plans are you fomenting?"

"For the present situation, why, that we must take Kanarsmot as quickly as possible. Drak should be back by now and I want to go home to Vondium."

"And I." I looked at her, and I smiled. "You could always go—"

She did not say anything; but before I could go on she took off her slipper and threw it at me. I caught it. It was warm and soft.

"Very well. You won't go home by yourself."

"You could go. Nath can handle affairs here."

"That is true. But I feel responsible. I want to clear the area this side of the Great River. After all, the villains to the east seem to have settled down in our country. If they respcct the line of the river it will prove valuable."

"You are, Dray Prescot, as cunning as a newborn infant."

"Ah, but," I said. "There is no one more fitted by nature to work cunning than a baby."

She smiled at this, and I knew her memories mingled with mine, and the warmness enveloped us.

Presently we had to get back to work. The army had not suffered the ghastly scale of casualties I had at one time envisioned. But we had not got off scatheless. The final nikvove charge, slap bang through the middle and to hell with anything that got in the way, had relieved a lot of pressure. Karidge and his zorcamen had behaved splendidly. The cavalry was pursuing; but the enemy were not a fleeing force for they had withdrawn onto a further considerable body of reinforcements and then presented a front. They were still in play. The cavalry harried them, and parried their cavalry probes. We had not been worried by their flying machines but in the successful accomplishment of that our small saddle-bird force had been fully stretched, so that no aerial cavalry had played a part in the battle.

Nath was most wrought up about the late arrival of the flank force. When I pointed out to him that they had been too early they would not have had an exposed flank to charge into, he sniffed, and agreed, and said with devastating logic: "But had they been on time, as you ordered, majister, the flank would have been there and we would not have been so hard-pressed."

We had not grown hard and callous over casualties. We mourned good men gone. But more and more the truth, unpleasant at first glance and then, with greater acquaintance, acceptable with a kind of glow of abnegation, was borne in on us that for what we sought to do even death had its part to play. These murky philosophical waters led us on, inexorably, to a continuation of the heady and almost intoxicated feelings the people of Vondium had felt during the protracted Time of Troubles and later, when we were penned up in the city. No one wants to die in the ordinary course of things, but if death comes to us all then a fighting man may choose his going over into the care of the gray ones on a battlefield. That, surely, is his right. And, do not forget, we were an all-volunteer army.

The arguments against this kind of thinking, involving manic pressure and self-hypnotism and twisted logic that goes against the grain of life-enhancement, were well known to the sages of Kregen. There is no proprietary right to life-thinking. But we all felt that our lives were well spent in the attempt to provide a free land for our children.

So I was able to read the casualty returns and see the familiar names leap out at me from the long lists with a calmness that no longer surprised me. No, we of Vallia are not callous in these matters.

Nath said as I lowered the last list: "We lost Yolan Vanoimen, I am sorry to say." Yolan Vanoimen was—had been—Jodhrivax of the Second Jodhri of the Kerchuri. "A stinking Rapa bit his throat out."

Nath looked down at his hands. I said nothing.

After a space he went on: "The Rapa was brave, you have to say that. He went down with four pike heads piercing him and a Hakkodin axe severing his wattled neck."

"I am sorry that Yolan Vanoimen has gone," I said at last. "He was in line for Kerchurivax of the Eighth. We have to pay a heavy price for what we believe in."

The mineral oil lamps glowed and the camp tent was crowded with our familiar belongings. But I felt the chill. I tried to shake it off. The Eighth Kerchuri would have to find a new commander. We were forming a new Phalanx in Vondium, the Fourth. The Kerchuris were numbered throughout the whole Phalanx force. The Jodhris were numbered through their Phalanx, the First to the Sixth and the Seventh to the Twelfth. The Relianches, the basic formations of a hundred and forty-four brumbytes and twenty four Hakkodin, were numbered through their Kerchuri, the First to the Thirty-Sixth. Later we made adjustments to this numbering.

The aftermath of battle is not kind. Useless to dwell on that. We gave the army a breather of four days during which time the additional units I had summoned from Vondium flew in. After that we pursued the campaign. From information received from the local people, who rallied wonderfully after the battle, we learned that the commander of the enemy army was on Ranjarsi the Strigicaw. He was a Rapa, one of those beaked and vulturine diffs of Kregen, and he showed great skill in fending us off and leading us a dance. But, in the end, with our enhanced forces, we pinned him against the Great River.

The Fourth Kerchuri of the Second Phalanx had joined us, so we had a full phalanx in action. More bowmen and archers and cavalry swelled our ranks. Second Kanarsmot was a fearful debacle for the invaders and Kapt Ranjarsi the Strigicaw was lucky to escape across the river with the remnants. The waters of She of the Fecundity rolled red.

We did not pursue across the river, and we trusted the invaders got the message. Larghos the Left-Handed, a spry, clever, completely loyal Pallan came up from Vondium to take over the command in the area. I trusted him, along with his comrade, Naghan Strandar, to deal with many of the higher details of the government, the army and the law. They worked with the Lord Farris and made a capital team.

Leaving sufficient forces to ensure that any fresh attempts

to invade across the river would be crushed swiftly, we turned toward Kanarsmot itself. This still held out against the small screening forces so far pitted against it, the garrison, of mercenaries, commanded by a Fristle called Fonarmon the Catlenter. He had dubbed himself, no doubt with Ranjarsi's blessing, the Strom of Kanarsmot.

We disabused him of that idea.

The plan I outlined was to take the place by a *coup de main*. I had no desire whatsoever to sit down to a protracted siege. So, on the night chosen, when for a space only two of the smaller moons of Kregen rushed across the dark sky, we set off. Infiltraters within the walls overpowered the guard at the West Gate and we poured in, a silent host, and set about securing the town, house by house.

Other forces went in over the walls. After that the garrison awoke to their peril and we came to handstrokes.

Over the southeastern walls of the town the citadel had been built with its footings in the waters of the river. The mercenaries fought well, earning their hire, and slowly withdrew to the citadel. The massive gates closed with a couple of ranks of our bowmen trapped inside. We knew we had seen the last of them. Other bowmen dropped with yells into the moat or withdrew from the hail of arrows that sprouted from the battlements. By that narrow margin had we failed to take the citadel.

I said: "I regret the men we lost there. But as for the citadel, well, the cramphs are mewed up inside and we can leave them to rot. I will not lose more good men in unnecessary attacks."

That seemed sound common sense, by Vox.

Dawn was breaking and illuminating the clouds with fringes of gold and ruby, orange and jade. Someone let out a high excited yell. We all looked up.

High against that paling sky the rope arched. It curved like a whip. It fell all quivering down the wall and its length dangled an invitation at the end of the bridge which the mercenaries had been unable to draw up. The next moment helmets tufted with the maroon and white of the churgurs of the Fiftieth Regiment of the Nineteenth Brigade appeared on the left-flank gate tower.

Kov Vodun shouted by my side.

"Those are my men up there." He threw off his cloak.

In the next instant as he started forward across the bridge I was flinging my leg over the zorca to dismount.

Delia's voice, warningly, said: "Dray."

Korero, whose shields were uplifted against the occasional arrow, said, "Majister. . . ."

"You can't expect me to sit here and watch!"

Then a whole bunch of men ran over the bridge, yelling, and with Kov Vodun in the lead they began climbing the rope.

"By Zair!" I shouted. And I was running, too, running like a fool over the planks of the bridge where arrows stood thickly, and taking my turn to grip the rope and so go hand over hand up like a monkey. Korero, with four arms and a tailhand, had no difficulty in swarming up the rope after me, carrying his shields and giving me an assist from time to time. We tumbled over the battlements into a scene of confusion.

Those two ranks had done their job, and there could not have been above fourteen men between the two sections, in jamming the winding mechanism of the bridge and of clambering up the stairs of the left-flank gate tower. They had been unable to prevent the closing of the gates. But their dropped rope gave us an alternative ingress.

The tower top blazed with action, as swords clashed and spears flew. The paktuns, a mixed bunch of diffs with Fristles predominating, fought savagely to hold us back from the battlements. Our way down the gate tower was blocked; but once along the ramparts we could expand. The way into the citadel would lie open. Thc garrison knew that and fought like leems to hurl us back over the walls to shattered destruction on the ground below.

Very few of our men had climbed the rope with their shields. Vallians still had not fully mastered the art of shield play and had not slung the crimson flowers over their backs. I ripped out my drexer, the straight—or almost straight—cut and thrust sword, and plunged into the fray.

Over the clangor everyone heard the fearsome yells from the tower, dwindling. For a paralyzed instant the action froze . . . The soggy thumps sounded eerily loud.

"The rope has broken!" bellowed a hulking Deldar from the nearest group who had just climbed up. "We are on our own!"

"Not for long!" I fairly shrieked over the fresh hubbub. "Into them! We must open the gates!"

This was the red hurly-burly of action very far removed from sitting a zorca in the rear and methodically working out which way a battle should be run. We were up at the sharp end and if our wits and our sword arms failed us we were done for.

"Flung stuxes flew into our ranks."

The party of mercenaries blocking the stairway resisted our efforts. They were fighting men. Many of them showed the gleam of the pakmort at throat, or looped into the shoulder of the war harness. We charged into them and were thrust back, struggling desperately.

Our numbers were thinning. Flung stuxes, those thick and heavy throwing spears with the small cross quillons set back from the head, flew into our ranks. Men shrieked and died, blowing bloody froth, vomiting. I hurdled a sprawled bleg, three of his legs missing, and launched myself at the mercenaries. Their swords flamed. It was all a mad business of cut and hack, of duck, of thrust, of parry, and recover.

I do not think, I seriously do not think, we could have done it. Looking back at that scene of carnage it seems to me the enemy were slowly overmastering us. We fought; but we were few and they continually fed reinforcements up from the garrison so that we faced what appeared to be an unending stream of foemen.

And then . . .

And then!

By Zair! But to think of it brings that excruciating tingle in the blood, sets the pulses jumping, shows it all again in splendor.

A shadow dropped down over us, a twinned shadow from the twin suns. An airboat hovered, for she could not settle with that seething mass of struggling men below without squashing friend and foe alike. From the voller leaped men. I saw them. Over the coamings they jumped, roaring into action. I saw their yellow hair flying free, for the Maiden with the Many Smiles was not in the sky. I saw the height of them, seven foot, each fighting man. I saw their weapons, those long single-bladed Saxon-pattern axes. Oh, yes, I saw them as they smashed into the mercenaries and the axes whirled in that old familiar way, ripping arcs of silver and red.

Warriors of Ng'groga, they were, tall sinewy axemen, and there was about their work the fierce controlled power of the typhoon.

At their head, urging them on, slashing with cunning skill, opening a path through the enemy—at their head, in the lead, roared on that tall familiar figure that meant so much to me.

"By Zair!" I said. "If only Seg were here now!"

With that and with renewed heart we swept the enemy from before the stairway. They were sent screaming to topple over the battlements of the tower. The stairway was cleared and men raced down, yelling, striking this way and that with lethal axes. The gate was opened.

After that—why the army poured in and in next to no time the citadel of Kanarsmot was in our hands.

Delia found me as I walked out of the open gate and over the bridge. Walking was not easy for the arrows and the corpses. The Sword Watch were busily engaged in the citadel in rounding up prisoners and discovering what portable property there might be worthy the consideration of a guardsman of the Emperor's Sword Watch.

"Oh, Dray! When you climbed the rope—"

"Did you see him?"

She smiled and the world of Kregen took on a roseate light. "Yes. I saw him. And here he is, walking up just as though nothing had happened." She was looking past me and as I turned so Delia ran by and threw herself at that tall, yellow-haired, grimly ferocious axeman. He clasped her in his long arms.

"*Inch*!"

He looked at me over Delia's brown hair and I swear he had to swallow before he spoke.

"As a comrade of ours would say, Dray—Lahal, my old dom."

"Lahal and Lahal a thousand times, Inch."

And I strode forward to clasp his hand. He had had to swallow before speaking. Damned if I didn't, too. . . .

CHAPTER EIGHT

Vondium Dances

Inch's adventures would fill a book of their own. We left affairs in the capable hands of Larghos the Left-Handed and prepared to return to the capital. Inch kept on looking about and uttering exclamations of surprise—at the flying sailers so different from those with which we had fought the Battle of Jholaix, at the Phalanx, and this and that. He was delighted to be back, and when, in an odd moment, we found him solemnly standing on his head, reciting the Kregish alphabet backwards and at the end of each recital clapping his heels smartly together, we smiled fondly. Inch and his taboos! If he fell over when he clapped his heels together, he'd have to start all over again.

We did not ask him which particular taboo he had broken. When you got to know Inch of Ng'groga, the Kov of the Black Mountains, you did not bother to question his taboos and simply took delight in his presence.

He told us that after he had been sorcerously flung back from the Pool of Baptism to his native Ng'groga, in southeastern Loh, he had been forced to spend some time atoning for all the mass of broken taboos he felt sure he had left strewn in his wake. Then, with due ritual and protocol and a mass of taboo-legitimized formalities he had wed his Sasha.

Delia clapped her hands.

"Wonderful, Inch, delightful. Congratulations. Is she with you?"

"Yes. I left her in Vondium—"

"Oh?" I said.

He looked at me—by this time he was sitting at a table in a decent chair and we had forbidden squish pie to be brought any closer than an ulm—and he smiled.

"I know you think I am a clever fellow, Dray. But it would take Ngrangi Himself to have known you were here at

Kanarsmot. No, the moment we heard in Ng'groga of the troubles in Vallia I set off." Across in the continent of Loh they had few if any airboats and travel would be slow and news hardly come by. "I took the liberty of going via Djanduin. I found the people wonderfully hospitable when they discovered I was acquainted with their king."

"Acquainted," I said.

Inch laughed at that. "Oh, yes, Ortyg Fellin Coper and Kytun Kholin Dorn are great fellows. They greeted me right royally and gave me splendid fliers."

"Fliers . . ."

"Well, of course. By Ngrozyan the Axe! You didn't think I'd come empty-handed? I enlisted a parcel of likely rogues, all friends of mine, or friends of friends, and we look forward to a rollicking time, I can tell you."

"How many?"

Five hundred or so—of course fifty of 'em are mindyfingling about somewhere in Pandahem, probably. One of the fliers broke down. And I sent half of 'em up to the Black Mountains under command of my second cousin, Brince, to sniff around and sort out any mischief up there."

Delia glanced at me. Kov of the Black Mountains, our comrade Inch, with responsibilities there he took most seriously. Yet—he had flown first to Vondium. . . .

All the same, the situation had to be explained to him, that same situation that had so puzzled and infuriated Seg.

Also, there was about Inch a new and refreshing air of determination, of a positive approach. He was still the same gangling affable fellow; but clearly discernible in his talk and his movements this new positive attitude to life marked off a change that had taken place in him, also.

I said, "We no longer employ mercenaries in Vallia." I saw his face. "Oh, there are still many paktuns in employ, of course, they have not all packed up and gone home. But as a part of the new imperial policy Vallia is going to be liberated by Vallians."

If he had stood up, flouncing, and shouted, before he stalked out, I could not have blamed him. This sounded like the basest ingratitude on my part. But Inch just stared at me, and scratched his nose, and pulled a long lock of that yellow hair.

"Yes. They told me something of the sort in Djanduin. If you've managed to persuade Kytun that he must not bring a horde of your ferocious Djang warriors to Vallia—well, the reasons must be cogent, most cogent indeed." He gave a little laugh. "But, by Vox! What a sight that would be!"

"Aye." I said. "It would indeed."

There was a great deal to be talked about and histories to be filled in. Larghos the Left-Handed came in to finalize his orders and the position as we saw it then. He had known Inch as the Kov of the Black Mountains before the death of the emperor, Delia's father. But when Nath came in, fresh from organizing the movements of the Phalanx, I braced myself up. Nath had not easily accepted Seg Segutorio. The last thing I wanted was friction between my comrades and my trusted lieutenants. Some emperors and dictators use antipathies between their subordinates to divide and rule; to me that is inefficient and, to boot, indicative of a society I have no wish to be a part of.

When the formalities were made, Inch, very gravely, said, "It was my misfortune not to have been with you, Kyr Nath, when you led the first Phalanx that the emperor has spoken of. I grieve that I missed so much. But I am here now and my axemen are under your command for the rest of this campaign."

He cocked an eye at me and I wondered if he was bracing himself to break a few of his taboos for which he would have to do remarkable penances later. "I understand we no longer employ mercenaries. But these fellows are not paktuns. They are friends of mine, out for what rascally fun they can find and a little loot if that comes their way. We shall be going up to the Black Mountains before long."

How difficult to judge when men and women talk in apparently open and frank ways just how much of the truth they are telling! Deeply thinking people do not rush into confidences the moment acquaintance is made with strangers. But I felt I knew Inch. He was a blade comrade. His words rang with truth, at least to me, and I knew that Delia also heard that truth.

Nath smiled.

"You are most welcome, kov. Like Kov Seg, you have been much spoken of in your absence. The Hakkodin will marvel at your axes."

"They will that," I said. And then I added, warningly, "But I think it takes a native Ng'grogan to swing that axe in just that way. We continue with our Vallian axes, Nath—do you not agree?"

"Assuredly, majister. And, anyway, I fancy some of my axemen could give Kiv Inch's men a gallop for their zorcas."

The conversation eased after that. I was not fool enough to imagine that perfect comradely harmony would exist between Inch and Nath immediately and without a little time for rubbing off the sharp corners. But, at the least, a start had been made.

There remained the last parades and the music and the marching and the distribution of bobs, and then we took off for Vondium. News came in from Seg that he had inflicted a minor defeat on the enemies facing him, that the clansmen were arguing among themselves over what to do, and that given a little more time he rather fancied his chances at driving them into the sea. Nath read the message and said, at once and without preamble: "Let me go up there right away, majister, and join Kov Seg. We have the strength now—"

Farris looked troubled.

"My sailing fliers can—"

"Of course, Kov Farris!" broke in Nath, eagerly. "And we can drop right on them and discomfort them utterly."

I'd heard this before. I pointed at the map, indicating the southwest.

Nath said: "I know, majister. But the Fourth is coming along nicely, we have fresh regiments of churgurs and archers. And, above all, the southwest is quiet now."

"Quiet. But what are they up to down there?"

"I," said Inch, "would greatly like to see Seg again."

There were a few other pallans in my rooms and each gave his opinion, honestly, for what it was worth, and all knowing I would have to make the final decision.

The notion that Vallia was some gigantic Jikaida board returned to me. One moved the pieces here and there and sought to contain strengths and to camouflage weaknesses. If you wonder why I hesitated to take the obvious step and rush up with all the forces at my disposal and smash the clansmen back into the sea, one reason was the ever-present threat from the south. Also the northwest remained a vague area of conflict in which racters fought Layco Jhansi's people, and where Inch would soon plunge with his axemen into the Black Mountains. No—the reason lay in that recent conversation with the Star Lords. I had been snatched summarily from Vallia before. This time I waited. I knew I was to be called by the Everoinye. It was absolutely vital that Vallian affairs remained in honest and capable hands. Seg and Inch, Nath and Farris, all the others, would shoulder their burdens while I was away.

If this was a doom laid on me then I waited for the stroke as I had waited in the dungeons of the Hanitchik.

The happy sounds of laughter outside and the clanging crash as the three-grained staffs of the guardsmen of the Sword Watch presented heralded the joyous arrival of Delia, smiling, with Sasha, who looked radiant.

"The plans are all prepared and everything is going to be wonderful!" cried Delia.

I, I must confess, gaped.

"And the first dance is to be a mandanillo," said Sasha. "And you, Inch, are to lead off with me."

So I remembered. Tonight all Vondium celebrated. The palace was to see a great ball and the lanterns would bloom colors to the night sky and the tables would groan with food and everyone would dance and sing and laugh as the moons cavorted through the sky between the stars, until the twin suns, Zim and Genodras, awoke to send us all to sleep at last.

"Let us dance the night away," I said. "And in the morning, with Opaz, we will decide."

The dances of Kregen are spectacles that would drive the gods to tripping a measure. Everything conduced to laughter and pleasure. Every girl was beautiful. Every man was a hero. We sang and danced and drank and ate, and we kept it up as the Maiden with the Many Smiles cast down her fuzzy pinkish light, and She of the Veils added her more golden glow, as the Twins endlessly revolved above. The stars blazed. The torches and the lanterns filled the air with motes of color. The orchestras played nonstop, all the exotic instruments of Kregen combining to provide the right music for each dance.

And the dances!

Useless for me to attempt to describe them all. They delighted the senses and they fed the soul.

The sounds of plunkings announced the mandanillo and Inch and Sasha led off in that gliding, dreamlike dance. This was followed by more of the stately dances, in which the lines of men and women interlink and revolve and weave their magical patterns that woo the very blood in the body to the rhythms. As the night wore on so the dances grew wilder. Your Kregan loves a riotous rollicking dance, full of blazing passion and jumping and kicking and high jinks. In groups, in couples, the brilliantly attired revellers gyrated through the palace and into the grounds. In the avenues and boulevards the people danced and sang. The kyros filled with the rhythms, and the patterns of the dances cast kaleidoscopes of brilliance against the arcades and colonnades. The vener pranced in their boats along the cuts and the canal water glittered back in blinding reflections.

Oh, yes, we had a ball that night in Vondium.

The dance called the Wend carried people in swaying undulating lines through every corridor in the palace, it seemed, in a procession far removed from the solemn chanting religious festivals where the worshippers all chanted "Oolie Opaz, Oolie Opaz" over and over again. The Wend carried them singing the currently popular songs around and around: "Lucili the Radiant," "The Empty Wine Jar," "My Love is like a Moon Bloom," and dozens more.

As you will realize, they sang "She Lived by the Lily Canal," and "The Soldier's Love Potion," over and over.

Presently Delia drew me into the rose-bordered courtyard where Inch and Sasha and many and many another good friend laughed and waited, for we were to dance the Measure of the Princesses, often called the Jikaida Dance.

The ladies all wore their sherissas, those filmy, gauzy, tantalizing veils that float and drift dreamlike in the dance. The men wore masks, dominoes of silver and gold. The courtyard massed in its banks of roses was laid out as a Jikaida board, three drins by four, giving an area of eighteen by twenty-four squares. We all formed up, laughing and fooling, and the orchestra struck up the Jikaida Introduction and the choir started to sing.

Well, now. As the song unfolds the story, you have to suit your actions to the words. We were in the yellow party and we waved yellow favors. The blues, at the far end, waved their blue favors and taunted us, all laughing and joking, and every time some unfortunate made a mistake they were summarily ejected. We pranced around the board, hopping the blue and yellow squares, going through the contortions. No one cheated. There was no point in dancing else.

All too soon I missed a cue and forgot to wave my yellow favor aloft when I should have, and the marshals, killing themselves with laughter, attired in their white regalia, turfed me off the board.

"Dray! You empty-head!"

"It is all too clever for me, my love—but go on, go on—the blues gain on us."

For, indeed, there were far too many yellows gathered in the shadow of the roses, chattering and scoffing and doing their best to upset the blues still in the dance.

What a picture it all made! The gleam of the lanterns, the impression of the shadows of the trees above, the scent of the Moon Blooms, the music twining into our very beings—yes, Kregans know how to enjoy themselves. Be very sure the wheeled trolleys containing their racked amphorae were everywhere to hand.

In the end the yellows just piped the blues, and Delia smiled and gestured to Sasha, who accepted the golden flower of triumph. We clapped, for Sasha was rapidly proving a popular figure among us.

After that we had the Spear Dance, full of leaping and twisting and jumping the flashing spear blades. The Yekter followed and then there were more dances in which the participants enacted the stories of the songs.

Then, I walked to the orchestra I had spent a few burs with, doing my best to introduce them to the rhythms of the waltz. During my sojourns on Earth I had become addicted to the music of the waltzes that grew every year in popularity. The breadth and humanity of vision of the newest waltzes were a far cry from the early Ländler and I carried the tunes in my head. This is possible, and by repeated practice the orchestra chosen could reproduce the music most wonderfully. It had proved an altogether different kettle of fish with Beethoven; but even in this I persevered. So, now, to those evocative strains, Delia and I led out in the Grand Waltz of Vondium.

Soon the whole company were gliding and swaying and the music rose and a great sense of well-being filled me that was tinged with the sadness of coming parting.

We danced out from the lantern-lit areas and lightly followed the avenues of rose bushes, dancing under the Moons of Kregen. The feel of Delia in my arms, the scents of the flowers, the intoxicating strains of the music, the sense of a whole city enjoying itself, released the pressures and tensions of the times. And then Delia looked up and gasped.

"Dray—an airboat!"

Instantly my right hand darted to the rapier, for, dance or no dance, no Kregan goes abroad at night unarmed unless he has to.

The airboat landed on a wide terrace before the palace where the dancers and carousers scattered away for her. We heard the startled exclamations and then the laughter and the cheering. We stood, together, close. We saw.

From the voller leaped a tall, powerful, dominating man. He landed lightly and instantly turned to assist a women to step down, a woman who wore a tiered headdress of intertwined silver flowers that caught the lights and glittered. A monstrous shape rose up from the voller. The watching crowds stopped their laughter and cheering, and they fell back. The monstrous shape leaped to the ground with the liquid lethal grace of a giant hunting beast. Instantly a second appeared and leaped to stand, ferocious, beside the first.

Delia gasped. I held her and then she broke free.

She ran.

She ran along the rose-bowered walk, shouting.

"Drak! Drak! Melow! Kardo!"

She ran to greet her son and I smiled and felt the enormous weight lift from my shoulders.

Those two savage Manhounds of Antares, Melow the Supple and her son, Kardo, had been saved and brought back to Vondium by Drak, Prince Drak of Vallia, Krzy, and I felt the proper pride of a father.

And then I smiled a little smile. For Delia had not called the name of the woman who stood so close to Drak. She had not cried out in welcome to Queen Lushfymi of Lome.

But she would do that, I knew; for in Delia there is no room for pettiness. So I slapped the rapier back into the scabbard and hitched up my belt and started off between the roses to greet my son.

Now affairs in Vondium could take a different turn. Farris would be overjoyed to hand over the burden to Drak so that he could get on with his Air Service. I could take the army and see about winning a few battles secure in the knowledge that Drak was here. The moment we had Vallia in good shape he was going to take over as emperor. My heart was set on that. To hand over now, with all the problems still with us, would not be seemly. But, soon now, soon.

The blueness was at first merely a drifting mist that brushed irritatingly in my eyes.

In a summoning flutter of scarlet and gold, wings beating against the blueness, the Gdoinye flew down. The spy and messenger of the Star Lords cocked his head on one side, his beak insolently agape.

"It is time, Dray Prescot. The Star Lords summon you."

I felt my body would burst.

"Fool—" I managed to say.

"It is you who is the fool. You have been warned. See how considerate are the Everoinye, how tender of you—we have spoken aforetime—"

"Aye! And I have bidden you begone, bird of ill omen."

The blueness closed in, thick and choking. The Gdoinye uttered a last mocking squawk. The shape of the phantom Scorpion coalesced, huge and menacing. I caught a last parting fragrance of the Moon Blooms. The ground whirled away. I was falling. The coldness lashed in. The blueness, the swirling movement, the cold—and then the blackness.

CHAPTER NINE

Pompino

A hard abrasive surface scratched at my stomach and legs. The blueness and the Scorpion of the Star Lords had hurled me somewhere. My arms dangled. I opened my eyes. Light—a familiar opaline wash of radiance—reassured me instantly; the idea that I might have been transported back to Earth had tortured me, held me in a stasis that this simple opening of the eyes dissipated.

I was lying full length on the knobbly branch of a tree, my arms dangling into space, and bright green fronds tumbled about me as I moved. Swinging my legs over I sat up. The tree was not overlarge, and the leaves were very pleasant; but the bark was like emery paper.

How far the woods went on I could not see for trees.

About to jump down to the ground a glint of light off metal caught my eye and I waited, still, scarce breathing. In the direction which, by reason of the moss on the treetrunks, I took to be north, that wink of metal blinked twice more and then vanished. I was wrong about the direction being north, as I subsequently discovered. I waited for five heart-beats and, again, prepared to jump down.

A man walked out from under the trees opposite.

Like me, he was stark naked. Unlike me, apim, he was a diff, a Khibil. His shrewd fierce foxy face turned this way and that. His body was compactly muscled and he bore the white glistening traceries of old scars. A bronzed, fit, tough man, this Khibil, with reddish hair and whiskers, and alert contemptuous eyes. He bent and picked up a stout length of wood, a branch as thick as his arm, which he tested for strength before he would accept it into his armory.

At this I frowned.

He looked all about him and then padded off between the trees, going silently and swiftly like a stalking chavonth.

My business, I thought, could not concern him. He was in

no immediate danger and, anyway, apart from being naked and weaponless, looked as though he could defend himself.

A cry spurted up from the trees to my rear and I swivelled about. Just beyond the end of the branch on which I sat bowered in leaves, and running to fall on the grass, a young Fristle fifi yelled and blubbered. The Fristle who was hitting her with a slender length of switch wore a brown overall-like garment, and his whiskers jutted stiffly. His gray-furred arm lifted and fell and the switch bit into the fifi's gray fur.

The branch bore my weight almost to the end. Then it broke with a loud crack. I jumped. I fell full on the Fristle. We both collapsed onto the grass.

He came at me raging, slicing his switch. I took it away and clipped him beside the ear and he fell down. He lay sprawled, and his whiskers drooped most forlornly.

Instantly the little Fristle fifi was on her knees at his side, wailing and crying.

"Father! Father! Speak to me!" She shook him, and pulled him to her. Then she sprang to her feet. Like a flying tarantula she was on me, striking and scratching, shrieking.

"You beast! You rast! My poor father—a great naked hairy apim—monster! Beast!"

I held her off. I felt foolish.

"Your father?"

She was sobbing in my grasp.

"We are poor wood cutters. I broke the jar with poor father's tea." She tried to bite my finger. "It was ron* sengjin tea. He beat me for it."

"Tea," I said. I shook my head. "Ron sengjin. A broken jar and a father's chastisement."

She broke free, for I could not bear to hold her, and she dropped to her knees and took her father's head into her hands, crooning over him. Presently he opened his eyes and stared vacantly upward. I put down my hand and hauled him to his feet. He stood, groggily, shaking his head. I feel sure the Bells of Beng Kishi were clanging in there well enough.

"You fell on me from the sky, apim."

"I owe you an apology—but the switch was too severe a punishment for the crime."

"You fell on me." His eyes rolled. "From the sky."

A blaze of scarlet and gold flew down between us. The Gdoinye passed right before the staring eyes of the Fristle and his daughter. The cat-faced man and girl saw nothing of

* ron: red

that impudent bird. He perched on a tree and he squawked at me.

"From the sky," said the Fristle. He swallowed. "A great naked hairy apim. Fell on me."

The Gdoinye squawked again and ruffled a wing.

Knowing when to make myself scarce I left the Fristles to it. The father might have lost his tea; I fancied he had learned a little lesson, also.

"Remberee," I shouted back. And I plunged into the blue shadows of the trees.

With that curious little incident, over which many a man would have grown rosy red in the remembrance, to point me on to my duty for the Star Lords, I ran out from under the far trees and so looked down on my real work here.

And yet, even as I plunged on down the slope, I could not feel fully convinced. The horizon lifted mellowly from a patchwork of fields and woods, threaded by watercourses, and the glittering roofs and spires of a town showed less than a dwabur off. The air held that fragrant freshness of Kregen. I breathed deeply as I skipped down the slope into action. The length of wood I had snatched up would serve to crack a few skulls.

And yet, as I say, I was not fully convinced.

An ornate blue and gold carriage drawn by six krahniks was being besieged by a band of Ochs. The offside front wheel of the carriage jutted awkwardly from under the swingle tree, indication that the axle had broken. The krahniks stood, russet red and placid in their harness, chewing at the grass. Half a dozen Ochs were busily attempting to cut the traces and make off with the animals.

Half a dozen more were banging spears on the wooden panels of the carriage and yelling. A big Rapa was running about, his beaked vulturine face desperate, trying to fend the Ochs off. Another Rapa lay in the grass. He was not dead, for his crest kept quivering as he tried to haul himself up, only for an Och to give him a sly thwack and so stretch him out again. Now Ochs are small folk little above four feet tall with lemon-shaped heads with puffy jaws and lolling chops. They have six limbs and use the central pair indiscriminately as arms or legs. Usually, they prefer to work in as large a body as they can, numbers giving them strength.

The rest of the group, about ten or so, were all yelling and jumping about and trying to attack the naked Khibil. He was laying about with his length of wood, knocking Ochs over, sending them flying, whirling them away. It was all a crazy little pandemonium. I ran down, debating.

Often I have had to make up my mind just who the Star Lords wanted rescued. Was this Khibil in need of assistance? Or was he the aggressor and the Ochs required for the mysterious purposes of the Everoinye?

The Gdoinye, who had acted in so strange a manner, left me in no doubt.

He flew on before me and swooped at the Ochs banging on the coach. They could not see him. So I ran on down and stretched that group of Ochs out and turned to give the Khibil a hand.

There were only three left by then and they ran off as I turned on them. The rest left the krahniks and ran off, also, squeaking, their spindly legs flashing.

The Khibil swelled his massive chest and regarded me.

He held his length of wood cocked over his right shoulder. Deliberately, I allowed my length of wood to drop.

"Llahal, dom," I said cheerfully.

For a moment he hesitated, and I fancied he was fighting the inherent feelings of superiority some Khibils never master. Then: "Llahal, apim. You were just in time to assist me in seeing this rabble of Ochs off—they are not worth pursuit."

"Probably."

A noise echoed inside the carriage and I heard a whisper, quick and fervent. I moved slowly sideways so as to get a view of Khibil and coach together. The Khibil lowered his length of wood. Whatever the obi might be hereabouts it evidently did not include the immediate giving and receiving of a challenge it held in other parts of Kregen. I, of course, had no idea where I was. That I was on Kregen was the extent of my knowledge. The two suns were in the sky, and they were high in the meridian, and they did not jibe with my moss-and-tree deduction of the direction of north.

The Khibil shared my curiosity.

He said, "Tell me, dom, where are we?"

Before I could answer, a sharp female voice from the coach window spat out: "Why, you knave, in Kov Pastic's province, of course, and if you don't put your clothes on at once I will have the kov's guard arrest you the moment we reach Gertinlad."

The Khibil and I stared at each other for a space. His reddish whiskers twitched. I thought of the Fristle on whom I had dropped from the sky. I thought of the occasion when I had given a helping hand to Marta Renberg, the Kovneva of Aduimbrev, with her luxurious coach that fell by the way. And, too, I thought of an earlier occasion when I had been transmitted to Kregen by the Star Lords to assist Djang girls against Och slavers. The two instances were strangely mingled here. Again that sense of machination troubled me, and by machination I mean wheels within wheels and not the ordinary interference in my life by the Everoinye. So the Khibil's whiskers twitched. The woman in the coach was still screaming about our nakedness and her friend the kov.

The Khibil was the first to laugh.

And I, Dray Prescot, who had learned to laugh muchly of late in odd ways, I, too laughed.

The Khibil recovered first.

With the length of wood held just so he approached the carriage. He spoke up; but the note in his voice was of a fine free scorn tempered by social observance.

"Llahal, lady. We have no clothes. They were stolen by these rascally Ochs. But we have saved your life."

The woman was hidden from me by the jut of window; I could see her hand, thin and white, on which at least five rings glittered. Her voice continued in its shrill shriek.

"Onron! Give these two paktuns clothes! Bratch!"

The Rapa who had been running about, the one with the red feathers in whirlicues about his eyes and beak, went to the trunk fastened to the back of the coach and, presently, the Khibil and I were arrayed in gray trousers and blue shirts. I was beginning to have an idea of where I was, and not caring for it over much.

"See to the wheel," said the lady, and the window shutter went up with a clatter. A mumble of conversation began within the coach.

I looked at the Khibil, prepared to get on with fixing the axle, for I conceived that the Everoinye wished this hoity-toity madam in the coach preserved for posterity. If she was anything like the couple I had saved in the inner sea she might pup a son who would topple empires.

The Khibil said: "Lahal, apim. I am Pompino, Scauro Pompino ti Tuscursmot. When I saw the Gdoinye leading you on I realized you were a kregoinye." He sniffed. "Although why the Everoinye should imagine I would need help against miserable little Ochs, I do not know, by Horato the Potent."

I felt the solid ground of Kregen lurch beneath me.

A man, another mortal man, was talking of the Gdoinye,

of the Star Lords! He knew! He called me and by implication himself a kregoinye. I swallowed. I spoke up.

"Lahal, Scauro Pompino. I am Jak."

If I was where I thought I was the name of Dray Prescot would have that villain hog-tied and subject to an agonizing death.

About to go on to amplify the single name of Jak with some descriptive appellation—and it would not have been Jak the Drang for news travels where there are vollers—this Scauro Pompino ti Tuscursmot interrupted.

"You call me Pompino. On occasion it pleases me to be called Pompino the Iarvin."

"Pompino."

"Now we had best fix this shrewish lady's axle and then see her safely into the town, which I take to be Gertinlad."

"I agree. We are in Hamal, I think."

He shook his head as we began on the axle. The lady made no offer to get out of the coach, and the Rapas gathered themselves to help.

"No. I am not sure; but not Hamal."

Well, I thought, if you're right, dom, thank Vox for that.

The Rapa called Onron scowled. "Hamal? You are from Hamal?" His fist gripped his sword, a thraxter, and he half-drew.

"No, Knave," snapped Pompino. "We are not from Hamal."

"The Hamalese," quoth the Rapa, "should be tied up in their own guts and left to rot, by Rhapaporgolam the Reiver of Souls!"

"Quidang to that," said Pompino.

A soft clump of hoofs drew our attention as a party of men riding totrixes rode up. There were ten of them and their six-legged mounts were lathered. Their weapons glittered in their hands, apim and diff alike. Pompino grabbed his piece of wood and prepared to fight; but Onron shrilled a silly cackle and said: "Peace, Knave. These are the lady Yasuri's men, my comrades. They were decoyed away by other Ochs, may they rot in Cottmer's Caverns."

With the increment in our numbers we were able to repair the wheel and axle and so the coach started creakingly on its way to Gertinlad. Pompino and I rode perched on the roof, with Onron and his partner driving, and the totrix men resuming their function as escorts. We rolled through the mellow countryside and under the archway of the town and so into the familiar sights and stinks of a bustling market town and to an inn called the Green Attar. This was a high class hostelry such as would be patronized by a lady of gentle birth. The commander of her escort, a surly Rapa called Rordan the Negus, would have seen us off with a few curt words. He and his men wore half-armor, and were well armed with spear and bow, sword and shield. Pompino would have started an argument in his high-handed way; but Onron, who had carried the personal satchels from the coach into the inn, came out and yelled that the lady Yasuri would speak with us, and Bratch was the word.

So we jumped and obeyed on the run, which is what a serving man does when Bratch! is yelled at him.

As we went in Pompino said: "I think the Everoinye wish us to continue to take care of this lady. I admit it is not an assignment I relish, but the ways of the Everoinye are not for mortal man to understand."

I just nodded and so we went into the Green Attar and the smell of cooking and rich wines and stood before the table at which sat the lady Yasuri. The inn looked to be clean and comfortable, with much polished brass and dark upholstered chairs of sturmwood, with a wooden floor strewn with rugs of a weave new to me. We stood respectfully.

"You did well to drive off those rascally Ochs," said the lady in her high voice. "You will be rewarded."

She presented an outré picture, for she was tiny, and lined of face, with shapeless clothes that swaddled her in much black material like bombazine, shiny and hard, with a blaze of diamonds and sapphires, and with fine ivory lace at throat and wrist. She was apim, and her face looked like a wrinkled nut, with yet a little juice remaining. Her nose was sharp. She wore a wig of a frightful blond color. The rings on her fingers caught the oil lamps' gleam and struck brilliants into our eyes.

Pompino said: "We thank you, lady."

She glared at him as though he had offered her violence.

"I am for LionardDen. The kov here is my friend; but he is away in the north helping in the fight against those Havil-forsaken rasts of Hamal. The land is hungry for fighting men. You are mercenaries. I offer you employment to see me safely through to Jikaida City."

Pompino took a breath.

Before he could speak, the lady rattled on: "I can offer you better pay than usual. A silver strebe a day will buy a mercenary here. I offer you eight per sennight."

With a dignity that set well with him, Pompino pointed

out, "One does not buy a paktun. One pays him for services rendered." As he spoke I received the impression that he was a paktun, probably a hyr-paktun and entitled to wear the golden pakzhan at his throat. "But, lady—are the silver strebes broad or short?"

She cocked up her sharp chin at this.

This was, indeed, a matter of moment. Coinage varies all over Kregen, of course, just as it does on Earth; but the common language imposed, so I thought, by the Star Lords, and the wild entanglement of peoples and animals and plants mean a creeping universality makes of Kregen a place unique by virtue of its very commonality. A short strebe, the silver coin known over most of the Dawn Lands, is worth far less than a broad strebe, and every honest citizen knows very well how to value the two in the scales. They may carry the very same head of whatever king or potentate has issued them, and the reverse may show the same magniloquent declarations of power or current advertisement of political policy; but the short and the broad will not buy the same quantity of goods in the markets—no, by Krun, not by a long chalk.

Now the Dawn Lands of Havilfar form a crazy patchwork of countries, and they bear no resemblance to the ordered checkers of the Jikaida board. They are a confusing conglomeration of kingdoms and princedoms and kovnates and republics, and a map-maker's nightmare. The lady Yasuri hailed from one kingdom and while she was gone her king might be deposed, or her country invaded, so that when she returned she would have to vow fealty to a new sovereign—that was, if her vadvarate still belonged to her. The Dawn Lands, viewed from some lofty perch in space, must resemble a stewpot forever on the boil.

Watching the lady Yasuri I saw how she used her shiny black bombazine to armor herself against the world. She was more accustomed, I guessed, to soft sensil and languorous dresses in the privacy of her own quarters, and she'd probably doff that hideous wig. She presented a hard and shrewish front to the world out of fear or the desire to intimidate. She screwed up her eyes, and her white hand toyed with her glass. She made a great show of thinking deeply. Then:

"Broad."

Pompino nodded, still grave, still engaged in the negotiation of hiring out as a mercenary. But he did not attempt to increase the offer on account of his being, as I supposed, a hyr-paktun. He said: "But I am a Khibil. It would be nine for me."

"Done," said the lady Yasuri, promptly. "Nine for you, Khibil, and eight for the apim."

I was too amused to argue.

Most places of Kregen use the six-day week, which I, rather contrarily, call a sennight. So our pay would be useful. A Pachak here would receive at least twelve broad strebes, possibly fourteen. A Chulik would get the same. You would rarely find a Kataki as a mercenary although there were renowned races of that slavemaster people whose second method of earning a living was hiring out as mercenaries; and they would grump until they got their twelve. As for the Ochs, four or five at the most. Rapas and Fristles and the like would get the standard one strebe a day.

If they didn't argue it out, they'd get short strebes, too.

Pay is relative, of course, and I guessed that in these lands profoundly affected by the war with Hamal up north the price of commodities would have shot up. Perhaps this pay was not as excellent as at first sight it appeared. All the same, I contrasted these rates with those paid to the bowmen and archers of home, where a silver stiver was regarded as the small fortune paid to a Relianchun and where the bronze krad, a denomination of coin newly introduced by the Presidio, figured largely in the imaginations of the men come pay day. The krad, with, I hesitate to observe, an unspeakable likeness of the Emperor of Vallia on the obverse and resounding and inspiring slogans on the reverse, was regarded as fair and just. But, then, my men there in Vallia served their country and not for pay.

Even so, I did not think that the old Crimson Bowmen of Loh, who had formed the old emperor's bodyguard, had received a silver stiver a day. Their Jiktars and Chuktar had taken away their golden talens; of that I was very sure.

When Pompino and I, having made our respects to the lady Yasuri and the hiring being completed, returned to the courtyard of the Green Attar we became immediately aware of an offensive abomination going on there. The sights and sounds were sickening. A number of nobles put up here, for the place was renowned, and one of the members of a noble's entourage was being flogged.

The fellow had been triced up into the flogging triangle in a corner where sweet-scented flowers, brilliant and lovely, depended over the wall, forming a silent mockery of the obscenity going on in their shade. A thick leather gag had been forced between his teeth and secured by thongs around his head. He was flaxen-haired, strongly-built, and his tunic had been stripped down to his waist.

He hung in the leather thongs binding his wrists and ankles to the wood of the triangle. He hung limply, as though accepting what was happening, and then he would jerk, every muscle standing out ridged, and so collapse into that limp huddle again. So he hung and jerked, shuddering, and hung again, and then convulsed once more as the other lash slashed across his bloody wreck of a back.

A left-handed Brokelsh stood at his right side and a right-handed Rapa stood at his left. They took turns to slice the lashes down, black and whistling with stranded thongs.

"By Black Chunguj!" swore Pompino. "I never did like to see a man flogged jikaider."

For the Rapa and the Brokelsh between them were dicing the man's back up into a checkerboard of blood.

A Deldar, a heavy and thick-set man with the weight of years in the grade with no hope of ever making zan-Deldar and then Hikdar about him, spat and swore. "Hangi should have left the wine alone. It's doing him no good, no, nor us, neither."

The noble's guards standing and looking on glumly as their comrade was flogged jikaider—a cruel and inhuman punishment, even to me who had seen men flogged round the Fleet—wore harness much studded with bronze bosses, and with pale blue and black favors. They looked a hard-bitten lot.

Pompino made some remark, and the Deldar hawked up again.

"The notor is strict—aye, may Havandua the Green Wonder mete him his just desserts—strict. You can say that again about the notor, Erclan the Critchoith. Keep at it!" He swung away to bellow at the Rapa and Brokelsh who had desisted in their efforts to flay Hangi's back. "You know the score! Ten times six and six more! Stylor!" to the shaking Relt who stood with slate and chalk marking the strokes. "Keep a strick account!"

"Quidang, quidang," stammered the Relt, his weak beaked face betraying by its frizzle of feathers the state he was in.

The lashes thwunked down again, and Hangi jerked, and was still. There is no real mystery why such a beastly practice should be given a name that associates it, however, remotely, with the supreme board of Kregen. The contrast, it is said, explains the paradox.

"Stole Risslaca Ichor, did Hangi," the Deldar told us, his

face with the veins breaking around the nose sweating and empurpled. "A whole amphora. The notor's favorite, is Risslaca Ichor, always keeps a special supply, and Hangi found it, and Hangi drank it, and there's Hangi now, for all to see."

"Risslaca Ichor." Pompino sniffed. "A mere common rosé adulterated with dopa—"

"Fortified, dom, fortified!"

"So they say."

Then a profound change overcame the Deldar. He grew, if it were possible, even bulkier and more purple. The sweat sprang out in great pearly drops. "Keep at it, you hulus! Hit hard!"

So we looked up to the flower-banked balcony, and there stood the notor, this Kov Erclan Rodiflor. Square and hard and ablaze with gems, he stood braced on wide-planted feet, his hands clamped on his hips, his chin with his strip of black beard upthrust, and his square lowering face brooded on the scene below. Returning to Jikaida City, was Kov Erclan. A man who exuded authority and power, he possessed a dark inner core that gave him the yrium he would have taken had he been a gang leader and not a kov.

Like his men, he wore the pale blue and black favors, arranged in checkerboard fashion. Well, he looked down and we looked up and he saw neither Pompino nor myself in the shadows; his dark eyes were all for the flogging. I thought merely that I had met many men like that, and so we walked on, stony-faced past the guards, and when I next met Kov Erclan—well, that you will hear, all in due time.

Pompino and I thus became, for each of us once more, paktuns, hired mercenaries, bodyguards, men who rented out their skill with arms and laid their lives at risk to earn their daily crust.

Events moved with speed after that. The life of a paktun is mostly boring, and shot through with sudden and brief flashes of scarlet action. Often they are the last things that happen to him. We were outfitted, for it was all found, and donned bronze-studded leather jerkins, with gray trousers and calf-high boots. The weapons were thraxter, the straight cut and thrust sword of Hamal, stuxes, oval shields and a dagger apiece. The green tunic I was handed bore a rusty stain low on the left side, and a rip neatly sewn together, a rip about the size to admit a spear-blade. The trousers had been laundered clean, however, for which I was grateful.

Pompino made a face. "Dead men's clothes."

The helmets were of iron, and not bronze, iron pots thonged under the chin and with ear and back flaps. Holders at the crown bore tufts of green, black and blue feathers.

So equipped and astride totrixes Pompino and I rode out the next morning as part of the escort to Yasuri Lucrina, the Vadni of Cremorra, en route for LionardDen, Jikaida City.

From the rich lands around Gertinlad the way led us across rivers and through forests into country that grew impressively wild and menacingly forbidding. We were in the Dawn Lands of Havilfar. Here, in the ancient countries around The Shrouded Sea were situated those parts of the great southern continent that had been first settled when men arrived here in the beginning of history—so went the old stories. Both Pompino and I were firmly convinced that the Star Lords had sent us to ensure the safety of Yasuri. The whole operation, at least for me, was so markedly different from what had happened before that I deemed it prudent to follow events and to do my best to avoid the wrath of the Star Lords.

Of one thing I was profoundly grateful. Because of the differences this time, and the warning, there was no extra bitterness in me at the parting from Delia. Of course I grieved for the sundering, and vowed to return as soon as I could, echoing in the old way and the old days, I will return to my Delia, my Delia of Delphonc, my Delia of the Blue Mountains. But, this time, she was apprised of my disappearance, and she knew, now, what that fate was that dogged me. No moist-mouthed slimy minions of Quergey the Murgey could affront her now; she'd send that lot packing with a zorca hoof up their rumps. Sorrow touched me that I had not welcomed Drak and clasped hands with him. As with Melow the Supple and Kardo. But I felt the warm glow of satisfaction at the thought that Drak, Prince of Vallia, Krzy, was now there, in Vondium, and, Opaz willing, ready to take up the reins. Suppose he refused? Suppose he contumed the task of standing in for the Emperor of Vallia? He had told us that he would not become emperor while we lived, Delia and I, and I had brushed that aside as sentiment. I felt that Drak, who of all my sons was the strong, sober, industrious one, with that wild Prescot streak in him, too, was best fitted to run Vallia. Had I thought Zeg, who was now King in Zandikar, or Jaidur, who was swashbuckling about in connivance with the Sisters of the Rose, could handle the job better, then primogeniture, too, would have been kicked out with a zorca hoof up its rump. Primogeniture obtains on Kregen; but it is not an unbreakable rule. A man must fight for what he wants there, and it is what a man is and the spirit and heart of him that counts, not what his father is.

Or his mother, either. . . . For the ladies of Kregen are people in their own right, and fully aware of that, with minds that are their own. The ladies of Kregen count, as this Yasuri, Vadni of Cremorra, so sharply reminded us. Some of the women of Kregen there are who hate all men because they are men, as foolish a stance as to hate all calsanys because they are calsanys, or all roses because they are roses. But, then, some women do not deserve to be ladies of Kregen, anyway. . . .

There was little satisfaction to be gained in the situation where I was a puppet of the Star Lords; but it is useless to kick against the pricks when there is nothing one can do about that particular situation. I had slowly and cautiously been attempting to build a kind of structure of deceit against the Star Lords, and had intemperately gone against my own plans and been banished to Earth for twenty-one cruel years. Now I was trying a new tack. But, in the end, obedience to the Everoinye must dominate my actions. They were superhuman. Their powers were far beyond those of mortals, beyond those of the Wizards of Loh, beyond the Savanti. I trembled to dare to think that perhaps Zena Iztar might possess powers to match them.

As we rode I studied to learn what I could from what Pompino could tell me. He was of South Pandahem, a land of which I then knew little. He was married with two sets of twins and from what he did not say I gathered that he rubbed along with his wife, in a kind of habit-formed pattern, rather than taking any active joy from the marriage state. Well, two worlds are full of marriages like that. He was not at all displeased to be called out to serve the Everoinye. He talked well as we jogged along through the land that increasingly grew more ominous, with rocky defiles and overhanging crags leading on to wide plains where the sere grass blew. The country was pock-marked with tracts of badlands, and we were due to spend the night at a fortified posting house at the ford of Gilma. Gilma is a water sprite found in the legends of Prince Larghos and the Demons. Pompino told me that he did not like the Hamalese, a sentiment I could well understand from Hamal's ruthless conquest of Pandahem. But he could tell me little of the Star Lords.

He received his orders from the Gdoinye. When I introduced a casual remark about scorpions, he dismissed them as unpleasant but rarely seen creatures of Havil.

I told him I was from Huringa in Hyrklana. This city I knew well from my days as a kaidur in the jikhorkdun there, and so could fabricate substantial accounts to bolster my story. He eyed me at that.

"Queen Fahia grows too fat, so men say—and I mean you no disrespect, Jak. But men say she cannot live long."

I nodded. "So it is said."

Pompino clicked his tongue at his totrix. We were passing a stand of withered trees and the branches reached out like gray wraiths.

"Men say that the tragedy of Princess Lilah cast a shadow over the kingdom."

Princess Lilah of Hyrklana! I had sent spies to seek news of her whereabouts and all had reported failure.

"It is indeed a tragedy. I would dearly love to know where she is now, By Kru—by Havil."

The slip passed unnoticed.

Much of what we said I will report when the time is due; suffice it that Pompino, for all he was one of those Khibils who consider themselves a cut above ordinary mortals, proved a stalwart companion and in the manner of Khibils brave and resourceful and loyal. A task had been set to his hands and he would fulfil that task with his dying breath.

He did grumble: "What the confounded woman wants to go all this dolorous way to play Jikaida for is a conundrum I would not burden Hoko the Amusingly Malicious with."

There were so many burning questions I had to ask that mention of Jikaida passed me by then. . . . But Pompino knew only that he took his orders from a great scarlet and gold bird, that he was paid handsomely for his trouble in real gold, and that should he disobey he would be punished with exceedingly unpleasant penalties. We did not go into their nature.

"Why, Pompino? Why?"

He looked puzzled. "The gods are passing strange in their ways, Jak. Passing strange. But to serve the gods, to serve the Everoinye, is not that a great pride and does it not confer stature upon a man? Is it not, Jak, a High Jikai?"

I had never looked on rushing about pulling the Star Lords' chestnuts out of the fire as a High Jikai. That great word, that supreme notion of high chivalry and courage and self-sacrifice, seemed to me sacred to deeds writ in gold.

As I did not answer he scowled. "Well?"

"Yes," I said. "Assuredly."

Because he had been the first to pelt down all naked into action and drive the Ochs away he had quite naturally assumed the leadership of our twin mission. I did not bother my head over that. Let him imagine he carried the burden. Truth to tell, I was happy to allow it—and, equally, I liked him.

The posting house at the ford of Gilma was merely a single story house and surrounding wall all built of the gray stones carried down from the frowning hills. We did not change the totrixes or the krahniks, for we had not been pushing them and they were beasts of price. We set off early the next day and so came down the long valley into Songaslad, a town of thieves.

Over the border some sixty dwaburs off lay the country of Aidrin in which lay the capital, the city called Jikaida City. The journey was fraught with peril. It lay over badlands of an exceedingly bad badness. In Songaslad, the town of thieves, caravans were formed for mutual protection on the journey. The lady Yasuri sent her Rapa Jiktar to haggle for the price of a caravan's protection. Perforce, we waited, and set a doubled guard over our possessions.

We lost only a good saddle, richly inlaid, a carpet of high price, and a set of golden candlesticks whose theft almost gave the lady a fainting fit. Her companions, her handmaids in the coach with her, used burned twigs of Sweet Ibroi to revive her. We concluded a deal with hawk-faced Ineldar the Kaktu, the caravan master, forthwith.

So, a long straggling procession of carriages and wagons and riders and people trudging afoot, we wended out of Songaslad, the town of thieves, to cross the Desolate Wastes, and so win our way to Aidrin, and the rich country around LionardDen, Jikaida City.

CHAPTER TEN

Into the Desolate Waste

Many times have I journeyed in caravans across country inhospitable by reason of nature or man, and on each occasion I vow never again, and know even as I vow that the lure of the adventure will always drag me on. Each occasion is different. Kregen is a world of so many startling contrasts that the beauty and terror mingle and fill the spirit with wild eagerness or desolation, with burning ambition to win against all or a calm and joyous acceptance of the stupendous.

Nights under the stars! Ah—they are never to be forgotten.

The Caravan labored along, crossing rivers and winding down long defiles, gaining the far slopes and so rising to emerge onto the vasty plains where the mist lifted blue and eerie, like lantern smoke against snow.

The totrix of the lady Yasuri's given into my charge and whom I rode across the Desolate Wastes was a skewbald called Munky. I was careful of him. Accustomed I may be to walking barefoot across the awful places of Kregen, I was now far more of a mind to ride rather than walk.

Oh, yes, despite all my deeper concerns, I enjoyed that caravan across the Desolate Wastes to Jikaida City. And, if the truth be told, the land was not all desolate. Grass grew and the animals fed. There was water in swift silver streams. Every now and then we crossed stony deserts, or sandy deserts; but we prepared for them. The various places along the way were infested with drikingers and these bandits attacked us, as was their custom. We fought them off.

Here we saw why the Star Lords had provided two men—two kregoinye, I must now call them—to escort the person they had chosen to save for posterity. The Rapa escort fought well and earned their hire along with all the other caravan guards. But, one by one, they went down, by arrow or spear, sword or javelin. Soon my companion Pompino was given the escort command, with the rank of Jiktar, whereat he smiled at me, and I warmed to him, realizing how much and how little he valued these titles. But we saved the skin of the lady Yasuri.

It is not my intention to give a blow by blow account of that journey, much though the prospect tempts me, for this was a kind of holiday. It is with some of the people of the caravan that my interest lies, and therefore yours.

The lady Yasuri herself was going to Jikaida City to play Jikaida, and most of the other folk in the caravan were doing likewise, to play, to participate, to gamble or merely to make a profit on the game.

As is the way with such caravans, people tend to fall into clumps, who jog along together, for company, good fellowship and mutual protection. A deal of this can be put down to the speed of progress. The lady Yasuri's coach matched the speed of an ornate, topheavy creation of the carriage-builder's art, in blue and yellow, that swayed along next in line. This conveyance was drawn by six krahniks. In the caravan were so many of the various marvelous animals of Kregen it were vain to name them all; but there were Quoffas, calsanys, plain asses, hirvels, totrixes, and the like. There were few zorcas. Of course, being Havilfar, there were no voves. This blue and yellow coach with the black and white checkerboard along the sides contained Master Scatulo. In Master Scatulo's terms to speak his name was enough.

Master Scatulo—he trumpeted a host of names all attesting to his enormous prowess as a Jikaidast—permitted the lady Yasuri the graciousness of his company when we halted for meals. Yasuri hung on this young fellow's words—for Scatulo was young, brash, supremely self-confident and, by the reckoning of anyone you cared to ask; a remarkable player of Jikaida, a true Jikaidast.

His face was of a sallow cast, sharp and edgy, with deep furrows between his eyebrows, and eyes of a piercing quality that Sishi, the lady Yasuri's least important hand maiden told me with a laugh, he painted with blue-khol to enhance their impression of brooding intelligence. I believed this. It is known. Pompino guffawed and passed a most demeaning remark.

"He's real clever, is Master Scatulo!" protested Sishi. She, herself, was apim and a little beauty with dark hair and a rosy glowing face and ways that were still artless, despite the way of the world. I waggled a finger at her.

"Now then, mistress Sishi. Beware of clever men like this

Scatulo. Just because he says he is Havil's gift to the world, that he is a genius, doesn't mean he can—"

"I know what you're saying, Jak!"

"Just as well you do, Sishi," said Pompino. "For Jak speaks sooth. This Scatulo will get you—"

Her face was scarlet, Sishi burst out, "You're horrible!"

That, by Vox, was true enough; but had little to do with the subject in question.

There were other Jikaidasts in the caravan; not many. I gathered from sly remarks that a Jikaidast must be in the very topmost flight of his profession to be preferred in Jikaida City. Trouble was, Pompino and I could not flaunt our ignorance; everyone understood so well the significance of Jikaida City that significant details were taken for granted. We agreed to keep our ears open and learn.

The other person who jogged along with us and shared our fire and engaged in conversation was a Wizard of Loh.

Yes. Oh, yes, I well realize the surprise anyone must feel in so cavalier a treatment of a representative of one of the most powerful groups of wizards on Kregen. But Deb-Lu-Quienyin was a pleasant old buffer whose red Lohvian hair was much thinned by perplexed rubbing and whose lined face expressed a perennial surprise at the state of the world. But, for all that, he was a Wizard of Loh. He wore plain robes, with their dark blue only moderately embellished with silver and he wore a stout shortsword, which made me look in wonder.

"Aye, young man, a sword and a Wizard of Loh. Parlous are the days, and grievous the evil thereof."

"Aye, san," I said, giving him the correct honorific of san—sage or dominie. "You speak sooth."

He tilted his lopsided turban-like headdress to one side so as to rub his hair. Strings of pearls and diamonds decorated the folds of blue cloth; but he assured me they were imitation only. "For I have fallen on hard days, young man, and Things Are Not What They Were."

He rode a preysany, the superior form of calsany used for riding, and that indicated a slender purse. Munky jogged alongside the preysany well enough, for a few emphatic kicks indicated to him he had best mind his manners. Preysanys, like calsanys, do offensive things when they are frightened, Deb-Lu-Quienyin wanted to talk. I did not think he suffered from that hideous disease, chivrel, that wastes a man or woman into premature old age; but he was without doubt unlike any Wizard of Loh I had previously encountered. During the days of the journey across the Desolate Waste I heard a deal of his history.

He had been a powerful sorcerer, come from Loh as a young man into Havilfar, and set fair to making his fortune. He had been variously court wizard to kings and kovs in the Dawn Lands, and had spent a time in Hyrklana, whereat we reminisced for a space. Then he had become aware that his powers were failing. He talked to me like this, frankly, I believe, out of the misery in him. He maintained a dignified mien to the people of the caravan and they, being prudent, gave him a wide berth.

Some spark struck between us. I realized he told me much more than he perhaps knew, and I put that confidence down to the journey and the circumstances of the caravan and our traveling together through dangerous country. In the event, we got along capitally. He kept no famulus, for, as he said: "The last one grew too clever, and taunted me, and so left to set up for himself. And I do not have the wherewithal to pay an assistant."

He had a little tame Och slave who tended his clothes and cooked his meals and chattered away to himself, a scrawny bundle in an old blanket coat who walked, for Deb-Lu-Quienyin's purse could not stretch to a second saddle animal. His calsany was loaded with mysterious bundles, bowed under the weight, and there was no room for the Och, Ionno the Ladle. The Wizard of Loh cast glances of mingled covetousness and scorn at the Jikaidast, Master Scatulo, and sighed.

"Look at him, young man, Puffed With the Pride of the Masterful. Once I, too, must have been like that. And see his slave, the muscles, the strength—why, he could carry his master on his back all the way to Jikaida City if he had to."

Truly, Scatulo's personal slave was a powerfully built diff, a Brukaj with immense rounded shoulders and a hunched-forward head with a forceful face with more than a passing resemblance to that of a bulldog. The Brukajin possess legs rather on the short side, it is true; but they are determined, dogged, and I had been pleased to have them serve in any of the armies I had commanded on Kregen. As is to be expected from their natures they are superb in the defense. They are as dissimilar as one could imagine from the Tryfants, who attack with enormous elan, and in retreat merely rout, running every which way. The Brukajin are not to be confused with the Brokelsh, whose thick mat of coarse body hair complements their generally coarse ways of carrying on. I have good friends among the Brokelsh, and I was intrigued to notice the protocol that existed between the Brokelsh in the caravan and this slave of Scatulo's, this powerful but docile Brukaj, who was called Bevon.

Not for Bevon the Brukaj, as a slave, the privilege of a descriptive appendage to his name; Deb-Lu-Quienyin's slave chattering to himself in his brown blanket coat was crowingly conscious of his descriptive name, the Ladle. The Wizard of Loh was good-natured enough to be pleased at this.

"Since my accident, young man," he confided to me as we jogged along under the Suns of Scorpio, tasting the sweetness of the air, watching the ominous countryside. "I have not been the man I was. Time has Entrapped me in Her Coils."

I gathered that the accident, the exact nature of which he did not specify, although it sounded as though he had tried some magic too powerful to be contained, had deprived him of enough of his wizardly powers as seriously to jeopardize his life style. He could not, for instance, go into lupu and spy out events and people at a distance. There were other powers he had lost. He was resigned to them in a bittersweet way, talking of his misfortunes and of life in capital letters. He was a humorous old boy, not strong, proud as are all Wizards of Loh, and yet much on the defensive after the accident.

After a trifling brush with drikingers who drew off after the caravan guards shot their leader we found we had water trouble. The bandits had shot deliberately at the water barrels fixed to the wagon. The amphorae they smashed with ease. The wooden staves of the barrels resisted; but enough were pierced through to cause Ineldar the Kaktu, the caravan master, to put us all on quarter rations until the next water hole.

This caused trouble.

Two days later we were all hot, dusty, dry—and thirsty.

And an event occurred that brought me vividly face to face with the Meaning of Life.

CHAPTER ELEVEN

Prince Mefto the Kazzur

"By Horato the Potent!" exclaimed Pompino. "I am drier than a corpse's shinbone."

I said nothing but sucked on my pebble.

The caravan wended along, a brightly colored succession of carriages and wagons, with clumps of people, apim and diff, trudging along in the dust, and the outriders flanking us, their weapons ready. Ineldar the Kaktu had been wroth with his caravan guards, although, in all honesty, they had fought well and driven the drikingers off. But we all guessed we had not seen the last of those skulking rasts. Before we reached the water hole they would attack again—with a new leader in command, no doubt.

When a straggling line of black dots showed in the southern sky I felt the muscles beside my eyes tighten. At bellowed commands the caravan halted at once. Dust hung about us, slowly dissipating. Everyone stared aloft, to the south, away from the twin suns. Those flyers there must be flutsmen, out reiving, and if they attacked us we'd be caught between two foes. But, and I do not think the flutsmen missed seeing us, the big birds wheeled away in the air and soon vanished. Probably they were in insufficient strength to attack our caravan, which was clearly large and well protected.

This being Havilfar one would expect many flyers to be seen. That group was the only one we saw on the journey. The exigencies of the war being waged against mad Empress Thyllis of Hamal demanded hordes of flyers and the land here was almost denuded. The same was true of vollers and we saw not one. Some of the countries of the Dawn Lands manufacture their own fliers, and these were in constant demand and short supply. Hamal, as I knew to my bitter cost, had a stranglehold on that particular industry.

We were traveling generally westward toward the rugged chains of mountains running through the heart of Havilfar.

These were the same mountains that in their northern reaches the Hamalese call the Mountains of the West, and against which nestles Paline Valley. But that was around four hundred and fifty dwaburs north. We were about halfway between the River Os north of us and the Shrouded Sea to the south. In their southern extremities the mountains swing somewhat to the west and beyond them lie broad rivers and wide lakes, all terra incognito to me. The folk in the caravan called the mountains there—for they have a plethora of names, as common sense must indicate by reason of their extent—the Snowy Mountains.

We were within a day or so of the water hole and the drikingers had not attacked us again.

A group of brilliantly attired riders went past the caravan at a good clip, apparently reckless of our short water supply situation. They had ridden out in defiance when the flutsmen vanished. I had asked Sishi about them and their leader soon after the caravan had started on its journey.

There was no gainsaying their splendid appearance. There were some twenty of them, clustered about their leader. They were diff and apim; the leader was a Kildoi. He reminded me so much of Korero that I had started up, the first time I espied him as he cantered past on his swarth. He had the same beautiful physique, the same four hands and handtail, the same golden beard, glinting in the light of the suns. His eyes were lighter than Korero's and, when I got a good look at them, held a lurking distaste in their depths I recoiled from in instinctive antipathy. In this, he was poles apart from Korero.

The swarths they rode were powerful beasts but two or three hands less in height than those we had fought at First Kanarsmot. Their scales were of a more greenish-purple than the swarths we had defeated, which were of a more reddish-brown. The swarths' wedge-shaped heads which protruded from their bodies on necks that were extensions of body and head, diminishing in diameter from body to head, all in a smooth curved line, so that of neck, really, they had nothing, were decorated barbarically with metals and jewels. Their trappings blazed. From the front a swarth presents a picture of a massive humped mass with that wedge-shaped head thrusting down and forward, the jaws sharp and pointed, the teeth bared and serrated like razor-edged saws.

The Kildoi who led this brilliant and barbaric group wore link-mesh of that superb quality that is manufactured in the Dawn Lands of Havilfar. He affected a gilt-iron helmet. He wore a short slashed robe of white liberally encrusted with cloth of gold. His cape was short and flared spectacularly when he galloped. It was a bright hard yellow in color, edged in gold and silver. His feathers blew in white and yellow, fixed into a golden holding crest.

Yes, he looked magnificent, proud, barbaric, blazing with light under the suns.

"Who," I had said to Sishi, "is that man?"

Sishi knew all the gossip of the caravan, and the scandals, too. She had looked and her color mounted.

"Is he not splendid? So brave, so bold and handsome—"

"Who is he?"

"Why, everyone must know! He is Prince Mefto—Prince Mefto A'Shanofero, Prince of Shanodrin!"

As she continued to stare after the Kildoi and his companions I shook my head. Shanodrin was a country situated in the heart of the Dawn Lands, west of Khorundur. It was a full rich land with great wealth to be won from the rocks and rivers.

Then Sishi heaved up a great sigh.

"Oh," she said. "I do so love a prince!"

"And why not?" I said, I fear somewhat drily.

If there was one thing certain sure about Prince Mefto, he liked to show off. He and his swarthmen would gallop around the caravan like gulls circling a ship, affording visible proof to the people of their presence and the sharpness of their weapons.

And then Sishi, still enraptured with the dazzlement of the prince, said: "Prince Mefto—he is the best swordsman in the world."

Well, for all I knew, he could be. I will have no truck with this nonsense of proclaiming boasts about the best swordsman of two worlds. I have expounded some of my philosophy anent the perils of swordplay and the doom by edge or point that lurks—if expound is not too pompous a word. So I made some light quip, whereat Sishi flounced around, blushing, and tried to hit me with the length of sausages she happened to be carrying for the lady Yasuri's midday snack. With that deeply philosophic reminder, I went off to see about my duties as a paktun earning his hire.

The rich personages in their carriages had taken the obvious and sensible precaution of providing a supply of water for their own personal use. We knew Yasuri had her amphorae stacked in her coach, which we louts of her escort were not permitted to enter. Ineldar the Kaktu was cognizant of this trick, of course, and he did his best to share out the water on an equal basis. But, as Master Scatulo was not slow to point out with his sharp Jikaidast's wit, the caravan water was paid for and for the use of all. What he, Master Scatulo, happened to have in his coach was by way of an extra and, by the Paktun's Swod's Gambit! was none of anyone else's damn business.

These sentiments were shared by the lady Yasuri and the other upper crusties of the caravan.

Poor old Deb-Lu-Quienyin, for all he was an apparently dried up old stick, seemed to be in need of water, and I had fallen into the habit of sharing my ration with him. I am often wholeheartedly glad that I can scratch along with little to drink, although preferring unending cups of tea, and when it comes to push of pike and there is a serious shortage of drink—I can managed, somehow.

We had passed the stage where he would say how kind I was, and that people who assisted a Wizard of Loh usually wanted something in return, and now we would sip the water companionably and talk while our mouths were moist.

"Do you notice that our famous Master Scatulo usually talks in terms of Jikaida?"

"I had noticed."

"An affectation. He plays all day. He plays against his slave, Bevon the Brukaj, and always he wins."

"Well, he is a Jikaidast. They are professionals. They have to win to eat."

"True. But watch Bevon. He is a skilled player. I believe he makes stupid moves deliberately so as to lose."

"Scatulo would see that at once!" I protested.

"Maybe. Maybe he is too puffed up with pride."

It was not exactly true to say Scatulo played all day. The board would come out the moment we halted and the Deldars would be Ranked; during traveling periods he read from the many books of Jikaida lore he carried with him in his coach.

I had fallen into friendly conversation with Bevon the Brukaj and had learned some of his history. His gentleness seemed to me to sit strangely with his evident craggy toughness. He carried no sword, although he confided to me that he could use a blade, and as a slave was equipped with a stout stave to defend his master. I knew Scatulo had a sword in his coach that Bevon might use if pressed. The Jikaidast's orders to Bevon resounded with the ugly word "Grak!" It was grak this and grak that all day. Grak means jump, move, obey or your skin will be flayed off your back or you must work until you drop dead. It is, indeed an ugly word.

I said to Bevon one day: "Are you a Jikaidast, Bevon?"

"No, Jak." He fetched up a sigh. "I might have been back home but for my tragedy." He looked mournful as he spoke. Well, his story was soon told, and ugly in the telling thereof. He had been accused of a cowp, and, as you know, a cowp is a particularly beastly and horrible kind of murder, in which sadism and mutilation form part. The people had cried out against him and he had been locked away and would have been slain in lawful retribution. "Had I been guilty, Jak, I think I would have stayed and let them kill me. But I was innocent, so I escaped."

"I can't see how anyone could think you would commit murder, Bevon."

"The man who died had made advances to a girl with whom I was friendly. I do not know; but I think she slew him. But I was blamed. So I ran away to be a soldier and was taken up as a slave. I do not really mind, for my heart is not in life—"

"By Havil!" I said, incensed. "Now that is just not good enough. So you are slave. Why not escape when we reach Jikaida City—?"

"You know little of that place, I fear."

"I know nothing."

"They play Kazz-Jikaida there." Kazz is Kregish for blood.

That did explain a great deal. It also explained a little of Prince Mefto's vaunted nickname, for he was traveling to Jikaida City to play in the games, and his sobriquet was Mefto the Kazzur.

That splendid prince was pirouetting his swarth about a little to the side of the space where the caravan had halted. I looked at him, and grew tired of his antics, and resumed our conversation. Whenever Bevon found the time away from his master's Jikaida board we would talk, and he joined Deb-Lu-Quienyin and me at night around our fire. The Wizard of Loh regarded the Brukaj not as he did his own slave but rather as a potential Jikaidast who had temporarily fallen on evil times.

Often Pompino would join us, and, to tell the truth, we played Jikaida as well as Jikalla and the Game of Moons. This latter is near mindless; but it amuses many folk whose brains for whatever reason are not able to grapple with Jikaida or any of the other superior games.

So, as we neared the water hole and the drikingers had not

put in an appearance and we were hot and thirsty and fatigued, I fancied that we might find the damned bandits waiting for us at the water, mocking us, taunting us to try to reach the water hole against their opposition. Ineldar shared the thought, too, for he hoarded our water meanly. The caravan guards stood watch like hawks.

During a halt when the suns burned down we drank little if at all, for the sweat would waste the precious fluid. That last night before the water hole with the stars fat in the sky and the cooking fires burning with eye-aching brilliance, we took our water rations thankfully. What happened happened in a kind of copybook way, as though this were the moment I had been waiting for many seasons to arrive. When it did, I found I could not identify my emotions with any accuracy.

It turned out this way. . . . At our fire the lady Yasuri and Master Scatulo finished their meals and retired to their coaches. Bevon, Pompino, Quienyin and myself lingered for a space, for we had hoarded a little water and were about to share it out between ourselves. It was legal water; that is, it was ours issued to us by Ineldar the Kaktu. Sishi slipped past her mistress's coach to join us, giggling, for she had a little sazz with which to sweeten the water. She had probably stolen it from Yasuri, a procedure I regarded with both disfavor and applause. In return for the sazz, which would freshen the water and make of it a pleasant drink, Sishi was to receive her share. We would split the sazz five ways.

Ionno the Ladle might come in for a few mouthfuls, also.

To get the sequence right is not easy. In the starlight with the Twins just vaulting over the horizon and the flare of the fire we crouched around like conspirators. The rattle of a window shutter announced Master Scatulo's peevish voice.

"Grak, Bevon! Grak, you idle, shiftless rast! Bring some water—Pallan's Hikdar's Swod to Pallan's Hikdar's sixth! Bratch! You useless cloddish lumop, Grak!"

With a sigh, Bevon stood up, a massive bent shape against the starlight. Quienyin murmured that he was not enamored of Scatulo's notation. The fire struck sparks from a glinting figure that appeared, striding along between the caravan and the fires. I saw this was Prince Mefto. Bevon took up his goblet and started for Scatulo's carriage. Prince Mefto, leading his swarth, approached.

There was nothing any of us could say to halt Bevon and to persuade him that the water ration was his. His master had demanded it and Bevon was slave.

A fellow who had been slave a long time and grown cunning in slavish ways would have gulped the sazz down instantly and then whined that there was no water—and if he got a beating for it would regard that as quits doubled, once for drinking the water himself and second for depriving his master of it. But Bevon was gentle and unschooled in the devious ways of the world. And, too, there is every chance that he really felt his master required the sazz—oh, yes, absolutely. Something like that must surely have been in his mind in view of what occurred.

Mefto was swigging from a bottle. He resealed this and moving to the side of his swarth thrust the bottle away. He patted the swarth's greenish-purple scaled head. He saw Bevon.

"Hai, slave! Kraitch-ambur,* my swarth is thirsty. Give me that water."

Bevon halted.

Better he should have run into the darkness.

Prince Mefto frowned. We could see his resplendent figure reflecting our firelight. His lower right hand fell to one of his sword hilts.

"Slave, the water! Grak!"

"Master," stammered Bevon. "It is for my master—"

"To a Herrelldrin Hell with your master! I shall not tell you again, slave. The water!"

Bevon just stood, his dogged face perplexed, his massive shoulders hunched, it seemed, protectively over the goblet. Scatulo yelled again and Bevon jumped and Mefto reached forward to snatch the water and the goblet fell and the sazz-flavored water spread into the dirt.

"You onker! You stupid yetch!"

Prince Mefto was incensed. He whipped out the sword he gripped and with another hand patted his swarth affectionately. "My poor Kraitch-ambur! There is no water for you. But the slave will be punished!"

With that Mefto the Kazzur began hitting Bevon with the flat of his sword.

Desperately attempting to protect himself with upraised arms, the Brakuj was knocked over onto the ground. The Kildoi went on hitting him sadistically with the flat.

I stood up.

Pompino rose at my side and put a hand on my arm.

"No, Jak. He will take it amiss if you interfere."

* Kraitch-ambur: Thunder

"Had I my powers," sighed Quienyin, and took a sip of his drink.

Sishi was gasping and her hands were pressed fiercely to her breast, her face shining in the firelight.

Now Bevon was beginning to yell, the first cries of pain that had passed his lips. The sword rose and fell with wet soggy sounds. Bevon rolled this way and that, a huddled quivering mass, defenseless.

"No, Jak!" Pompino pulled me.

I shook him off and walked across to this gallant Prince Mefto the Kazzur.

"Jak! He will slaughter you!"

The prince paused in the beating to look across Bevon's prostrate and groaning form. His golden eyebrows drew down menacingly. His upper right hand dropped to the second sword hilt.

"Well, rast?"

I said, "Prince. You chastise this man unjustly—"

I got no further. Soft words were not the currency of Mefto the Kazzur.

He simply said, "Yetch, you presume to your death!"

He leaped Bevon and charged full at me, two swords whistling. Both were thraxters.

I drew my thraxter and parried the first blows. I gave ground, circling, already realizing I was in for a fight. To be forced to kill this fellow would lead to most unpleasant consequences, for he was a prince and I a hired paktun.

It seemed to me in the first few moments of the fight that I dare not slay him and must therefore seek to stretch him out senseless. He would have to be tackled as I tackle a Djang, with the added complication of his tail-hand. He was rather like a Djang with his four arms and a Kataki with his tail rolled into one. I have fought Djangs and Katakis, and one Djang can dispose of—well of a lot of Katakis.

This unpleasant cramph was a Kildoi.

Nine inches of daggered steel whipped up in his tail-hand and twinkled between his legs at me.

With a skip and jump I got out of the way. I did not slash the tail off. As we fought I fancied I had not sliced his tail off because that was the beginning of more trouble, that he had to be knocked out. As we fought I realized that he had not let me slice his tail off.

He was a marvel.

We fought. The blades flashed and rang with that sliding

screech. Oh, yes, he had three blades against my one; but that was not it, not it at all. I knew and he knew, after a space.

He drew back. He was smiling. He looked pleased.

"Whoever you are, paktun, I have never met a better swordsman. But I think you must number your days now."

The best swordsman in the world, Sishi had called him.

I didn't know if he was that. But I did know that I had, at last, met my match.

CHAPTER TWELVE

The Fight Beside the Caravan

Every swordsman must be aware that one day he may meet his match and so enter his last fight.

One reads so often of our intrepid hero who is so vastly superior as a swordsman, fighting other wights, and toying with them, cutting them up, with the outcome never in doubt. As you know I had always entered each fight with the knowledge that this could be the time I met my master. Oh, yes, I have cut up opponents, as I have related. One reads of the way in which the hero goes about his task. But now, here under the fatly glowing stars of Kregen, with the Moons rising and the crimson firelight playing upon the halted caravan, I was in nowise being gently admonished and taught a lesson, rather I was being sadistically tortured before the end.

With a convulsive snatch I managed to get my dagger out and into play. That made two blades against three. But this Kildoi was a master bladesman. The swords wove their deceptive patterns of steel. He knew every trick I essayed. He showed me three or four I'd never come across and only by desperate efforts I managed to escape, and even then I believe he let me, for the fun of it. Once a swordsman sees a trick he knows it—as I have said—otherwise he is dead.

I learned.

But I knew that he knew more than I did. And, all the time, his two left arms poised prettily and the hands hung gracefully. If he wished, he could bring two more blades into the fight.

Well, to take some ludicrous credit, after a space he hauled out a short sword with his upper left hand, and pressed me. I knew now I was fighting for my life and any thought of merely hitting him over the head was long flown. I rallied and fought back, and the swords clashed and clanged, and then, and I saw the fact as proof of something and as a final death warrant, his lower left fist pulled out a long dagger. So now he had five weapons against my two, and some of the smile was gone from his handsome face with the golden beard blowing.

Could Korero, I wondered, fight like this?

I'd have to see when I got back to Vallia.

And then. . . . The truth was I wasn't going to get back to Vallia. . . . Not after Prince Mefto the Kazzur had finished with me.

As some fighting men do, he talked as he battled.

"You are good, paktun, very good. I would love to talk to you about your victories, your instructors. But I am a prince and I do not tolerate your kind of conduct."

He cut me about the left shoulder and I swirled away and then used a risky attack to land a hit on his left shoulder. I saw the blood there, a smear in the light. We both wore light tunics, having doffed our armor. His face went mean.

"You think, you rast, you can better me? Me, Mefto the Kazzur, who fought his way to a princedom over the bodies of his foes? Fool!"

Well, yes, I was a fool, right enough.

I hit him again, a glancing blow across his face and severed a chunk of his beard.

Those two hits were the only ones I scored.

He pinked me again and I slid two of his blades and a third and fourth chunked a gouge out of my right side.

He was beginning to enjoy himself.

He didn't like the cut on his face. I hoped it left an ugly scar, the rast.

Swordsmen have their little foibles. He had me in his toils, right enough. But as we fought and I tried the old trick of dismembering him piecemeal, being unable to finish him with a body thrust, I began to pick up hints as to his favored techniques. The trouble was, it was not just that he had five blades, or that his technique was well-nigh perfect, but that he was just supremely good. He was not quite as fast as me; had he been I'd have been stretched lifeless by now.

So I began to work out a last desperate gamble that would break all the rules and would make or break. Truth to tell, I had little real hope. The moment I began the passage I fancied he would detect instantly the attack and know the correct counter. But desperate situations demand desperate remedies. I was bleeding profusely now; but all the cuts were shallow and I knew he but toyed with me.

He was chattering away as we fought.

"I joy in this contest, paktun! By the Blade of Kurin! You are indeed a master bladesman."

Maybe—but I was like to be a dead bladesman, master or not. . . .

With a sudden and ferocious passade he began an attack aimed at slicing off my left ear—I think. I defended desperately, and gave ground, and faintly I heard screams and guessed Sishi and Pompino were riveted by this spectacle.

Time for the last great gamble. . . . I positioned myself and a long arrow abruptly sprouted from Mefto's right shoulder, between those cunningly swiveled double joints.

He screamed.

He fell back, screeching, and he dropped all his weapons.

Another arrow hissed past my head and went thwunk into the painted wood of Scatulo's carriage. Without a thought I dropped flat and dived under the coach.

Well—yes.

The drikingers had played us and now they drove in to finish us completely and steal all we had.

Logic indicated they had chosen their time well. We were at rest, we were short of water, we were tired and apprehensive, and we ought all to have been asleep but for the sentries, and they, poor devils, would no doubt be sprawled with slit throats. The fight had given the bandits pause and some intemperate hothead had loosed at us and so the alarm was raised.

The drikingers were blessed by me, then, I can tell you.

And, to be honest and all the same—that second arrow would have pinned me but for the instinctive move I'd made when the first one shafted Mefto. Speed—that was all I had as advantage over Mefto, and it was speed of reaction that in the end had saved me.

The caravan roused and the paktuns turned out and Bevon took up his sword from Master Scatulo's carriage and we fought.

The fight was savage and unpleasant with much carving up of leathery hides and stripping of bright feathers; but at last we drove the drikingers off and collapsed, exhausted.

These skirling events were just those I had been missing as emperor in Vallia. . . . How far removed this brisk little encounter was from the ordered and planned evolutions of the Phalanx!

But, death attended both in equal measure.

In the morning we buried our dead or cremated those whose religious convictions demanded that ingress to the Ice

Floes of Sicce. Various gods were apostrophized for good fortune for the ibs of the departed. As for the drikingers, we found only three of them, twisted in death by the wagon wheels, and these, too, we buried. They had been lean hardy men, apims, with leathery skins and ferocious bunches of hair dyed purple, and with scraps of armor looted from previous caravans. Of the other bandit dead, they had been all carried off by their comrades.

So, groaning and protesting, the caravan moved off and safely reached the water hole and from then on the journey across the Desolate Waste proceeded as such a journey should—filled with alarums and excursions but with a happy arrival at the end.

The country opened out and grew fat and rich once we crossed the River of Purple Rushes. There was a ford and a strong fort and parties of warriors of Aidrin to escort us in. They greeted us in jocular mood, making light of our problems, telling us of the troubles that previous unfortunate caravans had endured. There were caravans that set out from Songaslas, the town of thieves, that never reached the River of Purple Rushes. White and yellow bones scattered over the Desolate Waste marked their endings.

From the fort by the ford Prince Mefto was carried swiftly ahead of us, with his men, to Jikaida City. He left the caravan. He had not spoken to me and was reputed badly injured—and at the time I suspected that an arrow in the cunning double-joint had done more harm than it would do to a fellow with only two arms to fight with. I had kept a strict watch for revenge; but nothing transpired. What honor code he followed, if any, I did not know. But I had the strongest—and nastiest—suspicion that I had not heard the last of Prince Mefto the Kazzur.

If I do not dwell overmuch on my reactions to that fight I think you will respect that. I had had a shock, all right; and, too, I had grown in understanding. In future, fights would not be quite the same again; but I fancied I knew enough of Dray Prescot to guess what he would do. One is as one is, and like the Scorpion, must hew to nature's path.

The Wizard of Loh, Deb-Lu Quienyin was overjoyed to have reached his destination safely.

"I shall seek out San Orien at once. He, I feel sure, I hope, will be able to cure me—to retrieve my powers."

Saying remberee to him I brought up the subject I had been harboring for long. "I am confident he will do everything he can to aid you, San. Tell me, do you know of a Wizard of Loh called Phu-Si-Yantong?"

"Dear San Yantong! I have not heard of him for ages."

Well, now. . . .

How Wizards of Loh kept in touch was a subject not for ordinary men. But old Deb-Lu-Quienyin barbled on happily about Yantong, the biggest villain unhanged, and I wondered if there could be two Wizards of Loh with the same name. But now, Quienyin would have none of that. He had not heard of Yantong for many seasons, and when last he had been in contact Yantong had been building up a useful practice in Loh. "Of course, I always felt he was marked for great things. There was an aura about him, despite his difficulty. I do hope he prospers."

There was no point in arguing about that; but I did pick up one or two useful hints from Quienyin. He was reticent about this "difficulty" of Yantong's, and would not be drawn, and I wondered if Phu-Si-Yantong was indeed the cripple he had pretended to be and that was his difficulty.

We watched Master Scatulo's coach trundling off to the superior inn where the Jikaidast would stay until, as Bevon put it: "He has established his credentials."

LionardDen, Jikaida City, was given over to one thing in life. Jikaida. The game consumed the people. Of course, they lived by it and it paid them handsome dividends. Their country of Aidrin was rich in worldly goods, the fields and mines and rivers yielded a bountiful harvest. People flocked from all over to play Kazz-Jikaida. There were enormous fortunes to be made. There were reputations to be made.

Standing saying remberee to the Wizard of Loh, Pompino said to me, "I do not fancy staying here overmuch. But it seems we may have to."

Quienyin nodded. "When a caravan returns across the Desolate Waste, I think. It is suicide to attempt the crossing alone or in small numbers. And all west of here across the lakes is dreadful, so I am told by those who know—leem hunters and the like."

I said: "D'you fancy the life of a leem-hunter, Pompino?"

Quienyin laughed and my fellow kregoinye made a face. "By Horato the Potent, Jak. No!"

"You could take employment in the games."

"How so, San?"

"Why, stout fighting men are always wanted. I, myself, do not care for Kazz-Jikaida. But it has its attractions."

"We will, I think find out a little more first," Pompino told me, whereat, feeling my wounds still a little sore, I nodded agreement.

Jikaida City certainly was beautiful, with airy kyros and broad avenues and with houses that were graceful and colonnaded against the heat and thick-walled against the cold. The climate, by reason of the lakes, was not too extreme this deeply in the center of the continent. Everywhere the checkerboard was used as decoration. One could grow tired of the continual repetition. Even the soldiers' cloaks were checkered black and white.

Quienyin shook his head. "If you go as a warrior you will be expected, as part of your duties, to act in the games. That is understood."

"I have no wish to be a soldier," said Pompino. Truth to tell, we two kregoinye were stranded here.

And there was not a single sight of a golden and scarlet raptor circling arrogantly above us, mocking us with his squawk.

The lady Yasuri paid us off, and she had the grace to thank us for our services. But paid off we were, and so were at a loose end. I said to Pompino: "I am for going back across the Desolate Waste. I have urgent business that will not wait."

"No business," he said sententiously, "is more important than that of the Everoinye."

One could not argue with that sentiment. But I was serious.

"If we can buy or steal a couple of fluttrells—"

"They are more precious than gold. And how many have you seen since we arrived?"

"None." There were volroks and other flying men abroad on the etreets of the city; but we saw no aerial cavalry. That there must be some seemed to me probable. I'd have a saddle-bird, I promised myself; but in the interim until I gained one we had to find something to do. So, as we had known, the games drew us.

"Anyway," I said as we hitched up our belts and went off to find a suitable tavern, "Ineldar the Kaktu will be taking a caravan back across the Desolate Wastes. We have only to sign on with him as caravan guards."

CHAPTER THIRTEEN

In Jikaida City

Before we patronized a tavern there was a duty Pompino and I must do vital to any good Kregan. We retained the shirts and trousers given to us by the lady Yasuri; but all else had been returned. We could feel the golden deldys wrapped in scraps of rag and tucked into our belts. Our first port of call was the armorers.

The fashion of rapier and main gauche imported from Valia and Zenicce into Hamal had not yet reached this far south into Havilfar. We chose good serviceable thraxters, and swished the cut and thrust swords about in the dim shop with its racks of weapons and armor. The proprietor was a Fristle. He stroked his whiskers as we pawed over his goods.

"Nothing better in Jikaida City, doms. Friendly Fodo—that's me—can set you up with an arsenal for the finest caravan across the Desolate Waste."

"Just a sword and dagger," I said, pleasantly. "And a brigandine, I think?" with an inquiring look at Pompino.

"I have this beautiful kax," said Friendly Fodo, giving the breast and back a vigorous polish. It was iron, with scroll-work around the edges. We did not even bother to inquire the price as we refused. We had to make our pay spin out until we found fresh employment.

The reason I had chosen a brigandine, in which the metal plates are riveted through the material, instead of an English jack, where the plates are stitched and threaded, was simply that even a cursory inspection of the workmanship of the jack Friendly Fodo displayed showed it was Krasny work, inferior. Pompino chose a brigandine and then he touched the forte of his thraxter. Neatly incised in the metal was that familiar magical pattern of figure nines interlocked.

"You're in luck, dom," said Friendly Fodo. "A high-class weapon. Came from a Chulik who died of a fever."

Examination of the thraxter I eventually chose for its feel

and balance revealed a tiny punched mark in the form of the Brudstern, that open-flower shaped form whose magic is whispered rather than spoken. I nodded, amused, and paid over the gold required.

Pompino bought solid boots and, after a moment's hesitation, I bought softer, lower-cut bootees. Walking barefoot is no hardship for me, an old sailorman, within reason.

Then, after a few other necessary purchases in the Arcade of Freshness, we placed our new belongings into a small satchel and rolled off to the tavern to begin the next important duty laid on a good Kregan.

Truly, Beng Dikkane, the patron saint of all the ale drinkers of Paz, smiled on Jikaida City.

We had a whole new city and its inhabitants to explore, a happy situation, and after the rigors of the journey Pompino certainly, and I, I confess a little wryly, without too many reservations, set about easing the dust from our throats and seeing what there was to be seen and generally winding down. The wounds I had taken, although superficial, itched nonetheless, and the soreness persisted. Pompino did remark with a twitch of his foxy face that, perhaps, that rast Mefto the Kazzur used poisoned blades. But that is unusual on Kregen.

Very soberly I said, "He has no need of that kind of trick. He is the best swordsman I have ever met." I drank a long swigging draught, for by this time we were on our second and the alehouse was filling up with mid-morning customers. "But he is a rast, more's the pity. All his prowess and skill has not taught him humility."

"He's a yetch who ought to be—"

"Quite. He is the best swordsman. But he is not the greatest."

"Yet, Jak, if I had his skill with the sword would I feel humble?" Pompino pondered that. "I do not think so."

"If you had been picked by the gods to be favored with a great gift, as Mefto surely has, would you feel arrogance over that? Or would you feel awe—and a little fear?"

Pompino stared at me over the pewter rim of his goblet.

"Jak—we are kregoinye. We have been marked!"

"By Havil!" I said, and I sat back, astounded.

After a space in which sylvie glided over to refill our goblets and Pompino spilled out a couple of copper coins, I said, "All the same. It is not the same—if you see what I mean. Mefto's gift and our tasks cannot stand comparison."

Pompino was staring after the sylvie and licking his lips.

"I'm surprised a place like this can afford to hire a sylvie—slave or not. They tend to—to distract a fellow."

That was true.

"We should, I think," I said, "find Ineldar the Kaktu and make sure he will hire us for the return journey. We must know when he is starting." I looked around and lowered my voice. "I begin to think we will not find a fluttrell or mirvol to steal in this city."

"Agreed. But another stoup first, Jak."

By the time we left to explore the city, Pompino was very merry. We quickly discovered that Jikaida City was not one but two. Twinned cities under the twin suns flourish all over Kregen, of course. The extensive shallow depression between low and rolling hills cupped the twin cities in a figure-eight shape. Between them rose edifices of enormous extent whose function was to house the games. We strolled along in the sunshine, admiring the sights, and Pompino kept breaking into little snatches of song, half to himself, half to any passersby who took his fancy. Despite myself, I did not pretend I was not with him. After all,he had proved a comrade.

Many of the more important avenues radiated away from the central mass of the Jikaidaderen and the buildings reflected the architectural tastes of many nations and races. In one avenue we saw a low-walled structure over the gate of which hung a banner, flapping gently in the light breeze, which read: NATH EN SCREETZIM.

Underneath, in letters only slightly less loud, was the Kregish for: 'Patronized by the leading Jikaidasts.'

Pompino ogled the sign owlishly. "Are you a leading Jikaidast, Jak? I can rank my Deldars and—and reach the first drin. But after that—" He paused to bow deeply to a couple of passing matrons, who eyed him as though the flat stones of Havilfar had yawned and yielded up their denizens. "After that, dom, why—it all gets confusing."

"Stick to Jikalla."

"No, no. The Game of Moons for me. Then the dice decide."

For some perverse reason I defended the Game of Moons. "And skill, also, Pompino. You can't deny that."

He staggered three paces to larboard, smiled, and lurched four paces to starboard.

"Deny it? I love it!"

"Come on. They'll have you inside with a sword in your fist before you can call on Horato the Potent."

He nodded his head with great solemnity, his face glazed,

his mouth slowly opening and then closing with a snap, only once more to drop open. I took his arm and steered him along the avenue away from Nath the Swordsman's premises.

Nath's place was not the only establishment we saw where the arts and skills and disciplines of fighting were taught. After my contretemps with Mefto I wondered—and not altogether in the abstract—whether or not I might benefit from a fresh course of instruction. One fact seemed clear to me from what I had pieced together of Mefto's career. As a Kildoi he was by nature possessed of formidable advantages in the fighting business. He had left his native Balintol seasons ago and had ruffled and swaggered his way through the Dawn Lands as a mercenary, rapidly rising through paktun to be hyr-paktun and privileged to wear the golden pakzhan at his throat. Then, with all the raffish and bloody accompaniments to revolution, he had taken command of a band of near-masichieri and with their help overthrown the old prince of Shanodrin and taken over the country, the titles, the wealth and the power. His legal acceptance had soon followed. By all the laws of Kregen, he was now Prince of Shanodrin. The revolution by itself would not have been enough—in law—to give him the right. The bokkertu had to be made. Then Mefto the Kazzur became Prince Mefto and could take the name of A'Shanofero as his own.

From what little I knew of the man I wondered why he had chosen a principality and not a kingdom. But, probably, he had his avaricious gaze already fixed on his next victim.

Looked at completely dispassionately, Mefto the Kazzur had merely done what I, myself, had done.

All the same, the idea of Mefto lording it as Emperor of Vallia sent a little shudder up my backbone.

"You ill, Jak?"

"Not as much as you, you old soak, Pompino."

"Don't get away from the wife enough, that's my trouble."

"Then may Havil the Green smile on us, and the Everoinye set another task to our hands."

"Amen to that, by the pot belly of Beng Dikkane!"

The twin Suns of Scorpio, the red and the green, are not called Zim and Genodras in Havilfar, but Far and Havil. Usually on Kregen Jikaida boards are checkered in blue and yellow or white and black. There are places where the red and green are used; Jikaida City was not, as far as I knew, one of them.

As we neared the imposing pile of the Jikaidaderen the walls assumed something of their true stature, and we saw the palace was large, perfectly capable of accommodating many laid-out Kazz-Jikaida boards. The place was a maze of inner buildings, a vast complex not, I suppose, unlike the jikhorkduns surrounding the amphitheatres and the arenas of Hamal and Hyrklana and other places. We strolled along, and Pompino was singing a charming if foolish ditty about a Pandaheem who kissed the baker's wife and went floury white to see the sweep's wife, whereat he became sooty black. The song is called "Black is White and White is Black" and I will not repeat it.

The city within Jikaida City in which we thus swaggered along was bedecked with yellow. The other city claimed the blue. They had names, long rigmaroles of high boasting; but folk usually called them just Yellow City or Blue City. I had to stop myself from joining in some of Pompino's songs. And, I wondered how long it would be before the Watch employed by the Nine Guardians would heave up to arrest us.

Each city was run by its own Masked Nine, and they had no kings or queens here. They did have a nobility, and from this aristocracy were drawn the Guardians of the Masked Nine. The system employed was a democratic one that extended only to these nobles and their families; but within that limitation they voted for office and did not fight for it. Jikaida drew the fires of the blood, so it was said.

As a secret ballot was used, the successful candidates remained anonymous, masked, inducted into office by their peers. This system had, so far, proved effective in preventing unrest from developing into revolution. The army and the Watch obeyed the orders of the Masked Nine Guardians and enforced their edicts. We had heard of punishments for disobedience that would give nightmares to a seasoned paktun. All was balance, force countering force, and, over all, the games of Jikaida dominated the twin cities of Jikaida City.

The truth would not be served in saying the inhabitants of Blue City and Yellow City hated one another. They were rivals, at times deadly rivals; but all their hostility was played out on the Jikaida boards. Yellow against Blue. Blue against Yellow. Their loyalties to their color city and their partisanship were alike intense. They were dedicated. The forces aloof from this rivalry, the religious orders, the army—and very few others, by Krun!—were still infected by the Jikaida fever and wore black and white checkerboarded insignia. Havil the Green was a noted deity here, with his temples and priests; but there were others, plenty of them in apparently equal prominence. On the surface there appeared no sign of

Lem the Silver Leem, for which I was thankful, although I kept my eyes open on that score.

Managing to drag Pompino off without further problems and keeping the Watch well in the offing, I found a suitable hostelry in the middle-sections of Yellow City called The Pallan's Swod. Here, after due payment, I was able to deposit Pompino in a bed and close the door on his snores.

Useless to detail my doings after that; they boiled down to confirmation of the absence of flyers, the vowed testimony from seasoned leem-hunters that only death by suicide awaited across the lakes, and that Ineldar the Kaktu would be returning when a caravan had been assembled and when that would be, by Havil, he had no idea. In the meantime he was going to drink up and visit the public games and have himself a good time and that was what Pompino and I should do. He'd be pleased to hire us as caravan guards when the time was ripe.

Then he lowered his flagon and laid a long brown finger against his nose. The uproar in the tavern around us masked our words from all but ourselves. He winked.

"That run in you had with Mefto the Kazzur. You are lucky to be alive. He is a marvel with his swords."

"Aye."

"You bear him no rancor?"

"Not for beating me. But, as to himself, as a man—"

"Agreed. Listen. Go to see Konec na Brugheim. He puts up at the Blue Rokveil. Speak of the king korf. Do not mention my name." He drew his finger down his nose and reached for his flagon. He looked at me, once, a shrewd hard glance, and then away. "I have spoken."

"Thank you," I said, not completely sure of what I should thank him for, but detecting his intention to help. He drank noisily and then bellowed for more wine, for the suns were declining. I joined him in a flagon of Yellow Unction, and then hied myself back to The Pallan's Swod to find Pompino not holding his head and groaning but cursingly trying to pull his boots back on and thirsting for more singing and amphorae of wine.

I draw the veil on that night's doings. But Pompino rolled back to the tavern with his head flung back and his mouth wide open, yodeling to the Moons of Kregen.

In the morning I took myself off to find this Konec na Brugheim at the sign of the Blue Rokveil, and to discover what secrets would be unlocked at the mention of the king korf.

CHAPTER FOURTEEN

Of the Fate of Spies

As the Zairians of the Eye of the World say: "Only Zair knows the cleanliness of a human heart." I had said I held no rancor against Mefto, and I believed that. But, humanly fallible as I am, perhaps a lingering resentment impelled me to watch my back with a sharper scrutiny even than usual as I walked gently along in the early morning opaline radiance of the Suns of Scorpio. That vigilance which may have been caused by bitterness and suppressed longings for revenge served me well on that morning I walked in Jikaida City to talk about the king korf to a man I did not know.

They picked me up a couple of streets from the hostelry and they paced me, fifty paces or so to my rear. They kept to the shadowed side of the street. There were four of them and they wore swords and were dressed in inconspicuous gray and blue, as was I, save that their favors were of a hard bright yellow. There were two apims, a Rapa and a Brokelsh. I walked on, placidly, and pondered the indisputable fact that no man or woman born of Opaz knows all the secrets of Imrien.

The decision I reached seemed to me common sense. With a succession of alterations in course and speed, and with a swift vanishing into the mouth of a side alley where a stall loaded with appetizing roasted chingleberries smoked in the early light, I lost them. I kept up a good pace, but not too obtrusive a bustle in the morning activity, and so circled the Jikaidaderen and came into Blue City. Would those rasts with their yellow favors follow here?

Finding the Blue Rokveil was simplicity itself; the first person I asked looked as though I was a loon and jerked his thumb, marked with ink, for he was a stylor, to a broad avenue lined by impressive buildings. The place was there, clearly signposted, and looked to be an establishment more properly called a hotel than a hostelry. Only persons of standing and wealth would gain admittance as guests. I walked calmly to a side gate where Fristle slaves were trundling amphorae and shrilling orders at one another, and went in. The yard led by way of odoriferous stables to a long gray wall, mellow in the light, clothed with moon blooms, their outer petals extended and the inner tightly folded. From over the wall came a familiar sound—the ring and chingle of steel on steel and the quick panting for breath, the scrape and stamp of feet seeking secure purchases. A wicket gate showed me men at sword practice. I half-turned, prepared to move on.

Hung on a wooden post just within the gate, and already burnished to a shining brilliance, a silvered iron breastplate was being lovingly polished up by a little Och slave. He had three of his upper limbs busily polishing away and with the fourth he was surreptitiously stuffing a piece of bread into his mouth between those puffy jaws. And good luck to you, my old dom, I was saying to myself as, being an old fighting man, my eye was caught by the sudden and splendid attack one of the energetic and sweating combatants within the courtyard essayed against his opponent in this early morning practice session.

The opponent, a strongly built Fristle, gave ground. The assailant, an apim with strands of extraordinarily long yellow hair swirling, leaped in, roaring his pleasure, his good nature blazingly evident on his round, cheerful, pugnacious face. The men at practice in there all wore breechclouts and sandals. The apim whirled his sword in a silvered pattern of deceptive cunning and the Fristle, ducking and retreating, must have felt that steel net whistling about his whiskers perilously close.

"Ha, Fropo! I have you now!"

"Hold off! Hold off! I'll slice your hair!"

"You dare!"

And with the speed of a striking chavonth the big apim, his yellow hair coruscating about his head in the light, leaped and struck—and the sword hovered an inch from the Fristle's throat.

"D'you bare the throat?"

"Aye, may Numi-Hyrjiv the Golden Splendor pardon me, Dav. I bare the throat."

With a great bellow of good-natured laughter the apim whipped his sword away and clapped a meaty hand around the Fristle's golden-furred shoulders. "You let me best you, Fropo, by thinking of my hair. It never gets in my eyes—ever."

Now they were at rest the two looked an oddly assorted couple, the Fristle and the apim. The apim, this Dav, was a splendidly built man, bulging with muscle; but I fancied his beginnings of an ale-gut might slow him down in a season or so if he did not temper his homage to Ben Dikkane.

So looking at these two as they snatched up towels to wipe the sweat away I saw reflections in the brilliant polish of the breastplate. The Och had dropped his piece of bread and bent to retrieve it. In the polished kax I saw four distorted figures. One was Rapa, one Brokelsh, and two were apims.

The Rapa lifted his hand and light splintered.

Even as I turned sharply away prepared to duck in the right direction, the big apim called Dav poised his sword and threw. It hissed through the air. It buried its point in the Rapa's breast, smashing through his leather jerkin, crunching into his bones, spouting blood.

In the next instant I had drawn and was running upon the Brokelsh and his apim comrades. With a clang the blades crossed. I was aware of the Fristle, Fropo, and the apim, Dav, running up. Somewhere, someone had shouted: " 'Ware your back, dom!"

The Rapa was done for, the dagger spilled into the dust. His viciously beaked face lay against the earth. But as my sword felt the savage blows of these would-be stikitches, I felt a new and wholly unexpected sensation—an unwelcome and treacherously deadly emotion.

I recalled that last fight with Mefto, and the way he had bested me. My blade faltered. The apims had sized me up and were pressing hard and somehow and, I think of its own volition, my thraxter leaped to parry their blows. But I saw again those five lethal blades of Mefto flashing before my eyes.

My throat was dry. I leaped and slashed the blade about and caught the Brokelsh in the side. The Brokelsh are a squat-bodied race of diffs, and he staggered and recovered and came for me again. Then Fropo's sword switched in and took the Brokelsh in play, Dav took one of the apims and I was left to face the last. Whatever my emotions had been, however the feelings had scorched through my brain, I felt the old secrets flowing along my arm and through my wrist and into my hand. I turned the sword over and beat and twitched and so lunged, and stepped back.

Fropo and Dav were standing looking at me. The Brokelsh and the other apim were coughing their guts out.

"It buried its point in the rapa's breast."

"You were a mite slow, dom," said Dav, in his affable way. "You need to sharpen up."

"Yes," I said. I took a breath. "My thanks—"

"Against them? The apim I took I know, Naghan the Sly, he was called. Look." Dav bent and ripped away the big blue favor. Under it the hard yellow showed. "They tried to cowp you from the back, the yetches. Well, they'll never report back to Mefto the Kazzur, may he rot in Cottmer's Caverns."

I said, "My thanks again. But I do not think they could have known you—who know them—would be here. They would not have been so bold."

"Right, dom. They would not. And," Here his big smile burst out. He wore a little tufty beard bisecting his chin, and he was burly, no doubt of that, genial. "And no Lahal between us. I am Dav Olmes. Lahal, This is Fropo the Curved."

"I am Jak. Lahal, Dav Olmes. Lahal, Fropo the Curved."

"And now I need three stoups of best ale, one after t'other," quoth Dav. "Instanter, by the Blade of Kurin."

So I knew he was a swordsman, and we went into the courtyard and found the ale and washed the dust away down our throats. And, for me, Dray Prescot known as Jak, the dust went down bitter with unease.

No need to ask where the sword with which Dav had made such pretty play had come from. The little Och was wailing away and scrabbling around picking up the scattered items of the harness that Dav had ripped to pieces from its hangings on the post. The beautifully polished kax had fallen with a crash. The gilt helmet with the brave blue feathers still rolled about, like a balancing act. Now Dav threw the sword at the Och, who caught it with the unthinking skill of the man who spends his life with weapons, free or slave.

"Thank you, notor, thank you," chattered the Och.

"That," said Fropo, "was the kov's own blade."

"Aye. And very fine, too. Now where is this ale?"

"The Och called you notor," I said. Notor is the usual Hamalian way of saying lord. We say jen in Vallia.

Before Dav had recovered from his gutsy laugh at my words, Fropo, with sudden seriousness, said: "Aye. This is Dav Olmes, the Vad of Bilsley."

A vad is a high rank of nobility indeed, and they had mentioned a kov. I said, "And the kov?"

Fropo sucked through his teeth. "Konec Yadivro, the Kov of Brugheim."

Ineldar the Kaktu could have told me I was going to see a kov, by Krun!

Dav had found the ale and after he had demolished the first stoup in two swallows, he said: "The kov and I do not parade our ranks here in Jikaida City. We have work to do that—" Here he took the opportunity of destroying the second stoup. Then: "By this little fracas I take it you have run afoul of Prince Mefto the Kazzur the yetch?"

"Aye." I told them I had fought Mefto, and lost, and had been saved by the drikingers. They expressed the opinion that I must be somewhat of a bladesman after all, not to have been slain in the first pass or two. And, I knew, I had stood like a loon, shaking, when I had crossed swords with these stikitches. Kov Konec and his comrades had reached Jikaida City a few days earlier in a caravan whose master was Inarartu the Dokor, the twin brother of Ineldar the Kaktu, and this explained Ineldar's knowledge, I thought.

The kov turned out to be a strong, frank-faced man with charming manners. I formed the opinion that he placed great reliance on the opinions and advice from Dav. Their estates, those of Brugheim and Bilsley, lay in Mandua a country immediately to the west of Mefto's Shanodrin. At once I realized the rivalry existing, and determined that it had nothing to do with me. Mefto could go hang; Vallia counted for me, and no where else. I was wrong there, of course.

However, I did take the opportunity in conversation of remarking that I knew a Bowman of Loh who swore that shafts fletched with the blue feathers of the king korf were superior to any other. I thought it tactful not to mention that Seg had also revised his opinion and had been heard to admit that the rose-red feathers of the zim-korf of Valka were as good. He wouldn't admit, as many a bowman felt, that they were superior.

"You know about the king korf, then, Jak?"

"A little. Not enough, kov."

"You call me Konec, Jak, here in Jikaida City."

"Konec."

"You have no love for Mefto?"

"He bested me. It was a fair fight—"

"A man with four arms and a tail?"

It rankled; but I had to say it, if only to show myself that I was not blinded by self-esteem. "It was not that, Konec. He is just simply superb. I think, perhaps, with other weapons he might. . . . But it would be a brave man who would go up against him, man to man."

"Aye," said Fropo, and he riffled his whiskers.

"His ambitions are overweening. He must be stopped before he brings ruin to all the Dawn Lands. It is here in Jikaida City that we stand the best chance, paradoxical though that may appear."

Dav chipped in to say, "If you are with us, Jak—"

I said, "There is the story in the old legends, true or false who can say after thousands of seasons? The legend of Lian Brewis and his enchanted brush. He was the artist for the gods, he could draw and paint so beautifully that his creations came alive, and peopled the world, and what the gods spoke of Lian Brewis created out of paint."

"The story is known over Kregen and is very beautiful," said Dav. "So—?"

"So when the evil gods grew jealous in their wrath they took up Lian Brewis. He was cut off in full flower, a plump, jolly, wonderful person. And the gods for whom he had created so much beauty arose likewise in their just wrath and placed Lian Brewis as that constellation of stars that adorns the Heavens of Kregen. He can never be forgotten." I looked at them, at their serious faces, and understood the intensity of their determination to halt Prince Mefto in his career of conquest. "Be sure the gods do not—"

"They will not," said Konec, and he spoke with power. "You may rest assured on that."

There was always the chance that the Rapa, the Brokelsh and the two apims had been sacrificed by their master just so that he might infiltrate a spy into the enemy camp. The trick is known. So I was not accepted whole-heartedly all at once, and of course my hesitation in dealing with my opponent added to the suspicion. But Dav was genuine and genial and my mention of the king korf, which was by way of being a secret signal, allayed much of the natural suspicion. They did not think that Mefto had penetrated that far into their schemes.

As for myself, I pondered just why I was here; how could these folk help me back to Vallia?

In the succeeding days I came to know them better and Pompino made the pappattu as my partner. We shifted quarters and Konec placed a room in the hotel of the Blue Rokveil at our disposal alongside the others. We spent the time practicing at swordplay, and, by Zair, I felt I mightily needed that sharpening up. The remembrance of Mefto's five blades seemed to have mesmerized me.

This party from Mandua were here ostensibly to play

Jikaida, and Konec was a player of repute. Their intrigues against Mefto were kept very quiet; but if assassination formed part of them, it stood little chance. Mefto was surrounded continually by his brilliant retinue of followers. He lay abed, recovering from his arrow wound. So Dav insisted we go with him to watch a well-touted game of Kazz-Jikaida. It was to be between rival factions of the twin cities, and was the usual Kazz game and not the Death game, that is, the pieces did not face certain death if they lost.

We went along to take our seats in the public galleries of one of the game courts of the Jikaidaderen and I watched the Kazz game—and I was not enthralled. There was a powerful fascination in Kazz-Jikaida, an appeal to deeply hidden emotions and a dark pull on the blood; but I kept seeing the magical blades and the scornful and triumphant face of Prince Mefto the Kazzur before my eyes.

CHAPTER FIFTEEN

How Bevon Struck a Blow

The game turned out to be the Pallan's Kapt's Gambit Declined. That was how the encounter began. Because this was Kazz-Jikaida, the precise and elegantly contrived moves broke down after a time when a piece refused to be taken. The game proceeded interestingly enough, despite that. One swod, a Chulik whose fierce upthrust tusks were banded in silver, fought very well, defeating two Deldars sent against him successively. This upset the right hand drins of the game as far as Yellow was concerned, and pretty soon Blue was sweeping through the center with a line of Deldar-supported swods and pieces. When the two Kapts were brought into play they swept aside a Chuktar and a Hikdar and, but for an interesting contest between a Hyr-Paktun and the Aeilssa's Swordsman, the game was over.

Here in democratic-aristocratic Jikaida City the piece around whose capture the game revolved was called not King or Rokveil but Aeilssa, Princess. Well, I liked the romantic ring of that, and having married a princess and having others of that ilk as daughters, I could not in all conscience find fault.

When the game was done, the sand already being raked neatly back into the blue and yellow squares ready for the next game—there being time for two encounters in that afternoon—Dav and I shouldered up to leave. Being Dav, his first thought was to discover the nearest alehouse.

With a flagon in his fist and his elbow on the counter, he said, "The pieces fight differently when it is a Death game."

I nodded, and drank. I was thirsty.

"How often do they—?"

"Very seldom for the public contests. Death-Jikaida is expensive. The inner courts. They are the places for the highest stakes and the most bloody of encounters."

"I have heard it said," I remarked, quoting Deb-Lu-Quienyin as we had talked around our caravan fire under the stars of the Desolate Waste. "That there is no skill in Jikaida where the outcome of carefully planned moves can be upset by mere brainless warriors fighting."

"So they say." Dav supped companionably. "But Konec says there is skill, albeit of a different kind. There is the skill of sizing up your opponent's powers and of arranging within the moves to place your best fighters to bear on the weakest of your opponent's, and of protecting your own lesser pieces."

"That Chulik swod with the silver-banded tusks—"

"In the next game he will be a Deldar, you mark my words."

"Chuliks are ferocious fighters. He'll be a Pallan yet."

"On the Jikaida board only, though! By Spag the Junct! The blue and yellow sand will drink much blood before they put him away in the balass box."

Pompino found us then and wanted to catch up with the flagons, and some of Konec's people arrived, and the alehouse began to liven up. We'd all put in some time in the practice court, and we lived and messed shoulder by shoulder, for Konec paid for everything in the Blue Rokveil with funds provided by contributions from Mandua against Mefto, and I'd practiced in a kind of daze. Dav regarded me as a better than middling swordsman. Pompino he rated much higher. I felt, in the turmoil that I couldn't plumb, that maybe he was right.

Now, with the flagons being refilled by Fristle fifis, who squealed as they did their work, well-knowing that the customers liked that, Dav broached the question. He opened up the reasons behind what had been going on.

"You are a fighting man, Jak. You are good. You could be better, I feel, if—but then, if we all knew that if, we'd all be Mefto the Bastards, eh?"

"I suppose so."

"Cheer up, you miserable fambly! I'm offering you a task you should joy in—we fight for Konec in Kazz-Jikaida. Will you join us?"

Pompino, who had just lifted a fresh flagon to his lips, blew a head of froth a clear six feet and into the cleavage of a fifi. She yelped. She put her finger down and wiped—and then she licked the finger, making a face. But she didn't deceive us. We laughed—even I laughed.

"All right," I said.

"We-ell," said Pompino.

"It depends on the size of the game we get into," Dav said, speaking to Pompino with intent to induce him. "Konec has brought first-class fighters; but we may need many more to make up the pieces. What say you? You know the pay is good, and the inducements offered by the Nine Masked Guardians add up to a handsome sum."

In Poron Jikaida, which is the smallest size reckoned to be worth the playing, there are thirty-six pieces a side. In Lamdu Jikaida there are ninety pieces a side.

In the end Pompino gave his assent; a qualified assent which, as he said, depended on getting the hell out of this city. We were both of the opinion that the Everoinye, having used our services, would not bother us again for a space and therefore we must use our own efforts to escape. For we regarded it as an escape. "There is no chance I shall stay once Ineldar the Kaktu begins to form his caravan," said Pompino, and he meant it.

"By Spag the Junct!" burst out Dav. "You eat Konec's food and sleep under his roof—"

"I shall pay," said Pompino, and his foxy face bristled. "I shall pay—you will see."

"Very well. We shall hire swods from the academies. The higher pieces are named. I think you two may be Deldars—"

"What?" Pompino was outraged. "I am a paktun—"

"We have hyr-paktuns with us in this, with the pakzhan."

Pompino stared furiously at me. I hate to see friends wrangling. "If you could at least give Pompino a decent harness it would—"

"The weapons and the armor are prescribed by law. It is all in the Jikaidish."

Well, by Vox, that was true. Each piece on the board was represented on the blue and yellow sands of Kazz-Jikaida by a fighting man. Each piece was equipped according to the laws of Jikaida as prescribed in the Jikaidish Lore, that is, in this sense of the Kregish word, the hyr-lif written in the jikaidish. Swods wore a breechclout and held a small shield and were armed with a five-foot spear. The Deldars wore a leather jerkin and carried a more effective shield. Mind you, the Jikaidish Lore provided for an amazing variety of equipments. One of the most important facts to remember about Jikaida is that the ramifications, combinations, extensions and sheer prolific variety of the game demand that before any game begins each player is aware of the exact rules under which the game is to be played. This is cardinal. Much blood has been shed because players were too stupid or lazy to make sure they agreed on the rules they were going to use before they started playing.

Pompino rubbed his whiskers.

"Arrange for me to have a sword, and, maybe—"

"It is difficult." Dav screwed up his face and then reached for the flagon. "It may not be possible to arrange the bokkertu for Screetz-Jikaida. But I will speak to Konec."

"Do so."

"Who is Konec playing?" I said to attempt to bring the conversation down a few degrees. It had been growing too warm.

"Some old biddy called Yasuri."

"Ha!" snapped Pompino. "I might have guessed."

"She didn't hire us to fight for her—she must be using the academies."

Dav nodded sagely. "I am told they train 'em here to fight in ways adjusted to the Jikaida board. It is cramped."

"Wise old lady Yasuri," sneered Pompino.

"Don't tell me the name of her jikaidast, Dav," I said. "Let me guess. One Master Scatulo, yes?"

Dav shook his head. "No."

I was surprised.

"She put great store by him. Fawned on him."

"If he arrived with you then he wouldn't have had time to Establish his Credentials."

"Bevon the Brukaj mentioned that," said Pompino.

We learned what that meant. Jikaidasts could earn fortunes here in Jikaida City. The great ones who could afford to come here and pay for the privilege of playing Kazz-Jikaida would all be devoted to the game, that went without saying; but they might not be quite as good players as they imagined. It was customary for each player to employ a Jikaidast to be at his or her elbow and to advise. A very conspicuous and ornate clepsydra marked off the time allowed for each move, and when the time was up the water-clock beat a resounding stroke upon a great brazen gong. In some games if a player had not made the move by then he was required to forfeit a piece. As for the Establishment of Credentials, this took place in the Hall of Jikaidasts.

The Hall was long and narrow. Along each side was ranged a column of Jikaida boards. The newcomer seated himself at the end board and played Jikaida against his opponent. If he won he moved up a board. There was a constant stream of Jikaidasts moving up or down—down and out to await their turn to begin the ascent of the ladder again, or up to the topmost table where they would have established their credentials and could then seek employment as advisers to wealthy players.

Master Scatulo, I fancied, would go up the ladder like a dose of salts.

As to my own chances of improving in the Jikaida pieces' hierarchy, I was not so sanguine. It was clear that the party with Konec, including Dav and Fropo, regarded me as a reasonably expert swordsman—they found it difficult to believe I had lasted even a couple of passes with Mefto—but were less than confident about letting me take the part of a superior piece. The Pallan, as the most important piece on the board, wore a full harness of that superb mesh steel. If he came up against a half-naked swod with a spear, the outcome would not be in doubt.

When I questioned the sanity of men prepared to fight as swods, the explanations I was given ranged from blind passionate partisanship for the Blues or Yellow, simple greed, a desire to get on in Jikaida, fear of retribution for a crime—there are many foibles and quirks of human nature that Opaz has given us and that remain dark and shrouded in our inmost beings.

Also, archers ringed the stands. If any piece, including a Pallan, shirked a fight and attempted to run, he would be shafted instantly at the signal from the representative of the Nine Masked Guardians who presided at every game.

As the archers posted up there were Bowmen of Loh; everyone knew they would not miss.

Some games of Kazz-Jikaida employed the rule that to make the powers of the superior pieces more representative of those the pieces really had on the board, more than one warrior took the part of a piece. Chuktars and Kapts might be represented by two fighting men, a Pallan by three. On other occasions all the pieces were armed in the same fashion. Once the stranger realized that Kazz-Jikaida was not quite like the Jikaida he had played as a boy against his father, or as a girl against her mother, then the anomalies were seen in their true perspective.

In the board game a piece landing on the square of a hostile piece captures. In Kazz-Jikaida the square is contested in blood.

To the death in Death-Jikaida.

In most games, but not all, the Jikaidish Lore states that when an attacking piece wins he may be substituted by a fresh fighter of the same force. If a defending piece wins he must remain where he is, on the square for which he has fought so valiantly—bleeding, dying, it makes no matter. Thus a successful defense, which is contrary to board Jikaida, is penalized. The Substitutes lined along the benches wait to go in.

Because like our Earthly game—coming possibly from chaturanga, shatranj—Jikaida has matured over the centuries and, also, because different folk play different rules in different parts of Kregen, there are many similarities and many divergencies. The swods—the pawns—move one square diagonally or orthogonally ahead, and take on the forward diagonal. If a Deldar stands on a square adjacent to a swod, then that swod, of the Deldar's color, cannot be taken by an opposing swod. This leads to fascinating situations which abruptly erupt into furious action.

This rule unique to Jikaida with its possibilities of Deldar-supported chains, is generally believed to have given rise to the traditional opening challenge of Jikaida: "Rank your Deldars!"

The jikaidish for this particular protection is propt, and as we left the alehouse to set off for our quarters and an enormous meal, Dav said, "When the propts collapse the blood will fly, by Spag the Junct!"

Because the prospect was both exhilarating and forbidding, making our fingers tingle, we swaggered and strutted, I can tell you, on our way to one of the six or eight square meals a day any Kregen likes to fuel the inner man. Pompino was more than a little put out by the unspoken imputations. His red whiskers bristled. But he was in the right of it. Our business was not taking part in blood games; it was in getting out of here.

As we walked along he kept rotating his head, looking, as I alone knew, for that magnificent scarlet and golden raptor of the Star Lords. He regarded the Everoinye with none of the scorn and hatred I had once shown them; they had treated him well and fairly and he repaid them in loyal service. In addition, he was possessed of a species of religious rapture at the idea that he was so closely involved with the doings of the gods.

Everybody in the twin cities talked in terms of the game, of course, and someone made a remark as we crossed into Blue City, that we had crossed a front. The Jikaida board is divided up into drins. Drin means land. Or, if you will, a number of drins are joined together to make the board. In general games a drin consists of a checkered board of six squares a side, making thirty-six in all. Six of these drins make up the board for Poron Jikaida, two by three. At the meeting of drins the line is painted in thicker markings. Some pieces have the power of crossing from drin to drin across a front on their move; most must halt at the front and wait until the next turn to cross.*

On the day appointed Konec led us to the Jikaidaderen where we were to play. The lady Yasuri had hired herself a Jikaidast off the top of the tree. Konec, in his turn, had taken into employment for this game an intense, brooding, nervous Jikaidast called Master Urlando, who wore a blue gown with yellow checked border. For the professionals blue or yellow meant only the angles of the game, for the opening move was decided by chance and not by tradition.

The game was an ordinary one and open to the public and the benches and covered arcades were filled. In the event Pompino gave in as much to his own estimation of himself as a fighting man as to outside pressures and took up his position as a Deldar. As I had expected, I was to act the part of a swod.

The game was not distinguished. We ranked our Deldars after the impressive opening ritual, where prayers were spoken and the choirs sang suitable hymns and the incense was burned and the sacrifice made. The ib of Five-handed Eos-Bakchi here in Havilfar was represented by the ib of Himindur the Three-eyed. For the first time I realized, with a pang, that five-handed really did have a strong and terrible meaning. So, with due propitiation made and the fortunes of Luck and Chance called upon, we took our places upon the blue and yellow sanded squares.

For a considerable period of the game I stood with a Deldar on an adjacent square and a swod—a Pachak with a brisk professional air about him, determined to get on—on the square to my left diagonal. He could not attack me by reason of the Deldar. We fell into an interesting conversation, although this was against the tenets of the game, and I learned of his history. I like Pachaks with their two left arms and their absolute loyalty in their nikobi to their oaths. Luckily for both of us we did not fight, the main action sweeping

* It is not necessary to understand how to play Jikaida to appreciate what follows. Dray Prescot relates in detail the description and rules of the game. A brief description of Jikaida is given at the end of this volume as Appendix A, together with sufficient rules for Poron Jikaida as to enable anyone to play an enjoyable game.

A.B.A.

up the left hand side of the board and then, as Konec plunged, angling directly to the center and the Yellow Princess. Konec was a bold player, ruthless when he had to be. Dav was acting as Pallan. He was thrust forward, crossing a front, plunging into a direct confrontation with the Yellow Pallan. The fight was absorbingly interesting; Dav won, the right wing Kapt and Chuktar swept in and, with a Hikdar angling for the last kaida, the triumphant hyrkaida was made by Dav, sliding smoothly in and, challenged by the Yellow Princess's Swordsman, defeating him in a stiff but brief battle.

The various shouts of acclaim went up, the Blue prianum, the shrine where the victory tallies were kept, notched up another win, and it was all over. I had neither struck nor received a blow. I bid a shaky remberee to the Pachak swod and we all went back to the hotel.

Anticlimax—no. For I had seen what went on in Kazz-Jikaida, and was not much enamored of it.

Konec said, "In two days' time I meet a fellow from Ystilbur. You will be a Deldar, Jak."

I nodded. There was little I felt I could say.

Pompino, who had had to beat a swod, told me he was not going to act again. We were standing in the shade of a missal tree growing by the wall of the courtyard and the shadows from the walls crept over the sand. The sounds of the twin cities came muted. The air smelled extraordinarily fresh and good.

"Ineldar is forming his caravan. I shall be one of his guards. You, Jak?"

"Yes, I think so."

"Excellent. By Horato the Potent! I cannot wait to get out into the Desolate Waste!"

A shadow moved among the shadows.

Our thraxters were out in a twinkling.

A voice said, "Jak? Pompino?"

Pompino pointed his sword. "Step you forward so that we may see you. And move exceeding carefully."

A dark form lumbered out into the last of the mingled light. Jade and ruby radiance fell about him. His hunched shoulders, his bulldog face, all the gentle power of him was as we remembered from the nights under the stars.

There was blood on his right hand.

Bevon the Brukaj said, "I have run away from my master. He abused me cruelly. And I struck a guard—I do not think

I killed him; but his nose bled most wonderfully, to my shame."

"Well, by the Blade of Kurin . . ." whispered Pompino.

"Will you help me? Will you take me in?"

The sound of loud voices rose from the street, approaching, and with them the heavy tramp of footsteps and the clank of weapons, the chingle of chains.

"Inside, Bevon. Pompino, find Dav. Explain. We cannot allow them to take Bevon."

"But—"

"Do it!"

Pompino took Bevon's arm and guided him into the inner doorway. Fixing a blank look on my face and sheathing my sword, I turned to the gate and stood, lolling there and picking my teeth.

CHAPTER SIXTEEN

Kazz-Jikaida

Over the seasons I have taken much enjoyment and indulged in merry mockery and silly sarcasm from that fuzzy look of blank idiocy I can plaster all across my weather-beaten old beakhead. But as the guards and the Watch strode up, clanking, I felt the pang of a realization that, perhaps, this stupid expression was truly me, after all.

"Hey, fellow! A slave, a damned runaway slave. Have you seen him?"

I picked my teeth. "Was he a little Relt with a big wart alongside his hooter?"

"No, you fambly—"

"I haven't seen anyone like that."

"A hulking stupid great oaf of a Brukaj—"

"Best look along by the Avenue of Bangles—they're all notors in here." I screwed my eyes up. "D'you have the price of a stoup of ale, doms? I'm main thirsty—"

But, angry and waving their poles from which the lanterns hung, flickering golden light, they went off, shouting, raising a hullabaloo. The black and white checkers vanished along the way and I, still picking my teeth, went back into the rear quarters of the hotel. They had given me no copper ob for a drink. They had cursed me for a fool, unpleasantly, and had there been time they'd have drubbed me for fun. Not nice people. I would not like Bevon to fall into their clutches.

After a quantity of shouting and arm-waving we persuaded Dav that Bevon wouldn't murder us all in our beds. As a runaway slave he was a highly dangerous person to have on the premises; but Dav's good nature surfaced. He was a man who knew his own mind, and he summed Bevon up shrewdly. Runaway slaves are not tolerated in slave-owning society for the bad examples they set. It was left to Bevon to say the words that got us all off the hook.

"Here in Jikaida City," he said in his pleasant voice, having got his breath and composure back and washed off the guard's nose bleed. "I am told that a slave may gain his freedom by taking part in the games."

"That is true, Bevon. But he has to act the part of a swod and he must survive a set number of games. It has been known—but is rare, by the Blade of Kurin."

"Enter me in the next game, and I shall be safe from Master Scatulo. My blood-price will be paid by the Nine Masked Guardians, for they always welcome anyone willing to take part in Kazz-Jikaida as a swod. You know that. I cannot be touched by the law until I am free or dead. That is the law."

Kov Konec, when consulted, agreed to Dav's proposals, and it was settled. I own I felt relief. Bevon seemed to me to be far too gentle a fellow actually to take up sword and fight; but as he said himself, rather that than being slave any longer.

The day of the game against the player from Ystilbur was set as Bevon's introduction to Kazz-Jikaida, and the authorities were notified. Also, this day coincided with the decision about the caravan out of here. Pompino was in no doubt.

"If we do not give our undertaking to Ineldar by tonight and conclude the bokkertu, he will have to employ other guards." Pompino stood with me watching as Dav stood facing a table on which a huge ale barrel was upended. The spout gushed ale into an enormous flagon. Dav stood there, hands on hips, his head thrust forward, licking his lips, and, I am sure, feeling the tortures of the damned. There was no ale for Dav on the day of Kazz-Jikaida.

Rather, there was no ale until we had won.

"I have promised to fight—" I said.

"Well, I shall not. They have been good friends to us, yes, I agree. But our duty lies elsewhere."

"I thought you said you didn't get enough time away from your wife?"

"True. But I've had enough time, now, by Horato the Potent!"

By just about any of the honor codes of Kregen there could not really be any faulting of Pompino's logic. I said, "I'll just play in this game for them and then I'll come with you to sign on with Ineldar."

"You might get chopped."

"Then the problem wouldn't arise."

Dav rolled across, wiping the back of his hand across his mouth just as though he'd demolished a whole stoup, and told us that the cramph from Ystilbur had hired the best the academies could offer. "Those rasts up there have gone in with the Hamalese, may Krun rot their eyeballs."

Very carefully, I said: "They are a small nation. They were overrun by the cramphs of Hamal, just like the folk of Clef Pesquadrin. D'you know what happens when a country is subjected like that, Dav? Put in chains?"

"Aye. And not pretty, either. But this Coner is half Hamalese, I'm told. There is a plot in this, and I don't like it." He frowned and shook his shoulders. "I've tried to warn Konec; but he sees this as merely another step in the games."

The many games of Jikaida all served to enhance or not the prestige of the various participants. There were league tables. This was the Two Thousand Five Hundred and Ninety-Eighth Game, and they played a Game a season, so that shows you. The champions went away from Jikaida City far wealthier than when they arrived; but also they took with them the intangible aura of the victor.

The twin cities lived and breathed Jikaida. That cannot be emphasized enough. Everywhere, in the taverns, along the boulevards, in the parks, people sat all day playing. Those who could visited the public games of Kazz. The highest nobility of Havilfar and anywhere else who were apprized kept strictly to their own private games, where Death Jikaida ruled. These were the games in which the highest honors were conferred. Everyone gambled, of course. I had heard stories of whole kingdoms being staked on the outcome of a single game. People bet on the results, on just which pieces would survive, how long it would be before certain positions were reached, how many pieces would be wounded or slain. They bet on anything.

Pompino said, "Plot or no, Dav, I'd put ten golden deldys on you; but no one will give me reasonable odds."

Dav said, "I've been lucky so far." The truth was, he was a fine fighting man, clever and quick with his blade, and the betting public had seen that and he commanded odds to gamblers.

Remembering how I had met a flutsman of Ystilbur in peculiar circumstances, a Brokelsh hight Hakko Bolg ti Bregal known as Hakko Volrokjid, I reflected that the Hamalese had all Ystilbur in their power. Perhaps some of the schemes of Konec also were known to them? Certain sure it was that the Hamalese, despite recent setbacks in the Dawn Lands, were intent on further conquest there.

So Konec led us off to play Kazz-Jikaida against Coner, and Pompino got himself a seat in the stands to watch. The day was fair. The preliminaries were gone through as before, with the rituals and the choirs chanting and the sacrifices and the libations, and mightily impressive it all was. Konec and Coner seated themselves on the playing thrones, one at either end, and we pieces marched out to take up our places on the board.

As a Deldar in this game I carried a shield of wicker and a five-foot spear. I had a leather jerkin. Dav, massive in his mesh, gave me a cheery word. Fropo the Curved, acting as a Kapt, strained his bulk against his lorica. Each piece was equipped according to the rules prescribed in the hyr-lif known as the Jikaidish Lore. I settled myself. Extremely beautiful girls, clad wispily in draperies of white and purple, danced about the board to carry the commands of the players to their pieces. Up on the throne dais each player had his Jikaidast at his side. The feeling of ages-old ritual, that this was the way the game should be played, the way it should be run, held everyone fixed in complete absorption. The fascination was there, like a drug, a dark compelling pull drawing on the deep tides of the blood.

Golden trumpets blew. The banners broke free. The first move was made.

Well, I will not go into it. It was a shambles.

We ranked Deldars and started off in fine style, and then we ran into disastrous trouble as a whole rank of swods was swept away. Red-clad slaves with litters and stretchers carried off the casualties. Other slaves raked the blue and yellow sand neatly back into the squares, and fresh sand was sprinkled over the blood. But Yellow surged on and on, triumphant, and we were pressed back, losing men like flies in winter.

The fighting men trained in the academies had been taught all the tricks of fighting in the admittedly limited space of the Jikaida squares. If a warrior stepped outside the square he was adjudged the loser, of course. If he stepped out too smartly, without giving of his utmost, if he shirked and sought that way out of the horror, then black-clad men ran onto the board. What they did ensured that pieces would fight, grimly and with thought only of victory.

Three swods I fought and dealt with them. Each little conflict took place on two squares, by virtue of the fact that the attacker and the defender occupied adjacent squares and the whole of these two squares could be used. Then a Hikdar came at me, whirling his axe, and I had a sharp set-to before I got my spear between his ribs.

Konec swung the play across to the other wing then and I

had time for a breather. The game had rapidly degenerated from the classical simplicity of the Aeilssa's Swod's Opening into a blood bath. Well, we Blues fought.

With consummate skill Konec made a space for fresh development in the center and a diagonal of pieces formed leading to Yellow's Right Home Drin. That would be Blue's Far Left Drin. Every drin has its name; everything has a name; I was concentrating on what I could see coming up. At the far end of the diagonal of pieces stood a Yellow Chuktar. The Yellow Pallan had been busy and was absent; the Yellow Aeilssa stood, just for the moment, vulnerable. But the Chuktar barred the way. An enchanting little Fristle fifi danced across from the Blue Stylor. He was positioned level with the board and beneath the player's throne to pass on the move orders. Konec moved a Blue swod onto the end of the diagonal line of pieces, and into the square diagonally off from me. So that meant I was sure what was going to happen.

Yellow made his move, a nasty threatener down the right wing, and then the fifi, who had been given my orders all ready, for Konec was a shrewd player, said to me: "Deldar to vault and take Chuktar."

I hitched up my belt and put my spear into my left hand. I spat into my right, not having an orange handy, and then took up the spear. Calmly, I started to walk along beside the diagonal line of men. This simulated the vault. What a sight it must all have been! The twin Suns of Scorpio blazing down into the sprawled representation of a Jikaida board, the blue and yellow squares a bright checkered dazzlement, the brilliantly attired figures of the pieces, the color, the vividness, the raw stink of spilled blood—and the tension, the indrawn breaths, the hunching forward of the spectators. The passions were being unleashed here. I walked gently along, and I held my shield just so, and the spear just so, for the moment I put my foot into the square occupied by the Chuktar we would fight.

Because I was coming down off the end of a vault, having leaped over a line of pieces, there was no empty starting square. I would come down slap bang on top of the Chuktar. We would contest the square in its own narrow confines.

The man representing the Chuktar was a Kataki. Unusual to find a member of that unpleasant race of diffs doing much else besides slaving, for they are slavemasters above all and know little of humanity—although Rukker had given certain glimmerings of humanity, to be sure—and this fellow was clearly in Kazz-Jikaida because of some ill deed. He was licking his lips as I approached. He wore an iron-studded kax and vambraces, and carried a good-quality cylindrical shield. His thraxter caught the light of the suns. I walked up to the right of the diagonal line of pieces, which surprised him, for any shielded man likes to get his left side around.

One thing was in my favor: that hyr-lif the Jikaidish Lore specifies what weapons may be used; the Kataki was not allowed to strap six inches of bladed steel to his tail. His lowering brows, flaring nostrils and snaggly-toothed gape-jawed mouth complemented his wide-spaced eyes. They were narrow and cold. His thick black hair which would be oiled and curled was stuffed up under his iron helmet. Formidable fighting men, Katakis, known and detested—and steered clear of.

As I marched up with my wicker shield and the spear, wearing a leather jerkin and helmetless, to face this armored man with his professional sword and shield, I reflected with some amazement that I must be very like a wild barbarian facing an iron legionary of Rome. So—act like a barbarian. . . .

When I got within three squares of him I launched myself forward in a bursting run, wild and savage. I went straight in, the spear outthrust, the shield well up. I saw his ugly face go rigid with shock and the thraxter begin to flick into line. But I was pretty desperate and I had to banish a phantom image of Mefto the Kazzur that sprouted shockingly before my eyes. Straight at him I sprang.

His sword clicked against the wicker and a chunk flew off, sprouting strands of painted wood. The spear went straight on, over the rim of the iron-studded breastplate, punched into his squat neck. He tried to shriek; but could not make a sound with sharp metal severing all his vocal cords. He flopped sideways and I hauled the spear out and lunged again and he went on down and stayed down.

We were playing Kazz-Jikaida, the ordinary game and not the Death Jikaida—we might as well have been for that Kataki.

The stands broke into a bedlam of noise and stamping; but I had not attacked until my foot was inside the square. And he had struck first—a last unavailing blow.

What Yellow's move was I have no idea. He made a desperate scrabbling attempt to get a piece back to defend. But on Konec's next move Fropo the Curved, as a Kapt, vaulted over the same diagonal and then pounced on the Princess. The Aeilssa's Swordsman stepped out to challenge, as was his right, and Fropo finished him off and—amazingly—Blue had won.

In the racket going on all about us, as the young girl who had taken the part of Yellow's Princess stood there with the tears pouring down her face, Fropo wiped his sword on the yellow cloak of the Swordsman and spoke cheerfully to me.

"I never thought you'd do it, Jak. A bonny fight. I was able to vault right home. Konec will be pleased."

"I doubt it, Fropo. We have lost a lot of good men."

At once the Fristle's cat face sobered. "You are right. Now may Farilafristle have them in his care. Good men, gone."

The final rituals were gone through and the Blue notched up another win in the prianum. Our player, Konec, also moved up in the league tables. We marched off. But it was hard. There were many gaps in the ordered ranks. Kov Konec's people had been drastically thinned. And that, I reasoned as we trailed off to our hotel, was the core of the plot against us.

The captured Yellow Princess was brought along in our midst; but she did not make up for all the good men lost.

CHAPTER SEVENTEEN

I Learn of a Plan

We held a Noumjiksirn, which is by way of being a wake, an uproarious and yet serious evening in which we mourned our vanished comrades. There was huge drinking and singing of wild songs and much boasting and leaping about and the odd clash of blade. Those who knew something of the history of the slain stood forth and cried it out, clear and bravely, and we applauded and drank to them, and called on all the gods for a safe passage through the Ice Floes of Sicce. The Yellow Princess sat enthroned on a dais in our midst, stripped of her yellow robes and chained. But this was tradition only; the days when the captured Aeilssa belonged to the victorious side were long gone, for that kind of boorish behavior smacked too much of the uncouth. She would be ransomed by her losing player, of course, and Konec would distribute a donative and pocket a tidy sum himself. This was just one of the perks accruing to a winning side.

The girl who had acted as our Blue Princess was the daughter of Nath Resdurm, a splendid numim who was a strom at the hands of Kov Konec. His lion-man's face bristled with pride as his daughter, Resti, danced the victory dance, taking a turn with every one of us pieces who had survived. The drink flowed. Dav took on a load. He danced and pranced with Resti, who laughed, her golden hair flowing, mingling with Dav's as they swirled across the floor and the orchestra Konec had paid for scraped and strummed and banged away.

Strom Nath Resdurm had acted as the other Kapt, with Fropo. We had lost all our Hikdars, our Paktuns and Hyr-Paktuns, all good fighting men laid to rest. Truly, the lion-girl Resti would not dance breathless with the survivors.

When Dav laughingly yielded her to a Deldar, who pranced her off across the floor, Dav bellowed his way across to the ale table and seized up a foaming stoup. He spied me.

"Aye, Jak," he said, and drank thirstily. "Aye—it takes strength to grasp a spear in that fashion—or skill."

"It did for the Kataki."

"But that bastard Coner has done for us. We are too few, now. And who else will fight for us?"

"Konec has only to hire pieces from the nearest academy—"

"Onker!"

I allowed that to pass. He was by way of becoming a friend, and in the passionate despair at plans gone wrong he knew more than he said and so cried out against fate. Or, so I thought.

"Yes, Jak," he said, after moment, with the uproar going on all about us. "Yes, you are right. We will hire pieces to fight for us. But Mefto—Mefto—" He drank and was swept up by a mob who shouted him into a song, which he sang right boldly, "King Naghan his Fall and Rise." The songs lifted, after a space, "The Lay of Faerly the Ponsho Farmer's Daughter," "Eregoin's Promise." We did not sing that rollicking ditty that ends in "No idea at all, at all, no idea at all." The mood was not right. And that perturbed me. So I started in my bullfrog voice to roar out "In the Fair Arms of Thyllis."

After the first couple of lines when they'd digested the tune and the name of Thyllis, Konec stepped forward, his face black.

"We sing no damned Hamalian songs here, Jak!"

"Aye!" went up an ominous chorus.

"Wait, wait, friends! Listen to the words carefully."

And I went on singing about Thyllis. That song is well known in Hamal, and is beloved of the Empress Thyllis, as it refers in glowing terms to the marvelous deeds of the goddess from whom she took her name and her scatty ideas. One day back home in Esser Rarioch my fortress palace of Valkanium, Erithor who is a bard and song-maker held in the very highest esteem throughout Vallia, being half-stewed, concocted fresh words about Thyllis the Munificent. The words were scurrilous, extraordinarily melodic, quite unrepeatable and extremely funny.

By the time I was halfway through the second stanza the people of Mandua were rolling about and holding their sides. I do not think Erithor ever had a better audience for one of his great songs. At least, of that kind. . . .

When I had done they made me sing it again, stanza by

stanza, and so picked it up and warbled it all through, again, four times.

Feeling that my contribution to the evening had been some slight success I went off to find a fresh wet for my dry throat. Kov Konec joined me, with Dav and Fropo and Strom Nath Resdurm. We all wore the loose comfortable evening attire of Paz; lounging robes in a variety of colors. Konec, for once wearing a blaze of jewelry, looked a kov.

"You do not care overmuch for the Hamalese?"

"Not much."

How to explain my tangled feelings about the Empire of Hamal? I had friends there, good friends, and yet our countries were at war. As for Thyllis, I felt sorry for her and detested all she stood for, and yet often and often I had pondered the enigma that she saw me in the same light as I saw her. Truly, the gods make mock of us when they set political and class barriers between the hearts of humans.

Of course, anyone of the many countries attacked and invaded by the iron legions of Hamal dedicated to obeying the commands of their empress, anyone suffering from oppression and conquest, would not see a single redeeming feature in Thyllis. That seemed only natural. Now Konec began speaking in a way new in our relationship. After all, I was merely a paktun, in employ, and he was a kov, conscious of his power and yet charmingly accessible.

"Mefto the Kazzur, who calls himself a prince. He is hated in Shanodrin by the people he claims as his. Only his bully boys sustain him against the people. Masichieri—scum."

"He never rode with less than twenty," I said. "But there were more in the caravan, that he uses in Kazz-Jikaida. When I fought him he had been visiting a shishi, I know, for Sishi told me. But when we fought I know there were others of his men in the shadows, laughing at my discomfiture." I went on, briskly. "That saved us from the drikingers."

"So assassination is difficult. Very. Stikitches have been sent—Oh, aye, Jak," at my raised eyebrows. "Honor is long gone from desperate men. And we of the countries of the Central Dawn Lands are desperate."

"Against a single prince hated by his people, dependent on hired swords?"

"No. You do well to question thus. Against Hamal."

"But—"

"Mefto is the key. Through him Hamal can extend her power where now she must fight."

I shook my head. "I believe you, Konec, for I have found

you an honorable man. But I have been told that Mefto is a real and regal prince, splendid in gold, beloved in Shanodrin—"

"Stupid stories of shifs, brainless giggling serving wenches."

There ensued a pause in this fierce half-whispered conversation then as we all drank, thinking our separate thoughts.

"A great one is coming from Hamal. A kov, or even a prince. He and Mefto meet in Jikaida City under the cloak of Jikaida. It will arouse no suspicion. Our spies have the story sure."

In the world of intrigue secure meeting places are valuable. Jikaida would explain even a meeting between a Grodnim and a Zairian. But as I listened to Konec talking, I began to see more than I had bargained for.

A pot-bellied ceramic jar of Neagromian ware sprouting wildly with the drooping tendrils of heasmons stood in its alcove and Kov Konec bent to partake of the fragrant aroma of the violet-yellow flowers. He swiveled his eyes to regard me, and I saw that he, like his men, was not a conspirator born.

"By Havandua the Green Wonder!" said Konec, standing up from the sweet-smelling plants, his face revealing all the passions struggling for utterance. "Mefto must be stopped! If his schemes and this rast's from Hamal succeed—well—" He paused, and his fists clenched. He had sworn by Havandua the Green Wonder. Well, you know my opinion of the color green; I enjoy its serenity, and it is the finest color for Rifle Regiments, and racing cars and Robin Hood and railway engines *and* passenger rolling stock; but it seemed my fate on Kregen had thrown me into opposition with green, through no will of my own. Men said that the sky colors were always in conflict. The red of Zim, or Far, and the green of Geondras, or Havil. Truly, I confess, the feeling of fighting for the Blue against the Yellow had come on me strangely and strongly; I would take yellow in Jikaida if I could.

"You are with us in this, Jak?" demanded Konec.

"You have not confided any plan as yet," I reminded him; gently.

If they still harbored any lingering doubts that I was a spy this was a good way to get a sword through my guts.

"Plan!" broke in Fropo, twirling his whiskers. "We are plain fighting men. We have our swords—"

"Aye," said Dav, with all the fervor in him.

The numim, Strom Nath, bristled up his golden whiskers in

complete agreement. Then he said, "But there is a plan. That is why we are here."

"Ah," I said, and waited.

Useless to sigh and think back to the brave old days when I was newly arrived on Kregen and would as lief bash a few skulls in as listen. Being an emperor—even a king or a prince or a strom—shackled the old responsibilities on a fellow. But I missed the skirling days of yore. That explained, I fancied, my acceptance of this enforced absence from Vallia. I needed to get the cobwebs of intrigue out of my head and the blood thumping around a body bashing into fights. Mind you, the last time that had been an unmitigated disaster, and I was not likely to forget Mefto the Kazzur in a hurry. Maybe I was getting slothful, complacent, too ready to take the easy way out.

I said, "If you have a scheme to do a mischief to Mefto and the Hamalese, I think I might be your man. If you trust me."

From what they said, and not only to me, I gained the impression, the reassuring impression, that they did trust me. They saw things in their own lights, of course; they had no real reason apart from our first meeting to suspect me. And Dav and the others, for all their geniality, would keep an eye on me, and cut me down, too, if I played them false.

The rest of the story made me feel again that sense of destiny taking me by the throat and choking all the sense out of my stupid head.

"By Makki Grodno's diseased left armpit!" I said, in a pause, "I am with you, a thousand times over!"

For what they said boiled down to this—Konec pulled his lip as he said, "The Hamalese are in trouble in Vallia, some island or other far north of here over the equator. I feel comradely sorrow for them. The Hamalese have withdrawn from their insanely ambitious attempts toward the west. Only a horrible death awaits any honest man there. Ifilion between the mouths of the River Os stands aloof." He eyed me. "And they have not struck at Hyrklana—"

They believed me to hail from Hyrklana. I said, "The island is relatively large and is wealthy. We have many troops. She would find it a toughnut, this bitch Thyllis."

"So—it is we here in the Dawn Lands and Vallia. Thyllis seeks to conclude a treaty with certain countries here who tremble at her name, with Mefto acting for her. By this means she will gain the alliance of powerful states. She will have at her disposal thousands of fresh men, professionals, paktuns, mercenaries, regulars. She will be able to advance against us, who await her coming, and free many strong armies to launch afresh against Vallia."

So I said what I said.

"Yes, Jak. The states will follow the strongest lead. Prince Mefto is the coming man, powerful, glittering, his charisma bright. If he can be taken out of the game, thrown back into the velvet-lined balass box, Mandua can take the lead. We stand firm against Hamal. The balance can be tipped."

"Jikaida—?"

"Precisely," said Dav Olmes, and he smiled, and quaffed.

They told me their plan.

Assassination had proved unreliable and a costly failure. Mefto went everywhere he was known with his bodyguard of swarth riders. They did indicate that they wished the gods had directed my sword between his ribs when we'd fought by the caravan; but, as they pointed out with the fatalism I recognized in them, no man could best Prince Mefto the Kazzur in single combat. So they would play in these Kazz-Jikaida games. And when it was the turn of Konec and his people of Mandua to meet Mefto and his people of Shanodrin, why, then, they would simply move their pieces up the board, and consigning the strict rules of Jikaida to a Herrelldrin Hell, charge him in a body and before his pieces could react butcher him and have done.

That was their plan.

I said, after I closed my mouth and swallowed and so opened my crusty old lips again: "The Bowmen of Loh will not tolerate so flagrant a breach of the rules. They will shaft you all."

"Of course," said Strom Nath. "But Mefto will be gone and our country will face the future with hope."

"And you would all give your lives—?"

"If there was more we could give, that, too, we would willingly pay," said Konec, and there was no mocking his dignity as he spoke—although I wanted to mock this so-called plan. By Zair! What a lot! And what I had got myself into!

They were standing, all looking at me with a hard bright regard. Konec said, "You look—You are not willing to give your life to save your country?"

"Only if there is no other way. But I have as tender a regard for my own neck as I have for my country."

At that they would have grown angry; but I said: "Let me think. There has to be another way."

"You disappoint me, Jak," said Dav. And, in truth, he looked cast down. "I had thought you a man among men."

The time was not suitable for me to make the classic rejoinder to that one: "I'd sooner be a man among women." But, by Vox, there had to be another way!

Then I saw Bevon the Brukaj, drinking quietly to himself in a corner. He had acquitted himself well today and proved himself a fine swordsman, for that, he had said, was his weapon.

"Bevon," I said. "He was by way of becoming a Jikaidast. Let me speak to him. He has a head on his shoulders."

The arguments went on a long time; but they were tired and wrung out, and the drink was working on them, and, truth to tell, although I did not doubt for a single instant their burning determination to give their lives, they would welcome another and better way in which they did not face certain death. So we parted, amicably, with my promise that if we could not discover a method of dealing with Mefto, I would join their party and take part in their suicidal plan.

The clincher came when I said, "Your force has been reduced. You are too few to get at Mefto in a body and fight off his men; and they will fight, mark it well."

"D'you think we don't know that!" said Dav, and the agony in him twisted in me, too, for him. . . . "And there is no one here we may ask or trust—save you, Jak the Nameless."

"And yet you would still have gone on?"

"Aye!"

After we left the Noumjiksirn with the bokkertu of the ransom of the Yellow Princess duly finalized, I met Pompino. He came into the room we shared looking the worse for wear. He threw himself on the bed, and yawned, and said, "By Horato the Potent! If I had a golden deldy for each copper ob I spent tonight I would be a rich man."

"Lucky you."

He regarded me, sharply enough, and sat up. "I have to see Ineldar the Kaktu first thing. He has kept open two places, but he will not hold them past the Bur of Fretch." That was two burs after the suns rose. "We must be up betimes."

"I shall not be taking a place in Ineldar's caravan guard."

"What?" He scowled at me as though I'd sprouted a Kataki tail. "You don't mean that? What of the Everoinye—"

"There is a task I must do—"

"You said you were desperate to go home—back to Hyrklana."

"I was. But now—"

"You are going to act as a piece in Kazz-Jikaida!"

"Yes."

"Fambly! Onker! You'll be chopped. What in Panachreem can?"

"There is a duty I owe which must be honored. A task has been set to my hands and I must do it."

"Ah!" He suddenly understood, or thought he did. "The Gdoinye has visited you. You have a service for the Everoinye—?"

"No. What I do is not for the Star Lords."

He looked shocked. "There is nothing in Kregen more important than laboring for the Star Lords!"

"Yes," I said. "There is."

CHAPTER EIGHTEEN

Of an Encounter in an Armory

Pompino shared my view that the Star Lords had acted in a way far different from their usual abrupt course when they had set us the task of protecting the lady Yasuri. For one thing; we had both been aware that the threat of the Ochs was more apparent than real. I had been warned of the impending mission in a new way, although Pompino told me that he usually received some prior notice. We felt that the Ochs had been laid on in some way so as to introduce us to the lady Yasuri and secure our employment with her.

"Her escort under that rascal Rordan the Negus returned in time. We did a good job, but—"

"Yes, the escort would have just been in time. So the Star Lords set that up for us. Not like most of the times I have been dumped down unceremoniously right in the thick of it."

Pompino was intrigued. I told him a little of some of the occasions when I had done the Star Lord's bidding, and he expressed astonishment. We were up early and making his preparations to leave. I would be sorry to see him go, and I felt he shared that opinion of me; but nothing he said could make me change my mind. We drank early-morning ale companionably together as we watched the suns rise.

"So you actually arrive when the action has begun?"

"Too right. Usually I have to scout around pretty sharpish for a weapon."

He shook his head, his foxy face surprised.

"When I am called the Everoinye place me carefully, and I can size up the situation and take the best course."

"Ha!" This, of course, merely confirmed my own early opinion of the Star Lords that had been changing over the seasons. "If I don't get stuck in pretty sharpish I'd be done for." Then, to be fair, I added: "Well, most of the time."

We talked around this puzzling fact—puzzling to Pompino although to me merely a part and parcel of my life on Kregen—and then he came out with a sober observation that shook me.

"I had a comrade once, a fine man, a Stroxal from a town near us in South Pandahem. We never went on a task together; but we talked. One day he just disappeared and never showed up again. He was, I feel sure, slain on a task for the Everoinye." Pompino looked shrewdly at me. "I think, Jak, that sometimes the Star Lords send a kregoinye to work for them and he fails. He is slain and does not do their bidding. Then, it is an emergency. They have to throw someone in as a last desperate attempt—"

"By Zair!" I burst out. "So I am the forlorn hope!"

"When all else fails they put you into the ring of blood."

I felt the seething anger boiling away and I held it down. After all, wasn't this just another reminder of my powerlessness? And then a thought occurred. "Hold on a mur, Pompino—the Star Lords have thrown me back in time, into a time loop, so that means they can choose the moment to put me into the action."

"I think that after the action has begun they cannot affect the course of time—I, too, have been through a time loop."

"Well, that is possible."

And, too, I had felt this so-called powerless ebbing of late. There was the rebel Star Lord Ahrinye to be taken into consideration. The Star Lords were not infallible, as I knew from my arrival in Djanduin. If what Pompino said was true, and it made good sense, I had another weapon against them.

"Well, Jak, time to be off."

He gathered up his gear and hitched his belt. He smiled at me, his fox-like face suddenly looking remarkably friendly.

"I have greatly enjoyed your company, Jak, by Horato the Potent. I grieve we will not travel the Desolate Waste together. Will you not come? There is still time. . . ."

"I thank you, Pompino, and I have enjoyed our time together. You are a good comrade. But my allegiance is with—is with another area that—"

"Hyrklana?"

I smiled. "Think it, dom, and do not fret."

Companionably we went out and through the crowded streets and past the boulevard tables where folk were already hard at Jikaida, the ranked armies of miniature warriors marching and counter-marching in frozen brilliance, and so came through the Kyro of Calsanys to the dusty drinnik where the caravans formed. The pandemonium was splendid.

The colors, the brillance, the movements, the stinks, the shouting and bawling—Kregen, ah, Kregen!

Ineldar had a go at making me change my mind; but he was in a hurry to get his motley assemblage into sufficient order for them to move off. There'd be confusion for a couple of days yet before he got them drilled. The Quoffas lumbered off, rolling, their patient enormous faces calmly considering the state of their insides, probably, indifferent to the pains of the journey before them. The calsanys were given a wide berth and their drivers wore bright scarves wrapped around their faces. The carriages and the wagons, the vakkas riding a wide variety of the magnificent saddle animals of Kregen, the swarms of people afoot, all moved along, jostling to find a good spot in the procession. A slave brought up Pompino's totrix and strapped his gear aboard. I shook hands. Pompino mounted up and stuck the lance into the boot. He shouted.

"Remberee, Jak! Come and visit me in Tuscursmot. I shall make you a great bargain from my armory."

"Aye, Pompino the Iarvin. I shall look forward to that." I waved. "Remberee!"

"Remberee!"

And Scauro Pompino ti Tuscursmot, known as Pompino the Iarvin, cantered off to take his place among the caravan guards.

With a deep breath that some folk might dub a sigh I turned away and swung off through the departing crowds. The dust hung. The stinks prevailed. Well, a little wet and then a trifle of business with Friendly Fodo. . . .

People were looking up. Pointing fingers strained skyward. I looked up.

An airboat fleeted in over the twin cities. She was a large craft with a high upflung poop and fighting castles amidships and forrard; but she was not as large an airboat as the enormous skyships of Hamal. But she was from that nation. Her purple and gold flags flew proudly, and in the Kregan custom she flew as many flags as she could cram flagstaffs in along her length.

So I knew who had arrived—not who, as far as name and rank and dignity went—but who in the sense that this was the great one of Hamal who came to talk the Dawn Lands into destruction with Mefto the Kazzur—and, with them, Vallia.

Some faint spark of the old Dray Prescot flared up then. Something that made me say, Dray Prescot, Lord of Strombor and Krozair of Zy. There was now a voller in Jikaida

City. So, perhaps, if I was lucky and bold enough and lived long enough, I had me my means of conveyance back home to Vallia.

Feeling ridiculously cheerful I slaked my thirst and then saw Friendly Fodo. I showed him the thraxter I had bought from him. The rivets of the hilt had frayed through the bindings. He made a face and stroked his shiny whiskers.

"Oh, a trifle, dom, a mere trifle, why that can be fixed for you in the shake of a leem's tail."

"No doubt. But I have a little more gold now—"

"Ah!"

The cupidity of him was transparent. Well, he had a living to make, and I had a weapon to buy on which my life would depend.

For a hoary old fighting man this dickering over weapons is always a pleasant business, and Friendly Fodo, assured of my gold, entered into the spirit of the occasion. A table was brought and laid with a purple cloth, and tea, ale, miscils and palines appeared, brought in by a slave Xaffer, distant and remote; but willing enough. I sat in the chair and partook of the goodies as Friendly Fodo paraded his wares.

No thought entered my head other than that I would buy a new thraxter. Fantasies are for fairy stories, sometimes for grim business men of the world, occasionally for poets. The thraxter, your hefty cut and thruster of Havilfar, is adapted to do its work. It is superior, even Vallians will tell you, to the Vallian clanxer. The drexer we had developed in Valka is far superior. I looked at the glittering and lovingly polished blades on the counter. I said, "You are cut off from the world, here in Jikaida City, behind the Desolate Waste—"

"Oh, yes, cut off. But the caravans bring in many strange articles from Havil knows where."

"There is a new fashion in Hamal," I said, and immediately added, "That pestiferous rast-nest. They have taken up fighting with a longer, more slender blade—perhaps—?"

He nodded, interested in talking shop.

"Aye, I have heard from the brethren in my craft. Rapiers, they call 'em. Whether they be as quick as they say—" He lifted his shoulders. "But I have not seen one, so cannot say."

"A pity."

We talked on, and I ate palines and examined the weapons. The Kregish for sword is screetz. I seldom use it in this narrative, for, like the Kregish for sea and water, it is not adapted to terrestrial ears. The same goes for princess. There are other Kregish words I do not use here for the same reason.

At last, seeing I was determined, Friendly Fodo brought out his better wares, blades he valued. These stood in a different class—and their price accordingly. But a fighting man does not care to set a price on the weapons of his trade; how to value your own life in terms of gold?

The best—that is the cardinal rule, the best you can afford.

In the end I selected a thraxter with a finer blade than most. The fittings were plain. There were secret marks on the blade, and Friendly Fodo claimed it had belonged to a kov slain in Death-Jikaida, although he did not offer any explanation of how it had come into his possession. The shop pressed in about me, hung with weapons and armor and glinting with steel and iron and bronze. The air hung heavy with the scent of the violet-yellow heasmon flowers. I took another paline, savoring the rich fruity flavor. The Xaffer brought forward a sturmwood box containing a blade; but a single gentle twirl told me the balance was untrue. This is, despite all, a weakness of the Havilfarese thraxter. When I say the blade of the example I chose was finer, I mean the lines were slightly more slender, the fullering that much more exact. I made up my mind.

"Fodo, can you have this blade fined down a trifle—I can draw you the lines. The curve of the cutting edge, so—" I traced a thumbnail down the blade.

He nodded, twitching his whiskers. "I can have that done in my workshop which is, as everyone knows, the finest in all Jikaida City."

"Good. If you will bring paper and pen I will draw it out."

Following my usual custom I had turned the chair as I sat down so that I faced the door. This is a habit, as you know. A shadow moved beyond the panels, and the brass bell chimed. I caught a glimpse of a hard bright yellow tuft of feathers vibrating ahead of the helmet beneath them, and I was out of the chair and back into the shadows of the shop past the counter, pressing up against a reekingly oily kax wrapped about a stray dummy.

The two Shanodrinese swaggered in, throwing their short capes back, laughing, making great play with the rings on their fingers. They wore armor. They guffawed, between themselves, talking of their prince in terms that betrayed respect and obedience but little affection. The two were masichieri, well enough, little better than bandits masquerading as paktuns.

"Hai, Fodo, you lumop! Where is the dagger you repair for me, eh? You useless rast!"

Not, as you will instantly perceive, a pleasant way to talk.

Fodo's Xaffer bustled forward in that indifferent way that strange race of diffs have, and produced the dagger. It was minutely scrutinized and reluctantly passed as serviceable. It would not have surprised me if these two specimens of Mefto's guard refused to pay, and broke Fodo's nose for him if he objected. But they rustled out the coins and made a great show of it, and then turned to leave.

I heaved out a sigh of relief. Oh, yes, I, Dray Prescot, hid and ached for these cramphs to begone. You will easily see why. Dav Olmes had cleared up the mess after the death of the four would-be stikitches and nothing further had transpired; but Mefto's men would still be wondering what had happened to their comrades. They had followed me, and therefore were obeying orders; but Mefto's men could not know I served Konec, at least, not yet, not until we met.

So they turned to leave and then one of them, the apim with the black moustaches and the lines disfiguring his mouth, saw the spread table, and the miscils crumbled on their plate and the dish of palines. He halted and, idly as I thought, picked up a paline and, as one does, popped it into his mouth.

His companion was a Moltingur, one of that race of diffs who, of the size of and not unlike apims, yet are diffs with a horny carapace across their shoulders, atrophied relic of wings, so it is believed. Their faces would be looked on as hideous on Earth, with an eating proboscis and feelers, and faceted eyes that loom large and blank and frighteningly ferocious. His tunnel mouth opened to reveal its rows of needle-like teeth that tore his food for the proboscis to masticate and swallow down. His words were hissed, as all Moltingurs seem to hiss whatever they speak, chillingly.

"You have a customer, Fodo. An honored customer, I think."

"Aye," said the apim. "By Barflut the Razor-Feathered, you are right, Trinko." So by these words I knew he had been a flutsman in his time.

"Just a customer—" began Fodo.

Now it was plain these two thought highly of themselves, as members of the entourage of Prince Mefto of Shanodrin. The clear evidence of the rapid departure of Fodo's customer must either have puzzled them and aroused their suspicious nature or piqued them because of the fancied slight. Either way, with gentlemen of that kidney, it did not matter. They were insistent on meeting this mysterious customer.

If I say, again, in the old way: I, Dray Prescot, Lord of Strombor and Krozair of Zy, I would add only that I would say those great words with a kind of sob, a despairing feeling of emptiness. Oh, yes, Dray Prescot could leap out and with drawn sword confront these two cramphs. Dray Prescot would have done that. The Dray Prescot who had not, as Jak the Nameless, fought Prince Mefto the Kazzur—and lost.

The naked thraxter shook in my fist. The blade had not been paid for yet. And the magniloquent thoughts clashed. The piece of paper and the pen lay to hand. What dreams I had had of getting Fodo to fashion this sword into a more perfect instrument of death—and how insubstantial and meaningless they appeared when I could not even leap forward into action and use that new blade!

"Sink me!" I burst out—but silently, to myself.

What might have happened Zair alone knows. I do not. I do remember that the thraxter was no longer shaking, and that I took a half step forward. The world was fined down to the shadows around me and the brilliant figures of those two men in their armor, tall and bright, and the hard yellow favors and feathers.

What might have happened. . . . The apim reached for more palines and he tossed one to Trinko, the Moltingur.

With a gulp that echoed, Fodo said: "It is a lady of reputation, come to buy a dagger for her husband. Her lover and his men await. It would be—" He hesitated.

The apim laughed.

Trinko hissed, "Passion and daggers and lovers. It is no business of ours, Ortyg." He flapped his yellow cape around and hitched his sword. Well, that familiar gesture can mean many things. But Ortyg, the apim, read his Moltingur comrade aright, and he laughed, and said, "So perish all blind husbands, may Quergey take them up. You are right, Trinko. Anyway," and he popped the last paline, "if there are men waiting. . . ."

"By Gursrnigur!" said Trinko. "You have the right of it."

So, their fists on their sword hilts, they swaggered out.

A space passed over before I emerged from the shadows. I did not ask Friendly Fodo the reason for his words. Perhaps he just did not like Mefto's men. Perhaps. Perhaps he had seen something in my sudden flight that revealed much to his shrewd Fristle eyes.

CHAPTER NINETEEN

"Vallia is not Sunk into the sea."

Events moved rapidly in the ensuing days although in ways that surprised me and, by Vox! that mightily discomposed Konec and Dav. My own emotions remained opaque and murky in relation to my feelings about myself. Eventually I had emerged from my hiding place and with no word of the two Shanodrinese between us had completed my business with Friendly Fodo. He would produce the finer lines in the thraxter blade and he would charge me well.

We heard reports that Mefto the Kazzur was recovered of his wound. His animal-like powers of recuperation aided in this sense of that certain possession of the yrium that aided him in his control of his people. But I wondered. Certainly, had one of my clansmen, or Djangs, been wounded in a wing, as Mefto had, he would not have dropped all his weapons. Those on the wounded side, yes, perhaps; but not all of them.

The day on which Konec's entourage visited the Jikaidaderen to watch Mefto and his people play a game comes back to me now as a day of suppressed passion and seething anger. We took our seats in the public galleries and settled down to study the play. The crowd was of the opinion that the prince would win, and resoundingly. This he did. We studied the way his men fought, their swordplay and techniques, tried to detect any weaknesses, and marked the men to whom he assigned the posts of most danger. On that occasion Mefto took part in only a single encounter. He and his Jikaidast worked the play admirably, and Mefto was able to put himself in as a substitute and deal with the opposing Princess's Swordsman. This man was a Rapa, beaked, proud, fierce and an accomplished bladesman. He had made a name for himself. But against Mefto the Kazzur he just did not stand a chance. As I watched the glittering blades and the dazzling, nerve-flicking passes, I stared hungrily, desperately searching for a flaw in Mefto's art. He appeared to me perfect at every point. When it was over the crowd applauded. At Konec's fierce urgings we clapped, too.

As the games were played and the positions on the league tables changed leading to the final tournament, the patterns of the final opponents emerged. We were at last advised of the day on which we would meet Mefto, for both he and ourselves had fought through successfully. The lady Yasuri, too, was well positioned with a handful of nobles and royalty from various countries. The play-offs would sort out the final positions. The wealth at stake in this session of games was breathtaking. As Konec remarked, dourly, "Let them keep their gold. We fight here for higher motives."

Yes. Yes, I know that sounds banal, juvenile almost, but if you had seen the burning determination of these people of Konec's and understood what they were prepared to sacrifice for what they believed in, I do not think you would mock.

One of the questions to be decided before a game could begin was the notation to be used. A simple grid-reference, or the English notation where squares are named from their superior pieces, were in use, as was the typically Kregan system in which each drin, having its own name, gives drin co-ordinates. Well. As you may imagine, Mefto in the preliminary planning stages insisted on using his system. Konec, who in other times might well have argued with the authority of a stiff-necked kov, gravely assented. We didn't give the chances of an arbora feather in the Furnace Fires of Inshurfraz what rules were used, just so we could get our swords at the cramph. But Dav screwed his eyes up.

"Do not agree too hastily to everything, Konec. The rast will suspect. I have the nastiest of itches that tells me he guesses we harbor plots against him—"

"You say so?"

"I do not say so. Just that I have this itch."

By this time I had formed enough of an opinion of Dav Olmes to respect his itches of intuition.

During this period when we all fenced consistently in the sanded enclosure at the rear of the Blue Rokveil I took much delight in bouts with Bevon. We used the wooden swords, the weight and feel nicely balanced to simulate the real article. With the rudis Bevon and I dealt each other many a shrewd buffet. He was a strong swordsman, blunt and workmanlike. His skill improved daily as he learned the tricks, his dogged face clamped with effort, the grip-jawed look lowering and determined.

Some of his history, clearly, he had not revealed, although he did mention that his uncle had been a paktun. I caught a glimpse of many a warm summer evening when uncle and nephew would steal away down to the bottom pasture and then go at it, hammer and tongs with their wooden swords; and, later, of the tall stories the scarred old mercenary would tell the boy. But, all the same, Bevon's main interest then and now lay in Jikaida, the purity of the game, the disciplined concentration that drove out every other thought, the sheer intellectual challenge.

"You hit a man shrewdly, Jak," he said once, after we desisted from a session and sought ale, wiping our foreheads with the yellow towels. "By Spag the Junct," he said, having picked up that beauty from Dav. "I swear your sword obeys your inmost spirit without thought. I never saw the last passage at all."

"It is a pretty one." I sliced the wooden sword about. "Look, like this. And, as to the sword and the spirit being one, yes, you have the right of it. Thought is too slow."

Although, I said to myself, I had thought when fighting Mefto the Kazzur. Aye, and the thought never put into practice. . . .

Bevon looked troubled as we drank. "This so-called plan. It is suicide, and that I do not like. Yet it seems I can see no other sure course."

"Well, there has to be. Or, as some of my friends would say: We must saddle a leem to catch his ponsho."

He eyed me. "Aye. And I have noticed that Kov Konec and Vad Dav Olmes speak with you in a way they do not with others. Me, they expect miracles from in Jikaida. But you, I think they see in you something that perhaps—" He paused, and drank.

I made no direct response. But it was true. For the simple paktun I appeared to be, these powerful men handled me with great attention. I know Konec listened to Dav. Perhaps they, at the least, could see something in this Jak the Paktun that was a faint and far off echo of Dray Prescot, Krozair of Zy.

I prayed Zair that this was so.

Some of the party from Mandua went to see Execution Jikaida. Most of us stayed away. When criminals were sentenced to death, as opposed to being sentenced to take part in Kazz-Jikaida, there still remained a chance. They took the part of pieces on the board. When they were taken, their execution happened, there and then, the taking piece striking them down. The Bowmen of Loh maintained order. And there was the chance that they might not be taken in a game. They could go onto the board, with many a wary glance to the position they had drawn, and hope. After all, many a game has been settled in just a few dramatic moves. . . .

One aspect of Execution Jikaida most unlikely ever to be found in Kazz-Jikaida was that, despite the blood-letting, real games of Jikaida still could be played. And one aspect of Kazz-Jikaida most unlikely to be found in Execution Jikaida—although sometimes this, too, was enforced—was the sight of the player taking his place on the board. Usually he or she would take the part of the Pallan, sometimes of the Princess. Mefto had taken part, gleefully, as we had seen.

When the player stood upon the board his professional adviser must be near him for consultation. So the Jikaidast was carried about the board in a gherimcal, a dinky little palanquin with a hood and padded seat and carrying poles. Too much ornamentation was generally considered vulgar; but there were examples finely decorated in precious metals and ivory and silks. Each would contain a conveniently slanted board with holes in the squares and pegged pieces for play so that the Jikaidast might keep track of what plans were afoot. Also there would be reference books, and, most important, shelves for food and drink. Slaves carried the gherimcal about the board, always keeping in close contact with the player and the pretty girls who carried the orders for the moves to the pieces.

In the game for which so much anticipatory apprehension was felt by the people from Mandua, there was no question but that Konec would play and act on the board. He would take the Pallan's part and Dav and Frodo would be Kapts. There was still some uncertainty as to the size game we would be playing, and Strom Nath might, if the game was a large variety, be a Kapt also; otherwise, he would be a Chuktar. They told me I would have to be a Chuktar, and I said that, by Havil, that was rapid promotion in any man's army, whereat they laughed.

Our nerves were fine drawn during this period. Men would suddenly laugh, and clap a fist to sword hilt, and so guffaw again, for nothing, and then turn away, and be very quiet.

Nothing was heard of the man the flier from Hamal had brought in; but Konec told us that he was confident that unless Mefto was stopped the alliance would go through and the countries of the Central Dawn Lands would fall like ripe shonages. I was not a party to the quarrel that occurred between Mefto and Konec when they met to finalize the bokkertu for the game; but the upshot was that Konec returned to tell us that it had been agreed the game would be Screetz Jikaida.

We pondered the implications.

On balance, we felt little had changed. We would have to hire men from the academies to take the places of our pieces, and they would be trained to the sword. In Screetz Jikaida all the pieces are armed with sword and shield alone, as the name suggests, and are naked but for a breechclout. There would be no spears or axes or different shields. Screetz Jikaida holds its own charm, as different and as bloody as Kazz Jikaida of the usual run.

Bevon was pleased. "Swords," he said. "Aye, that will serve."

But, all the same, we had deciphered no other plan in the mists ahead than the one which would encompass all our deaths.

In the last sennight before the game was scheduled zorcariders came in with news that the caravan that had arrived at the fort on the River of Purple Rushes would soon reach the city. One messenger rode straight to the Blue Rokveil and was closeted with Kov Konec.

When we met that evening for our usual lavish meal and general good-natured horseplay, Konec's mood was at once jovial and grim, as though he must plunge his hand into scalding water to snatch out a bag of gold.

"I have had word, certain word. Our spies have done well. If Mefto can be placed back in the velvet-lined balass box all Shanodrin will rise and expel his puppets and followers. The country is held in an iron grip; but with the threat of Mefto removed, the people will strike. Then Khorundur and Mandua will breathe easier, and the smaller states, the kovnates of Bellendur and Glyfandrin. We here, in Jikaida City, hold the key."

"We hold the sword, Konec!" growled Dav.

"Aye!" they chorused.

This news from the outside world affected me in a way different from these men of Mandua. I hungered to know what was happening in Vallia. I had not fretted over this absence, for there were good men there to run things, and Drak had returned. But, all the same, I wanted to know what was going on. There was a chance, a slender one, true, that some news of that distant island empire might have filtered down here, particularly as the people of the Dawn Lands must be aware that Vallia, far away in the north, stood shoulder to shoulder with them in the struggle against Thyllis.

Dazzling schemes of a great combination of forces marching from north and south on Hamal and crushing that empire until the pips squeaked rose in my mind. But they were dreams, dreams. . . .

Dreams, yes. But, one day, all of Paz, this whole island and continental grouping, must unite. It *must*. That was the task that, more and more clearly, I saw set to my hands—and as I often thought, with the blessing of the Star Lords and the Savanti. There must be a reason why I had been brought to Kregen. Oh, of course—the Star Lords employed me as a useful tool to pull their hot chestnuts out of the fire; but they had other kregoinye I had now learned. And the Savanti, those aloof and superhuman but mortal men and women of Aphrasoe, the Swinging City, had first summoned me to Kregen for their purposes to civilize the world. And, because I had got done as they wished, I had been thrown out of Paradise—well, that was no Paradise for me now nor had been these many seasons. But, I felt with a conviction I could not justify in view of what had happened and yet clung to with stubborn will, I was here on this marvelous and terrible world of Kregen for a purpose. I had to be. If not, then it was all a sham, all of it, save Delia and the family with whom I seemed to be at such odds, them and my friends.

And then, well, they say don't dice with a four-armed fellow.

The lady Yasuri had changed her accommodation to a better class of hotel called The Star of Laybrites. The name tells you it was situated in Yellow City. There had been some business of a Rapa attempting one of her handmaids. If it had been Sishi I fancy the Rapa was nursing a dented beak right now. Happening to be taking a short cut through Yellow City—and when I say happened I found, when I was there, I wasn't quite sure why I should be—I passed the hotel and gave a quick glance for the circlets of yellow painted stars along the arcade above. Why I had come here was made immediately plain to me.

People were passing along the avenue and giving me no attention, for I found I was wearing a blue favor. A figure staggered suddenly from a side alleyway that led to the rear of the hotel. He was stark naked. He was smothered in dust and unpleasant refuse, and straw stuck out of his hair. I recognized him at once. With a huge guffaw, and a quick snatch at the cords of my cape, I slung it off and swung it about his broad shoulders.

"By Horato the Potent! Of all the infernal—! Jak!" He grabbed the cape and pulled it about his nakedness and, at that, it only just hung down enough to be decent—just about. I still laughed. I knew exactly what he was thinking and the furious sense of frustration seething in that sharp foxy face.

And then, well, it was strange to experience this with someone else who experienced it, also.

A gorgeous scarlet and gold bird flew down the avenue and with wide spread wings cut in over the heads of the people who walked stolidly on with not so much as a single glance at the Gdoinye. Well, why not? They couldn't see this supernatural messenger and spy of the Star Lords.

Pompino the Iarvin looked up, and his face slackened off wonderfully, so that all the fury lines vanished, to be replaced by an expression of obedient wonderment.

"Pompino! Pompino!" called the bird, perching with a great feather rustling on one of the circlets of yellow stars. "You have been given no leave to abandon the Everoinye."

"But—" began Pompino.

"You know your task. You must hew to your path—"

"You stupid great onker!" I bellowed up at the bird. "What are we waiting on that stupid woman for? Let us depart from here—give us a fight, if necessary—you brainless bird!"

Pompino said something like: "Awwkk!" And he looked at me as though expecting me to be struck down in a blaze of blue fire.

Well, I might have been. But the way the Star Lords had been treating me and my recent thoughts on all the pressing work that needed to be done on Kregen braced me up powerfully.

"Dray Prescot! You onker of onkers! Hearken to your fate and submit—"

"Ask Ahrinye about that, fambly!"

"He is young and without caution, as you are. You fret on your Vallia. Rest easy on that score—"

"Rest easy! There is work to do there."

"And it is being done. Your cause prospers. But the Star Lords will not be baulked and they call upon you for a higher service."

Pompino was goggling away at me and at the Gdoinye. He'd been flung back here, just as I had been flung back to the scenes of my labors for the Star Lords when I had taken myself off. He must be annoyed; yet he could only goggle away at me as though staring at a demon from Cottmer's Caverns.

"Tell me about Vallia, you bird of ill omen."

"Why do you struggle against the Star Lords when they seek only your good? They have treated you with great kindness and you repay them with abuse and you miscall me most devilishly. Yes, your Vallia is safe as you left it. Nothing has gone wrong—"

"Has anything gone right?"

"Of course. Do you think you are irreplaceable?"

"No."

Pompino put a hand to his eyes. He was swallowing nonstop.

"Do the business here and ensure the safety of the lady Yasuri. The business of Mefto is yours alone." The scarlet feathers riffled. People were walking past all the time and no one cast so much as a glance in our direction. The Gdoinye lifted into the air. His wings beat strongly. As he had so often done he squawked down at me most rudely. And then he screeched out: "Dray Prescot, get onker, onker of onkers."

Well, we shared that, at the least. We'd established that kind of comradely insult between us, and I pondered his words.

Pompino gathered himself together. He pulled the cape more tightly about himself. It was green, I noticed, with yellow checkered borders. He stopped swallowing. He straightened his shoulders. The Gdoinye lifted high, flirted a wing, swung away and vanished over the rooftops across the avenue.

"The damned great fambly," I said.

"Jak." Pompino stopped shaking. "Jak—to talk to the Gdoinye like that—I've never heard—you might have been—I do not know. . . ." He shook his head, goggling at me. Then: "But, Jak, he was talking about someone called Prescot. It seems to me I have heard that name—"

"Some other fellow," I said. "More likely, two other fellows. And the Gdoinye and I have an understanding. We rub along. But, one day, I'll singe his feathers for him, so help me Zair."

There, you see. . . . Stupid intemperate boasting again.

We sauntered away and Pompino looked halfway respectable. He said, "How did you come to be so close when I was brought back?"

"Thank the Star Lords for that. I had no intention of walking this way; but I am here. And the cape; it is not mine."

He shook his head and I marveled at how quickly he had once again reconciled himself to the Star Lords' demands.

"This lady Yasuri," he said, pondering. "What is so special about her that she is so cherished?"

"She may be an old biddy, but she's not too old to have children if she wills it."

"I'm not sure—?"

"I once rescued a young loving couple out on a spree and they had a child who overturned cities and nations. He is dead now, thankfully, along with many others." How Gafard, the King's Striker, a Master Jikaidast, would have joyed to be here! And how I would welcome him, by Zair!

When Pompino heard of the Sword Jikaida coming up with Mefto he put a lean finger up and rubbed his foxy face. He looked wary.

"I do not think this thing touches my honor."

"Agreed."

He stamped his foot. "You are infuriating! What in Panachreem—?"

"Look, Pompino; you must carry out the duties of a kregoinye and that does not include being chopped. The Gdoinye gave me leave to deal with Mefto, if it is possible. That can only mean the Star Lords have an eye in that direction. But your duty lies toward the lady Yasuri."

"Duty to her! Ha!"

"She looks like a little wrinkled nut, true. But if she took off that stupid wig and let her hair loose, and washed her face with cleansing cream, and wore shapely clothes, why, many a man would delight in proving his duty to her."

"With a nose and a tongue as sharp as hers?"

"They could both be blunted, given love."

"Well, if that is what the Everoinye plan, we are in for a long and tedious wait!"

So, half-cross and half-laughing, we strolled back to the Blue Rokveil.

"As San Blarnoi says," observed Pompino as we went in to find Dav and ale. "The heart leads where the eyes follow."

The incoming caravan was due to arrive the day before the game and, expressing a wish to go down and see the entrance, I was joined by Bevon and Pompino. The others all declined. I pressed Dav; but he excused himself. He had a girl to attend to. Well, that was Dav Olmes for you, big and burly and fond of ale and women and fighting. A combination of great worth on Kregen.

The scene when we arrived presented just such a spectacle of color and noise and confusion as delights the heart. Many cities of Paz boast a Wayfarer's Drinnik, a wide expanse where the caravans form up or disperse, and we stood under a black and white checkered awning and sipped ale as we watched. The Quoffas rolled patiently along, the calsanys and unggars drew up in their long loaded strings, men dismounted from totrixes and urvivels and zorcas, all thirsty, all glowing with their safe arrival. The wagons rolled in. A group of Khibils dismounted from their freymuls, that pleasant riding animal that is often called the poor man's zorca, a bright chocolate in color with vivid streaks of yellow beneath. Willing, is a freymul, and as a mount serves well within his abilities. Pompino eyed the Khibils and then strolled off to pick up what news there was. The dust rose and the glory of the suns shot through, turning motes of gold spinning, streaming in the mingled lights of Zim and Genodras. I sipped ale and watched, and at last saw a man I fancied mught be useful.

He was apim, like me, limber and tough, and as he dismounted and gave his zorca a gentle pat I caught the fiery wink of gold from the pakzhan at his throat. He was a hyrpaktun. His lance bore red and blue tufts. I rolled across carrying a spare flagon.

"Llahal, dom. Ale for news of the world."

He eyed me. He licked his lips. His weapons were bright and oiled. He stood sparingly against the light of the suns.

"Llahal, dom. You are welcome." He took the flagon and drank and wiped his lips. "Now may Beng Dikkane be praised!"

"The news?"

He told me a little of what I hungered to hear. Yes, he had a third cousin who had returned from up north. Told him that paktuns were being kicked out of Vallia. He'd never been there—fought in Pandahem, though, by Armipand's gross belly, nasty stuff all jungles and swamps down to the south. Yes, Vallia was, as far as he knew, still there and hadn't sunk into the sea. They'd had revolutions, like anywhere else, and a new emperor, and there had been whispers of new and frightful secret weapons. But he knew little. His third cousin had been hit behind the ear by a steel-headed weapon he'd claimed was as long as four spears. Clearly, he was bereft of his sense, makib, for that was laughably impossible.

"Surely," I said. "My thanks, dom. Rememberee."

This third-cousinly confirmation of what the Gdoinye had told me had to suffice for my comfort. Bevon and Pompino reappeared and we prepared to leave Wayfarer's Drinnik. And then the slaves toiled in.

Well. The slaves had struggled over the Desolate Waste on foot. They wore the gray slave breechclout or were naked. They were yoked and haltered. They stank. They collapsed into long limp straggles on the dust and their heads bowed and that ghastly wailing rose from them. The sound of "Grak!" smashed into the air continuously, with the crack of whips. The slavemasters were Katakis. We caught a glimpse of this dolorous arrival of the slaves and then a protruding corner of the ale booth shut off the sight.

"No," said Bevon, and there was sweat on his pug face. "No."

Pompino and I knew what he meant.

"I had news from home," said Pompino. "Well, almost home, from a town ten dwaburs away and they'd heard nothing so it must all be all right."

Such is the hunger for news of home that even the negation of news is regarded as confirmation of all rightness. We did not hurry back and stopped for a wet here and there and admired the sights. We wore swords, of course, and our brigandines, and if Bevon tended to swagger a little in imitation of Pompino, who is there who would blame him over much?

The avenue on which stood the Blue Rokveil was blocked by a line of cavalrymen, their totrixes schooled to obedience, their black and white checks hard in the brilliance of the suns. People were being held back, and a buzzing murmur of speculation rose. We pushed forward, puzzled.

"Llanitch!" bellowed a bulky Deldar, sweating. At his order to halt we stopped, looking at him inquiringly. He shouldered across and people skipped out of his way. Just beyond the line of cavalrymen the hotel lifted, its ranks of windows bright, its blue gags fluttering. People craned to see. The Deldar eased back to his men, keeping them face front. We moved to a vantage point and so looked on disaster.

They say Trip the Thwarter, who is a minor spirit of deviltry, takes delight in upsetting the best-laid plans. We saw the dismounted vakkas hauling out their prisoners. There were many swords and spears in evidence, and no chances were being taken, for these men being taken up into custody were notorious and possessed of fearful reputations. We saw Kov Konec being prodded out, dignified, calm, his hands bound. We saw Dav turn on a swod and try to kick him, snarling his hatred, and so being thumped back into line. The swords ringed in the important people of Mandua, Fropo the Curved, Strom Nath Resdurm, Nath the Fortroi and others. Only the lesser folk were not taken up.

We stared, appalled.

"Treason against the Nine Masked Guardians," a man in the crowd told us.

"A plot to murder them all in their beds," amplified his wife, a plump, jolly person carrying a wicker basket filled with squishes in moist green leaves.

"Lucky for us Prince Mefto discovered the plot in time to warn the Masked Nine. By Havil! I'd send 'em all to the Execution Jikaida, aye, and put them all in the center drin!"

We stood as though frozen by the baleful eyes of the Gengulas of legend.

Konec saw us.

With a single contemptuous jerk he snapped the thongs binding his wrists. He stuck both arms out sideways, level with his ears. Then he drew them in and thrust them out again level with his hips. He brought his hand around to the base of his spine and swept it in a wide circling arc up over his head. The pantomime was quite clear. Then—then he drew his forefinger across his throat, forcefully, viciously.

I remained absolutely still.

The guards leaped on him then; but he did not resist as they tied his hands again. He had delivered his message, a chilling and demanding message. His eyes blazed on me.

Between files of the totrix cavalry Konec and his people were led away to imprisonment.

The plot against Mefto the Kazzur was stillborn.

"What—?" said Bevon. He looked bewildered.

"It is all down to you, Jak," said Pompino.

We were alone and friendless in Jikaida City, and it was all down to me to halt this glittering Prince Mefto the Kazzur in his ambitions and to prevent the total destruction of Vallia. As this thought struck in so shrewdly there rose up before my eyes the phantom vision of Mefto, brandishing his five swords and beating down in irresistible triumph.

CHAPTER TWENTY

Death Jikaida

"You must be a fambly, of a surety," said Nath the Swordsman, screwing up his scarred face in hopeless wonderment. "But if you wish to act against Mefto, that is suitable for me. I do not give the lady Yasuri more than one chance in ten."

"You are finding the pieces for the lady Yasuri. Put me down on the list."

"And me," said Bevon, at my side.

Pompino had disappeared. I harbored no grudge; this was no affair of his and he was mightily conscious of his duty for the Star Lords. We stood in Nath the Swordsman's room that looked out upon the inner square of his rambling premises. Men and women were being put through their paces out there, and the quick flitter and flutter of swordblades filled the dusty area. The room was plainly furnished and contained as its centerpiece a finely executed picture of Kurin, delineated as some long-dead artist of Jikaida City had visualized him, blade in hand, in the guard position and, as this was Havilfar, covering himself with a shield. The picture served as the focus of a kind of shrine, with flowers and atras and incense burning, which exuded a stink into the room.

"The lady Yasuri was fortunate in the misfortune of Konec," said Nath. His gaze seldom left the people practicing out there, and he would suddenly leap up and go striding out, yelling, to reprimand some poor wight whose clumsy technique had aroused Nath's displeasure. The women out there were all strapping girls, of course, for they fight hard in Vuvushi Jikaida.

"Yes," said Bevin.

The league tables led up to the final tournament and Yasuri had placed third, because she had already lost to Konec. That was her only defeat. With the absence of Konec, who was due to play Mefto in the final, Yasuri had been switched in. We were here to act as two of her pieces. Neither of us could see any other way of getting to Prince Mefto.

I had, in my old intemperate way, started to make a sally toward his hotel and had fought a few of his folk trying to get through. I had not succeeded and the darker the veil drawn over that chapter of misfortunes the better. I had had the sense to wear a mask. Now we presented ourselves at Nath en Screetzim's premises and he welcomed us like water in the Ochre Limits.

Once we had been accepted, the formalities went through like sausages on a greased plate and very quickly we found ourselves joining the lumpen gaggle Yasuri had been able to find. We waited in a long, wide, tall hall with arrow-slits for windows far higher than a man could jump. We were in the heart of the Jikaidaderen. The game was to be a private one. The public would be able to see most of the other tournament games; but they would not be permitted here to see the final. That they were prepared to accept this indicates something of the obedience rife in Jikaida City. We rubbed shoulders with criminals, with men who had been delegated this duty, slaves fighting for their freedom and few, very few, men who fought for the lady Yasuri.

The atmosphere in that anteroom to the games clogged on the palate, the stink of sweat, the stink of fear—and the silly bravado men put on in times like these to mask their deeper feelings. Well, Bevon and I endured.

We studied the Jikaida pieces waiting to go on. We tried to pick the stout from the weak, the brave from those who would be unable to perform adequately through fear—everyone knew the penalty for running. I said to Bevon: "One or two will run, I think, and welcome a Lohvian shaft through them rather than a chopped-up death at the hands of Mefto's bully boys."

"Yet some look capable. That Chulik, he's here for slitting the throat of a Rapa. And that group of Fristles, and see those Khibils? They will fight."

Rumors and buzzes swept through the men. There was weak ale to drink and no wine. There was ample food. We understood that the lady Yasuri had obtained the services of a lady Jikaidasta whose name, we gathered, was Ling-li-Lwingling, or something like that. Bevon listened to the swift gabble of a Fristle, and turned to me. I did not know if he was laughing or cursing.

"Who do you think Mefto has as his Jikaidast?"

"Oh," I said. "Well, Bevon, now you have a personal grudge in it doubled."

"Aye."

Och slaves at last brought in the equipment. These formalities differed markedly for us from our previous experiences. Then we had been part of a noble's entourage, playing for his honor and glory; now we were assembled from the academies of the sword and from the prisons and stews. The bagnios supplied their freight. The lady Yasuri apparently relied entirely on the resources of Jikaida City for her pieces, for we saw none of the small bodyguard she kept up. As for the equipment, that was simple. A blue breechclout, a thraxter and a shield. Plus a headband decked with varying numbers of blue feathers and, for some of the superior pieces, blue favors on sashes. Bevon and I each received a reed-laurium* with two blue feathers. This marked us as Deldars.

The swords were thraxters and Bevon and I, by arrangement as volunteers, received our own weapons. The shields were laminated wood, bronze rimmed but not faced, and were smaller than the regulation Havilfarese swod's shield, being something like twenty-seven inches high by sixteen inches wide, and were rectangular.

The shields were painted solid blue with white rank markings as appropriate, and a fellow would take the shield fitting his position as a piece when he left the substitutes bench.

The lady Yasuri had been obliged to play blue, as she was filling in and, no doubt, overjoyed at her own good fortune. She was a Yellow adherent, I knew; but the glory and profit of winning meant more to her, and it is proper that a Jikaida player should take either color for the experience of the different diagonals of play.

Wrapping the blue breechclout about me and drawing the end up between my legs and fastening it off with the blue cord provided reminded me, with a pang, of the times I had gone through this first stage of dressing with the brave old scarlet. But now there would be no mesh steel, no kax, no leather jerkin; now the blue breechclout was all. Well, by Zair! And wasn't this what was required? Wasn't it high time I went swinging into action wearing just a breechclout and with a sword in my fist?

"By the Black Chunkrah!" I said. "I think Mefto—" But I did not finish the thought. Black and white checks filled the room and we were being herded out. The smell of fear stank

* reed: headband. laurium: rank.

on the air, and, also, the sweat of men determined to fight before they died.

We all received a goblet of wine—a thick, heavy, red variety like the deep purple wine of Hamal called Malab's Blood. I do not care for it; but, by Krun! it went down sweetly enough then, I can tell you.

The preliminary ceremonies went as usual, with the prayers and the chanted hymns and the sacrifices. When we came out of the long stone tunnel from the gloom onto the brillance of the board, the brightness of the light smote our eyes. Ruby and jade radiance drenched the playing board. This was a very select, very refined Jikaida board. There was no noisy hum from an excited crowd of plebs. Around the board and raised on a plinth extended a broad terrace, shielded by black and white checkered awnings. The thrones facing each other at either end were ornate. On the terrace were set small tables and reclining couches, and the high ones of LionardDen lolled there, waited on by slaves, sipping their drinks and daintily picking at light delicacies. They had chairs which could be carried around the terrace by slaves so that they might watch the play from the best positions. No action would begin until the representative of the Nine Masked Guardians was satisfied that all the spectators were in position for the finest view.

"By the Resplendent Bridzikelsh!" growled a Brokelsh near us. "Why don't they get on with it."

"There is all the time in the world to die, as Rhapaporgolam the Reiver of Souls knows full well," a Rapa told him.

The Brokelsh spat, which heartened me.

A Pachak hefted his shield in his two left hands. "I have given the lady Yasuri my nikobi," he said in that serious way of Pachaks. "And by Papachak the All-Powerful! I shall honor my pledge. But I think this is like to be the last fight for us."

The Chulik slid his sword neatly under his left arm and then polished up his tusks with a spittled thumb. "By Likshu the Treacherous!" he said. "I shall take many of them down to the Ice Floes of Sicce with me."

"Numi the Hyrjiv fights with us," said one of the Fristles. "But I wish I had my scimitar instead of this thraxter."

So, as we waited to march out with our backs as straight as we could contrive and take our places on the board, we called upon our gods and our guardian spirits. This is human nature. And how the exotic variety of Kregen can respond! Truly is it said, on Kregen are joys for all men's hearts.

As we marched out we presented a spectacle at which, I suppose, many a person of limited intellect would scoff, dubbing us a collection of menagerie-men. Yet we were all men, all human beings, and we marched out to fight for our lives.

Even the Chulik shared some reflection of those feelings.

And, there was among our number a single Kataki.

"By the Triple Tails of Targ the Untouchable!" The Kataki swished his bladeless tail about like a leem in a temper. "Would that Takroti would slit all their gizzards!"

"Careful with your tail," snapped one of the Fristles. "By Odifor, you nearly tripped me."

The guards stepped in with upraised bludgeons to separate out the violently bawling combatants in the ensuing melee. Truly, we presented a horrifying and a pathetic spectacle as we marched out.

As we stepped onto the board we saw that the Princess's square was already occupied. The woman standing waiting wore a long white gown of sensil, lavishly embroidered with blue and yellow and black and white checkers. An enormous crowning plume of blue feathers rose above her head, surrounded by tufts of blue. She glittered with gems. As I passed her, and the carrying chair for her Jikaidasta, I saw her face. Most of the lines were gone, her flesh filled out, and I guessed many of those lines had been caused by apprehension for the journey across the Desolate Waste. Her hair was a dark brown, curled, and I caught its perfume. Her shape in the white sensil was a world away from the shape in the shiny black bombazine and lace.

She saw me and a muscle twitched in her cheek. But she made no movement and ignored me. That suited me. I was not here to fight for the lady Yasuri, but to fight against her opponent.

The eight slave girls who carried the Jikaidasta's chair were Gonells. The male Gons habitually shave off their white hair, believing it shames them. But some peoples of the Gon race take a proper pride in the silver hair of their females, and these eight Gonells were splendid girls, well-formed, clad in wispy blue, and their silver hair shone lustrously, sweeping in deep waves to their waists.

The occupant of the carrying chair was invisible to me and the gherimcal rested on its four legs, carved like prychans. We marched past and so fanned out to take up our positions.

As the trumpets blew and the Suns of Scorpio shone down on us, we Ranked our Deldars.

The game opened with Mefto taking the first move and

soon his pieces were extending down the board toward us, like rivers of lava from a volcano. Our own lines extended toward Yellow. Truly, Mefto's pieces looked splendid in their yellow breechclouts and with tufty masses of yellow feathers. Their shields formed a field of daffodils. He had picked his best men, no doubt of that; they were brawny, tough, adept. Like us, they were a mixture of diff and apim, and they were confident of victory.

The beautiful girls in their wisps of clothing ran about the board carrying the orders to the pieces. Men moved in obedience and soon the opening clashes began. Swords flashed and blood flowed.

We played Death Jikaida.

It chanced that I was formed into a diagonal line with a swod each side, and there I remained. Mefto had not put in an appearance on the board. I could just see him in the Yellow throne, giving his orders and the stylor below repeating them to the girls who ran so fleetly, their limbs rosy and glowing, or brown or black and splendid in the light. The lines formed and pieces fought and were taken or took, to be tossed back into the velvet-lined balass box or to be replaced from the substitutes' bench. The opening proved to be the Princess's Kapt's Gambit Accepted, and my diagonal remained fast, the action taking place on the right wing.

The young swod by me licked his lips. He was apim, a lithely built lad, without the bulky toughness of the fighting man who has campaigned for seasons on end. Despite the regulations, we talked, as the pieces did. What could the representative of the Nine Masked Guardians do about that now? Have us all shafted?

There were things he could order and which the black-clad men would carry out; but this infringement of the rules was minor.

"I only borrowed the chicken," said this lad, by name Tobi the Knees. "Mother was starving and Father—well, I do not know what happened to him. I would have given the next chicken back, as I always do."

So he had been taken up by the Watch and condemned, and sent to the academy to be trained for Kazz-Jikaida. He came from the teeming sections of the city in which many poor folk eked out a precarious living. There were too many of these poor quarters. The contrast between their squalor, and the lavishness of Yellow or Blue City, condemned the Nine Guardians—at least, in my eyes. As for the Foreign Quarters, where visitors who were impartial as to color stayed, they were as palatial in their hotels as the palaces of the City nobility. Tobi the Knees was not alone in his misery.

"I was going to be a wheelwright—always get work as a wheelwright. And I can shape the wood perfectly. But, mother was ill and I lost my job, and—"

"You borrowed a chicken."

"They got the feathers back!"

"I see."

"And they showed me this sword and this shield and I can make a pass or two. But I still don't understand it all."

"Keep the shield up and keep sticking the sword out, Tobi. You'll make a bladesman yet."

"But I—" He swallowed. He was keeping up a brave front and smiling and swishing his thraxter about; but he was scared, frightened clear through to his ib.

A flash of legs and a wisp of purple drapery and a girl's clear voice saying: "Swod to vault to Prychan D Four."

Prychan Drin was the third drin toward Yellow on the left of the board. Dermiflon was the home drin on that side, and then Strigicaw Drin. These drins do not appear in Poron Jikaida. Tobi the Knees looked. He gripped his sword. Then, without a word to me or the girl he walked up along the diagonal line. Prychan D Four was unoccupied. Tobi came down off the end of the zeunt and stood on the square and looked around. He was right out in the front of the Blues.

I just hoped Yasuri and her lady Jikaidasta knew what they were doing.

D Four is a blue square.

Over on the right of the board Mefto made a bold advance, vaulting a Hikdar down through Neemu Drin to the end of Wersting Drin, and as Yasuri brought a Hikdar across to Boloth Drin to cover, so Mefto advanced a Chuktar. I began to think the crucial action would take place over there, on the front between Wersting and Boloth Drins. I hoped so. I didn't give a damn who won this silly game; I owed Konec and his comrades from Mandua and I owed Vallia to make sure of Mefto when he appeared on the board.

The charming little girls with their blue or yellow feathers who carry the orders are equipped with long light wands of red-painted wood wrapped in blue or yellow streamers. With these they tap the pieces on the shoulders if, as so often happens, the men are staring in sick fascination at the fighting. So I felt the tap, and turned, and the girl said: "Deldar to Prychan E Three."

I vaulted. This placed me diagonally ahead of Tobi. He

greeted me as though we'd met on an Ice Floe in You Know Where.

The next instant Yellow's orders were carried out. A fellow wearing the Yellow favors and feathers stalked across the squares from Krulch Drin toward me. Mefto had decided to put an end to this advance.

I recognized the Yellow piece at once. He was acting the part of a Chuktar; but I had last seen him eating palines in Friendly Fodo's Weapons Shop. He halted for a moment on E Two, for as a Chuktar he had come straight on, and then, instantly, flung himself on me.

As his sword beat down on my upraised shield I fancied I'd stir him up a little.

"Why, Llahal, Trinko. Fancy meeting you here."

His muscular body shielded with that shiny carapace across his back bore on, and his Moltingur face, all eating proboscis and feelers and terrifying faceted eyes, showed shock. I thumped forward with the shield, let the thraxter snout to the side and below. The resistance was soggy, and then the blade slid in. I stepped back.

He toppled over and his tunnel mouth emitted a long hissing wheeze.

The slaves in their red tunics ran out with a stretcher and carted him away. Other slaves raked the blood and sprinkled fresh blue sand. There was no lifting uproar from the refined onlookers lounging in their chairs along the terrace. Yasuri made her move.

The red wand touched me again and the blue streamers tickled my face.

"Deldar to take Hikdar on Prychan C Three."

This fellow, a Rapa, had watched the previous contest with his blue-feathered beak stuck high in the air. The yellow feathers in his reed-laurium outweighed his racial feathers. I stalked across and we set to.

He was good—all Mefto's men were good—and the shields gonged like pale echoes of the Bells of Beng Kishi before I slid him and so stretched him out on the blue sand.

The red-clad slaves bore him off. Still there was no sound from the terrace and I did not expect any. They were connoisseurs up there, lolling in their fancy chairs and sipping their wines.

Yasuri, as was her privilege because I was the attacking piece, recalled me then. I trailed off to the substitutes bench with a word for Tobi as I went.

"That's how it's done, Tobi. Keep your chin tucked in and your shield up. Jikai!"

"It is to you the Jikai, Jak."

What could I say? I gave him a hard nod of encouragement and walked slowly back across the blue and yellows.

Up to this point the game had been reasonably equal, for Yasuri's scratch team had fought like wild leems when it came to push of pike. But the tension would increase with each succeeding move, as the pieces drew closer together and the skillful maneuvering gave way to the blood bath.

The palanquin of the lady Jikaidasta rested quietly near Yasuri, who, as the Aeilssa, had not so far been forced to move. As I walked back Yasuri looked at me. "Well done, Jak. I give you the jikai." Only lower and upper case initial letters can attempt to indicate the quality of meaning in the same word here.

"Watch his center, lady. I recall Scatulo favored a thrust—"

A voice spoke from the palanquin. The golden cords of the carrying-chair's curtains loosened. The voice said: "Go to the substitutes' bench, tikshim, and do not presume." And the curtains at the side parted and a woman's face looked out.

Red hair, she had, a glowing rippling auburn mass piled atop a small face, a pale face with the sheen of ivory of Chem. Her eyes were blue, and direct and challenging. Small her mouth, and scarlet, and pursed above a firm rounded chin. Beautiful? Yes, beautiful, like a stalking chavonth, lissom and slender and feline. Even then I did not liken her to a leem.

I halted stockstill at once. I was very near her chair. The silver-haired Gonells waited, stupidly transfixed by the blood and violence—and, at that, not stupidly. It was we who partook of the blood and violence who were the truly stupid. So I stood, not going to the bench as she had so impolitely ordered me, using that word tikshim that so infuriates those to whom it is addressed, being considerably worse than the condescending "my man" of Earth.

"I was talking to the lady Yasuri." I spoke softly.

The Jikaidasta's face resembled a mask at first sight; the sheen of ivory of Chem, the delineation of line of lip and jaw and nose, the flesh firm and compact as though carved from that smoothest and mellowest of ivories. But, as I stood there, a trifle lumpen and boorish, a faint mottling of color appeared on her cheekbones. She had a most perfect bone structure, fine-drawn, distinct, and in no single place could be seen any sagging of flesh. The effort with which she controlled herself was quite admirable, quite; here was a lady used to having her own way, and highly conscious of her own worth.

"Do not allow the blood to rule your head just because you have won two encounters. This is a game to win."

"You think you will win it—against Mefto?"

"If the creatures we have to fight for us do as well as you then perhaps. Nothing else will do."

I felt the pang in me. What I had done—would that be any use against Mefto the Kazzur?

And then, well, I was a trifle wrought up. So I said, "You are the Jikaidasta they call Ling-li-Lwingling. You are from Loh."

Three men in black appeared on the board heading in our direction. I will not describe the instruments they bore.

Yasuri said: "Be off with you, Jak."

"Aye, my lady." And then, before I went, I said: "We shall win today, by fair means or foul."

Ling-li-Lwingling, of Loh, let the side curtains fall back into place and I trotted off to the substitutes bench. I think, if the three men in black had followed me and attempted to use their instruments I would have dealt with them, not recking the consequences; but they looked malevolently, and then turned away.

The man chosen to replace the piece I had acted on the blue square was a Khibil. Yasuri was bringing her left flank into play with a nicely calculated precision of timing that, had this been other than Death Jikaida, would have placed Mefto's pieces in a cramped and unfavorable position. I fancied the lady Jikaidasta's hand was in this strategy. But this was Death Jikaida. Mefto sent a hulking swaggerer of a fellow, acting as a swod, to deal with the Khibil Deldar. The Khibil was carted away, dripping blood on the sand. The victor bore ghastly wounds and Mefto would quite clearly replace him. Yasuri responded by switching her attack, hoping to get our Chulik into action, and then—and at last, at long last—a response was elicited from those languid watchers on the terrace.

With the accompaniment of a long sigh susurating around him, Prince Mefto the Kazzur strode onto the board.

Useless for me to race toward him. I had almost the length of the board to go, and long before I reached the rast I'd be shafted by those vigilant Bowmen of Loh. No, I had to be on a square and near the cramph before I could break all the rules and leap for his throat. He stood on his square and looked about. He preened himself. Well, he was a master bladesman and I would not deny him that. While I would admit I did not know his full character and guessed there was good in him, somewhere, he did seem to me to vaunt his prowess, to take a dark pride from his own gift that, somehow, repulsed me. This is subjective. May Zair forgive me if I swagger in the same way. I do not think I do.

And, this was strange. The great swordsman I have known usually revere their gift, assessing it humbly as a gift of the gods, however much sweat they distribute in training and understanding the Disciplines. Perhaps I was still sore and vengeful, still filled with resentment. I sat down, and watched as Mefto went to work.

Tobi the Knees stood next in line. Mefto declared his move and pounced. He did not slay Tobi in a simple quick passage as he could have done. He toyed with him, and feigned alarm that he was under pressure, and poor Tobi thus drawn on pressed hard, and was cut, and then cut again, and so, all bewildered and uncomprehending, was sliced into pieces.

I suppose the old intemperate Dray Prescot would have leaped up and gone hurling forward. He'd have swatted the flying arrows away in the old fashion as the Krozairs of Zy do. But I do not think that maniac of a fighting man would have lived to reach Mefto the Kazzur, let alone have had time to cross swords with him.

The Dray Prescot that was me sat lumpen on the bench. But a change did come over me. As the remains of Tobi were carried away and the blue and yellow sand was sprinkled I felt I would not wait too long. And the game went badly for us. Our Kataki came up against Mefto, and his tail sliced this way and that, emptily, and Mefto laughed and his own tail-hand gripped the Kataki's bladeless tail as he sank his thraxter into his belly.

But our Chulik fought well, and dispatched his men, and Yasuri recalled him. We were being pressed back now, and over the lines of blue and yellow men the yellow of Mefto's pieces vaulted long into our home drins. That unique vaulting move in Jikaidish is zeunt, and the Yellows were zeunting in on us with a vengeance.

The carrying chair pressed close to Yasuri, and the two ladies argued long and fiercely over their next move, and the water dripped in the clepsydra and time fleeted away. The Blues out there began to cast anxious eyes toward the water-clock. The water dripped. The ladies conferred. Some of the pieces began to beat their swords against their shields. The hollow drumroll made no difference to the ladies. Still they talked. And the water dripped.

We all saw the long lenken arm of the gong lift ready to descend with a resonant boom against the brazen gong. Then a purple wisp of gossamer and a flash of spritely legs and a girl was off to order the move. It was made before the gong struck. But even as the Chuktar order to move complied the gong crashed out—too late.

"Well," said Bevon next to me. "I do not wish to be on the board if the ladies do that again."

"Nor me, by Odifor!" quoth the Fristle next to us on the bench. Sweat stank on the air, and both ladies used perfume bottles. Move followed move, and it was clear that Mefto had sized up the play and was ruthlessly pushing everything forward, not caring for finesse, just using the superior skills of his fighting men. Our ranks thinned. It was soon perfectly clear that we were going to lose, for a set-up was approaching in which the Yellow Pallan could sweep down in a long zeunt and coming off the vault turn sharply and so pin the Princess. Yasuri saw it and was helpless. Her every move was beaten by superior swordplay.

Yes, I know—this was an example of the futility of Kazz-Jikaida, and a confirmation of the pure Jikaida player's views.

But, do not forget, this was Death Jikaida.

As the final move in Mefto's play was made, a long and satisfied sigh rippled up from the terrace. The men and women up there, sipping their delicate wines, perfumed lace at their noses, appreciated what they were seeing.

Prince Mefto acting as the Yellow Pallan, made the last zeunt in person. He came off the vault opposite the Princess and his next move would capture her. She threw in our Chulik. He did well, he fought bravely; but he died. He died on Mefto's blade.

Now it was Yellow's move. As the winning defender, Mefto could not replace himself; but everyone present knew he had no intention of doing that. He was unmarked. Glitteringly in the sunshine he stood there, a golden figure of superb poise and accomplishment.

He made his move.

In a loud, ringing voice, he called: "Pallan captures Aeilssa. Hyrkaida! Do you bare the throat?"

Yasuri drew herself up, a diminutive figure yet shining and

oddly impressive in her long white gown with the tall blue feathers nodding over her head.

"I do not bare the throat! *En Screetzim nalen Aeilssa!*"

The Princess's Swordsman!

Her prerogative, available only in Kazz-Jikaida, and she had taken it—as, indeed, she must. Mefto knew that. He smiled. We all saw that smile, small and tight and filled with genuine pleasure. Mefto was a bladesman who loved to fight, who enjoyed his work, and who had never met his master.

The man who had been waiting all this time as the Princess's Swordsman started up. His face was green. He was apim. His eyes protruded grotesquely, and glistened like gouged-out eyes on a fishmonger's slab. With a shriek he threw his shield away and ran. He had no idea where he was running. He just fled from horror.

In a blundering crazed gallop he ran over the blue and yellows and the long Lohvian shaft skewered him through the back and another pierced him through the throat and as he fell a third punctured into and through one of those ghastly staring eyes.

His shield still rocked on its face in the mingled sunslight.

Bevon stood up.

"I think I shall see what I may do against this—"

I pulled him by his blue breechclout.

"Stay, Bevon the Reckless!"

So it was I, Dray Prescot, Prince of Onkers, who stepped forward and picked up the fallen shield with its proud marks of the Princess's Swordsman and walked straight and purposefully onto the blue and yellow squares of the board of Death Jikaida to face a man I knew had the beating of me in swordplay.

CHAPTER TWENTY-ONE

The Princess's Swordsman

Traditionally in Kazz-Jikaida whenever the Princess called on her Swordsman to fight for her the drums rolled. Black and white checkered tabards, black and white checkered drum cloths, all rippled and flowed as the drummers plied their drumsticks. The rataplan hammered out. Long thunderous rolls and flourishes, repeated and repeated, roared and boomed over the Jikaida board. And I walked forward, almost in a dream, feeling the blood in my head and the weight of the shield and the heft of the sword and the grip of the sand beneath my naked feet.

These were physical feelings. They bore in on me. They were tangible and real, like the sweat that beaded my forehead and trickled down my face from under the reed-laurium, like the taste of blood and sweat on the air. Physical, material impressions: the glitter of burnished steel, the gloating faces of the privileged onlookers as they crowded from their chairs to catch a closer look at this climactic butchery, the waft of a tiny breeze on my heat-soaked face—how refreshing that breeze, how vividly it brought back pungent memories of other days, of the quarterdeck of a seventy-four, of the scrap of decking of a swifter, a swordship, and the wind in my face and all the seas of two worlds! But I was pent in this stone-walled enclosure, this amphitheatre of death, and I recalled the Jikhorkdun of Huringa, and felt again the concussion of blows given and taken, and the leem's tail and the blood, and all the time as these jangling memories sparked through my head so I walked quietly and steadily out over the blue and yellows to take up my position beside the lady Yasuri.

"En Screetzim nalen Aeilssa! Bratch!" She called again, briskly, for she had not taken her gaze off Mefto, and did not turn, and she waited for her champion to stand at her side.

"I am here, lady," I said, and she turned, and saw me.

"Jak. Fight well. Fight well to the death—"

"Aye, lady, I shall fight as well as I am able and as Zair strengthens my sinews and gives cunning to my fist. And to the death, as it seems. But, lady, I do not fight for you."

She flinched. What she had thought I do not know. But she flinched back, and a look of pain crossed her face.

"This is a game to you, lady. A mere pastime, lady. So that you may wear the diadem of triumph, lady. But the drums roll and blood will be spilled and men will die, and not for your sake, lady."

The curtains of the carrying-chair rustled back. The ivory white face looked out and the glory of the suns caught in the red Lohvian hair. "Still your tongue, tikshim. You are condemned to fight, so fight and do not chatter."

I regarded her as I stood there, waiting for the drumroll to end. I did not look at Mefto—not yet. Ling-li-Lwingling put a hand as white as her face, as slender as a missal, to the golden cord and her fingers toyed with the golden tassel. I knew who she was, now—rather, I knew what she was. The drums rolled. And I said: "Ling-li-Lwingling. By the Seven Arcades, woman, you are a Witch of Loh!"

"Yes, Jak the Condemned. I am a Witch of Loh, and better for you to—"

"Save your pretty threats, Witch. I would give you the Sana; but other and more pressing matters await."

Her red red mouth widened. I did not think she knew how to smile.

"Your fears for Vallia are well-founded—you will fight for the lady Yasuri—and you will fight for me!"

I felt the whole enormous expanse of the Jikaida board tilt beneath me, and coalesce into the single square upon which I stood. I noticed it was a yellow square. Ling-li's smile slowly died and her face resumed that fixed foreboding expression as though expertly carved from solid ivory of Chem.

The long-drawn drumroll ended.

Absolute silence engulfed the Kazz-Jikaida board.

And I looked squarely upon Prince Mefto the Kazzur.

Arrogance and power and pride, yes, of course, they were all there, stamped upon him indelibly by his own prowess. I tried to see more. Men and women are more than mere bundles of flesh and blood hung on bones and walking the world in the light and darkness; this Mefto was a man, a five-handed Kildoi, and yet a human being. His presence smote me as a shell, a hard and shiny yellow carapace concealing the humanity within.

The vivid sensory impressions bombarding me as the drumroll rattled to silence contained all of the physical world; I dare not seek to pry into the world of feeling, of emotion, of fear or courage. I was here. Was not that enough?

Yet feeling decided all. Physical sensations were colored by the emotions, so I tried to look past the blue and yellow and the waiting silence and the spectators and the Jikaida pieces, past Yasuri and Ling-li and Mefto, tried to peer into the darkest depths beneath myself.

To find oneself. . . . In that moment even the central core of existence sought its meaning. I was a Krozair of Zy. Did that matter so much?

Mefto's voice lifted, high and hard and challenging.

"I know you, apim!"

I said nothing.

Perhaps, had the question been put to me, I could not have said anything.

But, at the very end of that somber tunnel there might be a light. It was just possible. All I had to remember was one single fact in all the universe: I was Dray Prescot.

That was all.

I am Dray Prescot.

Mefto twirled his sword with great dexterity, shoved up his shield and with a jovial bladesman's bellow, charged.

We fought.

Useless to try to peer past the physical—the feelings must come of their own accord. Our blades met and scraped and clung and parted. The power in his muscles was a dynamic force. It was sword and shield against sword and shield. Oh, yes, he had two left hands to grip his shield and thus afford a superior leverage; but as we fought and circled, and sought the openings, and thrust and recovered to the gong-notes of steel on shield, so I accepted my fate. My only advantage, I thought, lay in that belief I had that I was a shade faster than he was. That was all. But he was a marvel. Often and often have I said that about swordsmen I have fought; but this Mefto the Kazzur was a marvel among marvels.

This marvel went about cutting me up as he went about cutting up all his victims, as he had chopped Tobi the Knees. But I resisted. The thraxters flamed in the mingled streaming lights of the Suns of Scorpio. The sand beneath our feet spurted blue dust; for we fought for the square on which the Blue Princess had taken her stand, the Princess's Square, and this would be hyrkaida when I lost.

For I felt I would lose.

The feeling appeared to me like a strange object in some precious golden-bound balass chest, to be taken out and examined and pondered over. A new experience. A thrilling vibration along nerves and sinews, a dark space in the mind. . . .

Although I took no notice of her, I knew that Yasuri, who had moved back from her square, would be watching this combat with glowing eyes, her lip caught between her teeth, and, probably, her hands clenched over her breast. What the Witch of Loh, Ling-li-Lwingling, was doing I did not know, nor cared; setting out the pieces for a new game, probably.

Mefto the Kazzur sliced me along the right bicep; not deeply enough to hurt, just to draw blood, just to open the scoring. I had not touched him. He cut me again, and I found his thraxter a leaping silver flame, torturing, dazzling, infuriating. I kept myself inwardly, holding in to myself. We circled again, seeking the advantage that was not there, for the circumscribed lines of the blue square hemmed us in with honor. The technique—more a trick, really—I had pondered during the fight by the caravan might serve. But Mefto must be primed before I could use that last desperate throw.

Thinking clogged reactions; the sword must live with the body and become a part of the living being, free and uncontaminated by lethargic thought. But Mefto's reactions and skill negated the usual unthinking skill I exerted. Where he had been trained and who his masters had been intrigued me and I would one day visit Balintol myself. But, then, that was foolish, a child's dream of an impossible future, for I was due to die here, on the blue sand, chopped and bloody and done for.

As the combat went on and time stretched out and I was cut and cut again, a distant howling sound drifted in fitfully. The lethargic watchers on the terrace were responding, and losing all their languid affectation. The blood-sport caught them up in its choking coils.

With an infinite patience I accepted this punishment and worked on him. I found certain weaknesses I do not think he suspected existed. Certainly, I became sharply aware of several glaring deficiencies in my own technique. He feinted a thrust and as my shield flicked to cover and I went the other way, he allowed the almost imperceptible tremor of his body to force my instant unthinking reaction to drive me back. My own skill recognized that body tremor, and reacted to it, and so his original thrust slid in past my shield and sliced a ribbon of flesh from my ribs.

The next time he tried a variation of that I did not react as he expected, and his thrust missed and I leaned in and nicked him on his lower right arm. He sprang back, furiously.

"So you think to best me, Prince Mefto the Kazzur, apim! I have thrashed you before and this time—"

Well, sometimes I have a merry little spot of chit-chat when I fight. I did not reply, then, to his taunts.

The swords clashed again and I felt the power as he sought to overbear me and I resisted and, for a half-dozen heartbeats, we struggled directly together, body against body.

His strength was a live ferocious force. He compelled my sword arm down, and down. And I resisted, and so thrust him back, and slid his blade and sliced at him as he flinched and dodged backwards. I chopped only a strand of his hair. His face, which had been jolly and filled with good humor at indulging in the sport he liked best, lowered on a sudden, and his brows drew down. If this pantomime was meant to frighten me, well—by Zair, I will not lie.

For he bore in now with a more deadly intent.

Useless to attempt to describe the passages of that fight in detail, but it was talked about for season after season as the greatest encounter seen on the Kazz-Jikaida board.

He had taken a gouging chunk out of my shield and the wood splintered away from the bronze framing. Now his blade smashed down on the rim and wrenched the bronze into a distorted ribbon. With a few skillful blows as I defended myself he chopped half the shield away. His own yellow shield bore the marks of my sword; but it remained intact.

And, all the time, he kept up his chatter, taunting me, threatening me, deriding my efforts, sometimes patronizingly praising a last-minute defense that barely kept his sword from my guts.

"You fight well, for an apim. Truly, I admire your skill."

I grunted with the effort of parrying with the dangling remnant of shield. I would not throw it away yet, for it still served in a pitiful fashion, and if I hurled it at him he would merely duck, and laugh.

As he talked on, leaping and swirling and attacking and springing back and so coming in again, I remained silent.

My body was now a single shining sheet of blood. I felt no pain, for a Krozair of Zy, no less than a Clansman or a Djang, must refuse to acknowledge pain that will hamper his fighting ability. But I was weaker. I could feel that. Nothing could disguise the sluggishness in my limbs, no pushing away of pain and denial of torment could conceal my growing feebleness.

This Kildoi was a rara avis among fighting men, no doubt of that. So I must put in the last throw before it was too late.

With a sudden and shattering series of blows, with a wild smashing onslaught, Mefto came for me and I saw that this time he meant to finish me. I defended. I ducked and weaved and dangled the sorry scrap of shield before him and I flailed his blade away. Somehow I resisted and held my position in the blue square and he drew back, baffled. But my weakness was now on me. I was near the end.

So, positioning myself, I tried to remember who I was, that I was plain Dray Prescot.

He was talking again, not quite so jovially, clearly annoyed that he had not finished me in that passage.

"I said you were a fighter, apim. You have a little skill. I have joyed in our contest; but now—"

And then I spoke. For the first time.

I said: "I, too, have enjoyed this little swordplay. You have tried and you have failed. I have sounded you out." My voice was thick and my throat felt as though it was filled with all the sand of the arena. "But, now, Mefto the Kleesh, it is my turn."

And, instantly, I swept through the dazzlement of the attack I had long pondered, and thrust.

I'd have had him. I would have. But I was weak, too weak. The blows I had taken had punished me, and the blood that leached away took with it my strength.

He just managed to drag his shield across. His Kildoi face, handsome, handsome, with its golden beard and clear-cut features, drew down in shock. He knew he had been caught. He reacted with a primitive violence.

He dashed in on me and his shield collided with my own scraps of wood and twisted bronze. His bulk forced me on and over. I was down. Down on one knee, the dangling shield remnants held aloft in my left fist. For a space, a single heartbeat, I put my right hand and the sword flat on the sand, supporting myself, getting my wind, seeing the world revolving in black stars and icy comets.

He towered over me. He laughed. His thraxter slashed down. Somehow the remnants of my shield slid into the sword's path, and he lifted to strike again, and I forced up my right arm and gripped my sword and took the blows, refusing to go down.

"Die, you rast!" he screamed. "Die!"

The attempt to rise and stand on my own two feet was too much for me. I was on one knee, the shield held up and the sword feebly pointing, and I gasped and wheezed and fought to clear the black demons in my head and see through the leaping whorls of light and shadow encompassing me.

His passion controlled him now, and he struck and struck as though hewing wood. He had had a scare and he could not understand the emotions that corroded within him like poisons—so I guessed, seeing that never had he met his master. But, for all that, I was nearly done for. The pathetic bits of shield still held together and kept out his thraxter; but that was all.

So I tried to stand up. I made a last convulsive effort.

He saw that. He saw the way I lurched and recovered and struggled my foot under me and so started to rise.

"Rast! Yetch! Die!"

Toppling, swaying, I struggled with a despairing savagery to stand up. And I knew I could not. Mefto saw the way I moved, saw my body begin to rise, and it was clear he imagined I was about to stand up. Zair knows what kind of demon he thought I must be, after the way he had chopped me,. and the blood, and the punishment, and the state I was in. He thought I was going to stand up. That golden face contorted into a look of bestial unbelieving fury. He took three slow steps back, right to the very edge of the blue square, and then with a howl he launched himself at me.

And, then, Prince Mefto the Kazzur made his mistake.

The blows from his thraxter smashed down viciously on the chunk of shield I held aloft, twisted so that a remnant of bronze framing held against the blows. Mefto was a Kildoi. A Kildoi has been blessed by the gods with a tail hand. Mefto in his blind fury reached out with his tail hand and seized the rim of this infuriating frustrating chunk of shield, ready to tear it away and so leave me open for the last blow.

That hard brown hand gripped onto the bronze before my eyes. I saw the nails, trimmed and polished, the thin bristle of golden hair, the whiteness of constricting violence between the knuckles. The hand gripped and pulled. The shield moved.

With a final lurch I lifted halfway up, reached out with the sword, cut off that tail hand.

Prince Mefto the Kazzur screamed.

His golden body convulsed away, and he shrieked, a high

howling screech of agony and fury, of humiliation and despair.

Somehow, do not ask me, for I cannot say, I was crouched over his body as he twitched and convulsed on the blue blood-spattered sand. He held the gory stump of his tail in all his four hands, and he screamed and slobbered and cried.

I said, "Mefto the Kleesh. I have cut Kataki tails off before this, and those yetches did not cry like you do."

All that effort of speaking, of boasting, when I was bleeding to death, exhausted me, such is the stupidity of pride. There was little time. I lifted the thraxter, and it trembled. Mefto was wrapped up in his own horror and was not aware, not aware at all that the steel point hovered above his throat.

He was a master swordsman, he could hand out the punishment with a laugh; but he could not endure punishment. He was the best swordsman I had so far encountered; he was not the greatest by a very long way.

I raised the sword a last inch, grasping the hilt in both blood-stained hands. I took a ragged breath. I started to bring the sword down, to plunge it through Mefto's throat and on to bury the point deeply in the blue sand—and hands grasped my shoulders and the thraxter was taken away as a nurse takes away a baby's bottle and I was placed flat on the sand and there was noise and confusion and a needleman with his acupuncture needles and miles and miles of yellow bandages.

"Why—?" I tried to say.

Yasuri bent over me.

"Mefto's people resigned the game to save his life."

"Then," I gasped out, "Then I have failed!"

A stupid game, and its rules, had saved the rast to bring horror to the Dawn Lands and to Vallia, when a straight and simple fight outside the rules of Kazz-Jikaida—why had I listened to brave Konec and Dav? I should have—I should have—but the words went away and there was blackness like the blackness of Notor Zan. I awoke to see Yasuri looking down on me with the strangest of expressions on her face.

I felt light-headed and empty and very very thirsty. She told a slave girl to fill a goblet with water, and this I drank straight down. Someone with a reedy voice said: "No more for now. He is weak but will mend with care."

"I shall care for him," said the lady Yasuri, and I could see no lines on her face at all.

A shadow moved at her side and the lady Jikaidasta stood there in what must be a private room in Yasuri's suite at her hotel, The Star of Laybrites. Ling-li's pale face glowed in the reflected radiance and her blue eyes were very bright upon me.

"I must leave Jikaida City now. I did not aid you in the fight—Jak." She paused on the name. Then: "The Nine Masked Guardians maintain San Orien, who is a Wizard of Loh of great repute, to warn them of any sorcery practiced in the games. You fought your own fight—and won."

I could not shake my head, for it would probably have fallen off; but I wondered if it was possible for me to agree with her, that she might be right. Had I won? The crucial factor was, it didn't matter if I had won that fight or not.

Then there was a deeper rumble of voices, and shadows, and presently Kov Konec and Vad Dav Olmes stood by the bed. They were smiling with great broad smiles of triumph, for Prince Mefto the Kazzur had left Jikaida City, his stump tail bandaged, left it the very day after the fight, which was a sennight ago, and because there was no evidence against the people from Mandua they had been freed, and with an apology, too.

The words croaked from my throat. "And the rast from Hamal?"

"He remains. He plays in the Mediary Games, for there are always games of Jikaida going on in Jikaida City."

He smiled down on me, and Dav, with a finger to his nose, said, "Yes, the Mediary Games begin, and the lady Yasuri is the Champion, reigning Champion."

"And now the people of the Dawn Lands will take their own destiny into their hands." Konec's fist rested on his sword hilt. "The alliance between Hamal and Shanodrin never took place. I think, I hope, I pray, Prince Mefto is finished."

Maybe I did not know what the Star Lords wanted with the lady Yasuri. But I did know that, for me, the work I had had to do in Jikaida City was finished. There was nothing to keep me here now. Vallia called. If the Star Lords brought me back here, then I would have to think again. But the Witch of Loh, Ling-li-Lwingling, also, knew more than she allowed. This was all tied up together; but I had fought a fight, and, by Krun! I knew I had been in a fight. I lay back on the yellow pillows.

My way home to Vallia still remained in Jikaida City.

As soon as I could move I would be off.

The Hamalese flier would speed me across the continent and take me home. Home to Delia.

"Let us praise Dromo the Benevolent," said Konec. "We have won. It is all over now. The game is finished."

As I drifted off to sleep I said to myself: "For you it may be finished. But the game is not finished for me, for plain Dray Prescot who happens to be the Emperor of Vallia."

Appendix

JIKAIDA

The smallest form of Jikaida, known as Poron Jikaida, is here described. I should like to acknowledge the advice and interest of John Gollon of Geneva in the preparation of these rules for publication. I must also thank my son for his enthusiasm and expertise in playing Jikaida. He has helped to clarify game situations and contributed to the strategical shape of Poron Jikaida. As a matter of convenience the terminology of terrestrial chess is used when practical.

The board consists of six drins, arranged two by three, each drin containing thirty-six squares, arranged six by six. The dividing line between drins is called a front and is painted in more heavily than the other lines to facilitate demarcation.

The squares are almost always either black and white or blue and yellow, although other colors are known. On Kregen red and green are seldom used. The players have a yellow square on the right of the first rank.

Blue is usually north and Yellow south. Each player has two drins before him, his home drins, and the two wild drins in the center. From Yellow's point of view each drin is lettered A to F from left to right, and numbered one to six from south to north. Each drin has a name.

In Poron Jikaida the six drins are named and arranged:

Wersting	Chavonth
Neemu	Leem
Mortil	Zhantil

By using the drin name followed by the coordinates any square is readily identifiable, and this system has been found to be quick, simple and efficient.

It is possible to place artificial features on the board—

rivers, hills, woods, etc.—by prior arrangement between the players. Most often these are not employed, Jikaida purists contending that they interfere with the orthodox developments and powers of pieces in combination on the open board.

The object of the game is to capture the opposing King. This piece is variously called Princess, Aeilssa, Rokveil, and in Loh, Queen. When any piece is in a position enabling it to take the King the player calls: "Kaida." When the King cannot evade capture, "Hyrkaida." At any time he thinks he is in a winning position, a player may ask his opponent: "Do you bare the throat?" If his opponent does, he resigns.

Each player has thirty-six pieces, arrayed in his first three ranks. The pieces are: one King, one Pallan, two Kapts, two Chuktars, two Jiktars, two Hikdars, two Paktuns, twelve Deldars, twelve swods.

The King moves as in Terran chess. Notation: K.

The Pallan moves as Terran Queen plus Knight and may pass from one drin to the next, once only, during his move. The Pallan has the power of taking any friendly piece except the King. Notation: P.

The Kapt moves as Pallan, but may not take friendly piece. When crossing drin front must continue direction of travel. Notation: Ka.

The Chuktar moves as Terran Queen. May cross drin front once per move continuing direction of travel. Notation: C.

The Jiktar moves as Terran rook. Must halt at drin front and cross on next move. Notation: J.

The Hikdar moves as Terran Bishop. Must halt at drin front and cross on next move. Notation: H.

The Paktun moves as Terran Knight. Notation: Pk.

The Deldar moves and captures one or two squares in any direction, orthogonal or diagonal. A two-square move may not involve a change of direction and is not a leap. Notation: D.

The swod moves one square, straight forward or to the two forward diagonals and captures only to the forward diagonals. Notation: S.

The Paktun may leap twice on his first move. The Deldar may move twice on his first move, being able to move one, two, three or four squares, but changing direction only after the second square. The swod may advance or capture one, two or three squares on his initial move.

In these initial moves of Paktun, Deldar or swod, and in the case of the two-square move of the Deldar under normal circumstances, the move of such a piece ends when he makes a capture. The Paktun, for example, cannot on his initial move leap and capture, then leap again.

After his initial move, the swod moves and captures one square only.

In some areas of Kregen, Dray Prescot notes, players contend that the Deldar may only move and capture for a two-square move. Other areas allow a single square move without capture. These variations are considered interesting, and frustrating, as the piece's power cannot then extend to adjacent squares and would be limited to eight squares at a straight two-square range diagonally and orthogonally.

The Paktun crosses drin fronts in the normal course of his move. The Jiktar, Hikdar, Deldar and swod must halt at a front and cross on the next move. If the Deldar's normal two-square move is halted by a front after one square, he must halt and wait until a subsequent move to cross. The Chuktar and Kapt may cross a front once only during their move and must continue on in the same line of travel. The Pallan has this privilege; but also he may change direction at the front, (like light through the surface of water.) When a Pallan comes up to a front orthogonally he may continue straight on or take either of the two diagonals ahead. If the square adjoining the front is yellow on the hither side of the front, the two diagonals he may follow will also be yellow. If the square is blue, the diagonals will be blue. If the Pallan comes up to a drin front diagonally he may continue on the same diagonal or take either of the two orthogonals enclosing the diagonal. One of these orthogonals will always lie alongside the front. He cannot turn at right angles to his line of advance. The paktun-leap of the Pallan is his move and cannot be taken as well as another move.

A move through an interior drin corner would allow the player to move into any one of the other three drins.

Unless halted by a piece in the way, the Jiktar and Hikdar may move the full distance of a drin up to the front. The Pallan, Kapt and Chuktar, unless halted by a piece, may move the full distance of one drin and the full distance of the next. To cross a front, all pieces with the exception of those with trans-front movement and the Paktun must stand on a square adjacent to the front in order to cross.

There is no en passant capture in Jikaida.

There is no castling as such in Jikaida, but a near-equivalent is employed. If the King is not under attack and the square on which he will land is not under attack, and if the

King and the other piece involved are on their original squares (whether or not they have previously moved) once only during the game a player may switch the place of the King with that of a Kapt or a Chuktar. The King would then be moved to the square of the Kapt or Chuktar, and the other piece moved to the King's square. It does not matter if there are, or are not, pieces in the way, nor if the intervening squares are under attack. This move is known as the King's Fluttember. Because of zeunting, this rule is strategically less vital in Jikaida than the castling rule in chess, but nevertheless can be important tactically.

The use of drins and the power of pieces to vault make Jikaida unique. The Kregish word for vault is zeunt.

Any piece (some variations exclude the King) may move from one end of a straight unbroken line of pieces to the other end. The line may be diagonal or orthogonal and be of any length. The piece vaulting must stand on the square immediately adjacent to the end of the line, diagonally if a diagonal line and orthogonally if an orthogonal line, may move along the line and come to earth on the immediately adjacent square at the far end, diagonally if a diagonal line and orthogonally if an orthogonal line. Exceptions will be noted below.

A line for vaulting must consist of three or more pieces.

The pieces in the line may be blue or yellow or a mixture.

If there is a break in a line the vaulting piece must land there and finish his move. A piece may land on an opposing piece and capture anywhere along the line, providing he has already vaulted over at least three pieces, and he is not a swod landing on an opposing swod propt by a Deldar. (see below.)

Whenever a vaulting piece touches down, to capture an enemy, at the end of the line, or in a break, his move is ended.

The Pallan who may capture a friendly piece may do so in the normal course of a vault.

Any piece may vault across one or more drin fronts providing the line to be vaulted extends unbroken across those fronts. Pieces which would normally have to halt at a drin front when moving do not have to do so when vaulting. However, if a piece moves to a square abutting on a front and the line to be vaulted begins on the other side of the front he must wait until the next or subsequent move to vault.

Vaulting instead of moving normally counts as the player's turn.

Swods vault forward orthogonally or diagonally only.

If a line to be vaulted ends at a front the piece vaulting may touch down in the adjacent square as noted, or capture, over the drin front.

It should be noted that a vault may change a Hikdar's color.

In Poron Jikaida as usually played the Pallan is the only piece with the power of using two other features of the vault. The Pallan may, in his turn, move legally as specified in the rules, to the end of a line and in the same turn vault. The Pallan may make one change of direction when vaulting, but must follow a continuous line of pieces of three or more from one end to the other with a single bend in the line.

The Pallan may move diagonally to the end of an orthogonal line and vault, and vice versa. The change of direction can follow any single bend in the line.

A player wins by either checkmating (hyrkaida) or stalemating (tikaida) his opponent, or by baring his opponent's king, unless the opponent then immediately (on the move) bares player's king also, in which case the game is drawn.

If a Deldar stands next to a swod of the same color an opponent swod cannot capture that swod. Adjacency, to afford this protection, may be orthogonal or diagonal. In the Kregish, this protection is called propt. One Deldar may propt as many swods as he is adjacent to.

Dray Prescot points out that the idea of a rank of Deldars standing against an advance of swods, thus forcing heavier pieces into action, probably gave rise to the traditional opening challenge of the game: "Rank your Deldars!"

When a swod reaches the last rank of the board he may promote to any rank, including Pallan but excepting King, regardless of the number of pieces of the chosen rank already on the board.

The initial array of Yellow pieces from Yellow's point of view is: First rank: from left to right: Chuktar, Jiktar, Hikdar, Paktun, Kapt, Pallan, King, Kapt, Hikdar, Jiktar, Chuktar. Second rank: twelve Deldars. Third rank: twelve swods.

The initial array of Blue pieces from Blue's point of view is: First rank, from left to right: Chuktar, Jiktar, Hikdar, Paktun, Paktun, Kapt, King, Pallan, Kapt, Hikdar, Jiktar, Chuktar. Second rank: twelve Deldars. Third rank: twelve swods.

Kings stand on squares of their own color.

First move is by agreement, either color may open the game.

Variations

Whatever rules or variations of rules are used, it is essential that players are aware of them and agree before play starts. It is particularly important that the rules governing vaulting should be completely agreed upon.

These variations are similar to differences in chess rules on Earth before advances in communication and transportation allowed standardization. Poron Jikaida is the smallest form of Jikaida. (Jikalla will form the subject of an appendix in a subsequent volume in the Saga of Dray Prescot.) There are other sizes of board and numbers of pieces employed. Great Jikaida is the largest. Many forms employ aerial cavalry.

Jikshiv Jikaida is played on a board six drin by four drins.

Hyrshiv Jikaida is played on a board three drins by four drins. The Lamdu version of Hyrshiv Jikaida employs ninety pieces a side.

In the larger games with more pieces the power of the superior pieces increases with the additions, the Jiktar taking on the powers of the Chuktar for example. Some additional pieces are: the Hyrpaktun, who moves in an elongated Paktun's move, three squares instead of two before the sideways move. The Flutsman, who moves four spaces, diagonally or orthogonally, over intervening pieces, must touch down on an unoccupied square, and then move or capture one square orthogonally or diagonally. This simulates the flutsman's flight to his target and then the attack on foot. There are other aerial moves of similar character.

In some areas of Kregen the Hyrpaktun is allowed a single square move, like the King, to facilitate color changing.

The Archer moves one square diagonally and then as a rook. The Crossbowman moves one square orthogonally and then as a bishop. Trans-drin restrictions with the missile pieces vary. Vaulting rules vary considerably and have been the cause of great controversy. With the larger games the Pallan has the power of more than one change of direction during a zeunt, and may come down off the vault and continue moving. Sometimes the Kapts have the power of moving to a vaulting line. The pieces with a knight-like leap may come down off the vault to one side or the other, as though continuing their leap. This confers a very great power to these pieces, as they would then cover the entire sides of the vaulting line from three pieces away.

Trans-drin restrictions also vary, as, for instance, the Kapt being allowed to change direction at a front, and the Jiktars and Hikdars being allowed trans-drin movement. The Pallan may be allowed to cross two drin fronts, and this is particularly important during diagonal moves near the center of the board or where fronts meet. On the larger boards increased freedom of movement has been found to be essential, but this is often restricted to the home and central drins, and does not extend to the opponent's home drins.

The powers of the swods and Deldars also vary by agreement, and it is a pleasant game to play Poron Jikaida with two ranks of swods each. In Porondwa Jikaida there are two ranks of Deldars. The larger boards build on the basis of the Poron board, the additional drins of the Hyrshiv Board are as follows: From Yellow's point of view: The right-hand home drin is Krulch. The drins above that are Prychan and Strigicaw. Blue's home drins are Boloth, Graint, Dermiflon.

In notation it is usual to give only the initial letter of the drin, followed by the letter and number of the coordinates.

Prescot says an interesting variation developed in Vallia where the swods were called brumbytes and the Deldars were called Hakkodin; but he gives no details of the play, except a mention of the brumbytes being arrayed initially in three ranks of eight, and provided they are on adjacent squares being allowed to be moved three at a time. One assumes this privilege would end by at least the front of the opponent's home drins.

The above description is necessarily brief; but enough information has been given to enable the game to be played and enjoyed and some of the ramifications and developments to be explored. The construction of a board is a simple matter. It is suggested chess pieces are used where applicable, and the new pieces represented by model soldiers of a suitable scale and color. It is possible that a range of figures from the Saga of Dray Prescot will soon be available.

Finally, it is left to me to say, on behalf of Dray Prescot, enjoy your Jikaida and—Rank your Deldars!

Alan Burt Akers.

Don't miss the great novels of Dray Prescot on Kregen, world of Antares!

"Although Kregen has many aspects of Barsoom, it is more reminiscent of John Norman's Gor."—**Erbania**

☐ **TRANSIT TO SCORPIO.** The thrilling saga of Prescot of Antares among the wizards and nomads of Kregen. Book I. (#UY1169—$1.25)

☐ **THE SUNS OF SCORPIO.** Among the colossus-builders and sea raiders of Kregen. Book II. (#UY1191—$1.25)

☐ **WARRIOR OF SCORPIO.** Across the forbidden lands and the cities of madmen and fierce beasts. Book III. (#UY1212—$1.25)

☐ **SWORDSHIPS OF SCORPIO.** Prescot allies himself with a pirate queen to rescue Vallia's traditional foes! Book IV. (#UY1231—$1.25)

☐ **PRINCE OF SCORPIO.** Outlaw or crown prince—which was to be the fate of Prescot in the Empire of Vallia? Book V. (#UY1251—$1.25)

"For sheer pageantry and character development, Akers far outshines any other writer writing this type of story. . . ."
—Jackson (Tenn.) Sun

If you wish to order these titles,
please use the coupon on
the last page of this book.

Presenting MICHAEL MOORCOCK
in DAW editions

The Elric Novels

☐	**ELRIC OF MELNIBONE**	(#UW1356—$1.50)
☐	**THE SAILOR ON THE SEAS OF FATE**	(#UW1434—$1.50)
☐	**THE WEIRD OF THE WHITE WOLF**	(#UW1390—$1.50)
☐	**THE VANISHING TOWER**	(#UW1406—$1.50)
☐	**THE BANE OF THE BLACK SWORD**	(#UW1421—$1.50)
☐	**STORMBRINGER**	(#UW1335—$1.50)

The Runestaff Novels

☐	**THE JEWEL IN THE SKULL**	(#UW1419—$1.50)
☐	**THE MAD GOD'S AMULET**	(#UW1391—$1.50)
☐	**THE SWORD OF THE DAWN**	(#UW1392—$1.50)
☐	**THE RUNESTAFF**	(#UW1422—$1.50)

The Oswald Bastable Novels

☐	**THE WARLORD OF THE AIR**	(#UW1380—$1.50)
☐	**THE LAND LEVIATHAN**	(#UW1448—$1.50)

Other Titles

☐	**LEGENDS FROM THE END OF TIME**	(#UY1281—$1.25)
☐	**A MESSIAH AT THE END OF TIME**	(#UW1358—$1.50)
☐	**DYING FOR TOMORROW**	(#UW1366—$1.50)
☐	**THE RITUALS OF INFINITY**	(#UW1404—$1.50)

DAW BOOKS are represented by the publishers of Signet and Mentor Books, THE NEW AMERICAN LIBRARY, INC.

THE NEW AMERICAN LIBRARY, INC.,
P.O. Box 999, Bergenfield, New Jersey 07621

Please send me the DAW BOOKS I have checked above. I am enclosing $__________(check or money order—no currency or C.O.D.'s). Please include the list price plus 35¢ per copy to cover mailing costs.

Name ____________________

Address ____________________

City__________ **State**__________ **Zip Code**__________

Please allow at least 4 weeks for delivery